THE GREEN REVOLUTION DELUSION

The False Promise of Modern Agriculture

A Novel

Walt Davis and Tony Winslett

ISBN-10: 1499348363
ISBN-13: 9781499348361
CreateSpace Independent Publishing Platform
North Charleston, South Carolina

Death Wears Many Faces

As the Rapture
Death can wear the Saviors' face
Bringing, love, peace and eternal life

As Release
Death can wear a face of calm acceptance
Bringing conclusion to a full lived life

As Winter
Death can wear a cold but familiar face
Bringing completion to the annual cycle of life

As War
Death can wear a savage face
Bringing destruction, pain and loss of life

As Deception
Death can wear a fraudsters' face
Bringing the cruelest ruse of death disguised as life

Walt Davis 2010

Table of Contents

Chapter One: Thomas Bristol   1
Chapter Two: The State of the World – Corporate   9
Chapter Three: The State of the World – Human   19
Chapter Four: Rebirth of a Farmer   27
Chapter Five: The Way Things Were   35
Chapter Six: The Change   39
Chapter Seven: Bristol Farms Inc.   43
Chapter Eight: The World Outside   49
Chapter Nine: New Beginning   57
Chapter Ten: The Natural Way   69
Chapter Eleven: A Philosophy Forms   89
Chapter Twelve: The New Generation   95
Chapter Thirteen: A Death in the Cornfield   105
Chapter Fourteen: Backwards toward the Future   125
Chapter Fifteen: Beginning the Dynasty   137
Chapter Sixteen: The Specter Fades   147
Chapter Seventeen: The Foundation   161
Chapter Eighteen: The Road Back   167
Chapter Nineteen: Progress   185
Chapter Twenty: It Comes Together   193
Chapter Twenty One: The Wages of Sin   215

Chapter Twenty Two: Vindication   221
Chapter Twenty Three: Storm Clouds   227
Chapter Twenty Four: Allies Unite   231
Chapter Twenty Five: The Harvest   241
Chapter Twenty Six: Epilogue   249
Authors Note   253
Appendix   261
Author Bio   293

CHAPTER ONE
Thomas Bristol

Upper California coast 1849

"You dumb ox! I told you to hit him easy." "Cor! He's a big un and I didn't want to give him a chance to fight us!" "Well you killed him you stupid bastard and now we have to go find another in a hurry. If we don't get back to the ship with two hands before the tide turns, the Captain will have our hides off in strips. Roll him out of the road and let's go."

Thomas Bristol hurt! He tried to open his eyes to see why he hurt so badly but the effort caused the pain to become even worse and he passed into oblivion once again. Eventually, Thomas awoke to the feel of something cool and wet on his face; he managed to open his eyes but could see very little – it was dark. He seemed to be reclining in a semi-prone position propped up against something soft; the only light came from a small flickering flame on the floor to his left. Thomas tried to speak to the person who was washing his face with cool water; he wanted to say "Thank you" but only managed to make a croaking sound before once again falling asleep.

The smell of tea awoke him and he opened his eyes to see a small man in black pants and shirt squatting next to him. The man held a steaming bowl which he used to gesture towards Thomas as he asked, "Chai?" The tea smelled delicious to Thomas and he struggled to sit up. The little man put an arm around Thomas' shoulders and with an impressive show of strength, raised him to a sitting position. The sudden change of position made Thomas' head swim in an intense fit of dizziness but he closed his eyes momentarily and the spell passed. Thomas wanted to take the bowl and drink but found that he could not remain upright without both hands on the pallet behind him. Evidently the little man saw his problem because he set the bowl of tea down and reached behind Thomas to pull up a back rest. When Thomas leaned back, the little man handed him the bowl. Thomas sipped carefully and then drank the tea with relish; he could taste honey and some sort of citrus and when it was gone he held the bowl out and said, "Please, may I have more?" The little man smiled, took the bowl and left through the opening in what Thomas could see, for the first time, was a tent made of sail canvas. Thomas explored his body and found he was shirtless and had a large bandage on his head; no other damage that he could find but he was very weak. He still had a headache built for a horse but nothing like the searing pain that he now could only vaguely remember. He had no idea what time it was or even what day. As he struggled to place himself in time, he realized that the sunlight was coming from his right at a low angle and that he could hear the sound of surf coming from directly in front of him. The surf would be coming ashore on the north edge of San Pablo Bay so the sun was in the west and it must be close to sundown; the last thing he remembered was meeting, just at dusk, two jovial and very drunk sailors on the path up from the beach. He had been unconscious for at least twenty four hours.

His belt knife and the coin bag he wore around his neck were gone and his sea bag did not seem to be here; it probably was well out to sea by now. Thomas had to smile at the irony; he had jumped ship to get to California and had almost been shanghaied before he was off the beach. He cautiously ran his hand over the inside of his left calf and was pleased to find the dirk still strapped to his leg; repeating the action on his right calf found the leather purse strapped to that leg still in place. He had been in worse straits; if his head wasn't broken, he would be alright.

Thomas Bristol was born in Devon in the spring of 1823; his father was a gardener on the estate of Lord Sowell and Thomas grew up working the land with his dad. The two had batched in the little stone cottage that went with the job ever since his mother died when he was ten. Thomas liked working with the soil and with plants but he was a restless young man full of vigor and with his dad's permission went to sea when he was seventeen. For the next nine years Thomas learned his trade and sailed most of the seas of the world; he came back to Devon to see his dad as often as he could, letters were no use; though his mother had schooled Thomas a little before she died, Da could neither read nor write. Last fall, after being gone near two years, he returned to Devon to find another family in the cottage and his father dead. Thomas was sad but resigned – his father was old – his resignation turned to fury when he learned that the old Lord had died and the young Lord turned his father and two other old employees out to fend for themselves. His dad moved into a hovel at the edge of the village and did his best to support himself with odd jobs but it was too much; in the winter before, he took pneumonia and died. Thomas was not a violent man but the thought of his father thrown out like a piece of trash after a lifetime of service filled him with cold fury. Thomas waited in port until just before his ship was ready to sail; he rented a horse and met the young Lord as he was making his customary morning ride through the woods. Thomas did not kill the bastard but when he finally threw down his cured oak cudgel it was blood soaked; the young Lord was sobbing like a tortured baby and was no longer the handsome young nobleman. It would be months before he would be able to walk or even feed himself or wipe his own arse and it was highly doubtful he would ever be able to sire any little nobles. Thomas made it back to his ship just in time to sail; taking with him the young Lords purse and the knowledge that he could never return to England.

The light from the opening darkened and Thomas looked up to see the little man along with a younger version of him enter the tent. The young man nodded to Thomas and in fractured English, introduced himself as Jin Li and his father as Jin Tan. Jin Tan spoke to his son in Cantonese telling him to ask Thomas if he would like more tea. Both men started when Thomas said, in Cantonese, "My name is Thomas Bristol and yes, I would like more tea please." Thomas' Cantonese was as fragmented as Jin Li's English but they were able to communicate. Jin Tan brought Thomas his freshly washed shirt then went out and came back with tea for everyone and then again with bowls of rice cooked with bits of fish and greens of some sort. As they ate, Jin Li told Thomas that they had found him two mornings ago by the side of the path to the beach as they were going down to gather seaweed. He had a bad cut on the back of his head and had lost a lot of blood. They bandaged the cut as best they could; loaded him in the donkey cart they used to haul seaweed and brought him here. The wound was still bleeding so they had a doctor from the Chinese community come and sew up the cut; it was his opinion that Thomas would recover if he did not die in the first twenty four hours. Thomas spoke up to say, "You saved my life and have been out expense, time and trouble. I will repay you." Both Jin's objected that it was not necessary but Thomas said, "It is a debt of honor that I will repay when I am able."

Voices awoke Thomas next morning as the east was beginning to get lighter. He realized the pain had subsided and that he felt much better; he got to his feet and, after the world stopped spinning, joined Jin Li and Jin Tan as they drank tea at a small fire. Jin Tan gave Thomas tea and some rice cake and Jin Li asked if he would be alright by himself until they returned about noon? They had told him last night that they came to the beach to gather and dry seaweed to be used as fertilizer for their vegetable crops. They had several loads ready to be hauled the five miles to their farm. Thomas remained in camp while the Jins hauled three loads of seaweed and then went with them as they hauled a load of dried trash fish that they purchased from the wharf where the fishing boats docked. The two days of rest had done wonders; Thomas was much stronger and felt almost normal as he removed the bandage from his head so that sunshine and air could help the wound heal. He made the five mile walk to the Jins' farm without the need to rest. The farm was in the valley of a fresh water creek a few miles from where it flowed into San Pablo Bay. The Jins leased a small portion of the sixty acres owned by Don Pablo Garcia and had a ready market for all they could produce in the gold hunters that were swarming into the country. The Jins introduced Thomas to their families and insisted that they put the tent back up for him to stay in until he was completely well. He agreed but only on the condition that they put him to work. It was years since he worked in the garden but he found that he still enjoyed the experience. As he pulled weeds from a row of radishes, Thomas decided that he would remain in this valley and become a farmer. He also decided that he needed to spend more time with and study the techniques of the Jin family; Thomas had never seen a healthier or more productive garden. The Jins had cleaned out and repaired the old irrigation ditch that was built by mission Indians in the middle part of the last century; the ditch brought water from the creek onto Don Garcia's land and allowed the Jins to grow crops right through the dry season. All of Don Garcia's land had been irrigated at one time but when the mission closed, the Indians drifted away and the land went fallow for many years. If he was going to be a farmer, Thomas could not imagine a better spot for a farm or better teachers than right here.

Early the next morning Thomas went to see Don Garcia and when he returned, he had two deeds; one declaring that he owned the fifty acres where the Garcia home stood and one giving title to the other ten acres of the property to the Jin family. The young Lords gold had been put to good use.

CHAPTER TWO

The State of the World – Corporate

P resent time at headquarters of Genesis Alchemy International

"The meeting will now come to order; please take your seats so that we can get under way. Welcome members of the Board of Directors of Genesis Alchemy International, executives of Genesis Alchemy and invited guests; most of you know me but for those who do not, I am Jeffery Hostettler, Chairman of the Board of Directors of Genesis Alchemy International. This is an executive meeting of the board and attendance is limited to members of the board and guests who have received an invitation to attend and a blue lapel badge like the one I am holding. If you do not have one or the other of these credentials, I ask you to leave at this time. George, you have a question? No it is not possible for staff that has not already received clearance to remain. You will receive full minutes of the proceedings. Thank you and please close the door as you leave.

I assume that all of you have read the information packet sent to you which included minutes of our last executive meeting; are there any corrections or additions to those minutes? Does anyone wish to have the minutes read? If not do I have a motion for the minutes to be approved as printed? Thank you George; do I have a second? Thank you Dr. Gellibrand. All in favor say aye; any opposed? The minutes are approved. At this time I will turn the meeting over to Kent Corrigan, our chief financial officer, Kent."

"Thank you Jeffery and good morning everyone; if you will turn to page five in your booklet you will find an abbreviated quarterly financial report. I hope everyone has read the full report in the back of your booklet; I included this shortened version to more easily point out some very encouraging trends in our financial picture. Total revenues rose in every month of the quarter; we are selling more product both under our own label and through licensees and this trend holds for every one of our major products. Sales of our herbicide resistant corn, cotton and soybean seed have been especially strong and this of course boosts sales of our herbicides. It seems that the money spent educating farmers is finally beginning to pay off. In a recent in-house polling of major vendors, farmer acceptance of our GMO (genetic modified organism) products of all types is up. We have a sixty three percent increase over this period last year for seed and a forty two per cent increase over last year for our milk enhancing bovine growth hormone product. In addition, manufacturing costs are down substantially, due mainly to economies of scale in running larger batches of herbicide. With the market share that we control, I suggest that we begin to increase the price of our herbicide; a little higher cost is not apt to send farmers back to the cultivator and hoe after they have grown a clean crop with a single spraying of herbicide. I would also suggest that we add a warning on all of our seeds that the use of any other brand of herbicide will void our warranty; we can't be responsible for the results of the knock off products that are attempting to duplicate our success. Our financial picture is excellent for both income and expense with one exception which is legal costs; I see that Mike Justin, our chief legal officer is next up on the agenda so I will leave the explanation on legal costs to Mike. I look forward to a very nice increase in the size of our quarterly dividends."

"Thank you Kent, are there any questions for Kent? The Chair recognizes William Hunt, Vice President of Marketing." "Thank you Jeffery, I would question the advisability of increasing the price of either our GMO seeds or their accompanying herbicide at this time; we have been receiving quite a bit of negative press after the problems in Mexico and India. As you know, we in marketing follow what is being said about our company and our products very carefully; three years ago we were being lionized as saviors of the world but today we are seeing a significant and growing number of negative articles and news stories. These smears are not showing up in main stream agricultural publications – those people are too smart to antagonize the golden goose – but we are seeing a lot of rubbish being printed in publications that cater to the agricultural lunatic fringe – organic hippies and low input sustainability nuts. I am not really too worried about these; they reach a small audience with limited clout. I am more worried about articles appearing in various consumer oriented and health related journals alleging links of our product to various health problems in animals and lately in humans; these people do not have any research to back up their allegations but they are quoting a number of so called "experts" who appear to have credentials in their fields. My point in bringing this up is that we still do not have a majority of farmers using our products; I think it would be a mistake to raise prices until we get the hold out farmers hooked." At this point Chairman Hostettler interrupted, "Sheila, please pause your recording. William, I am sure that you did not intend to suggest that we promote addiction of any sort in our customers. Perhaps you would like to re-phrase your comment?" "Certainly, Jeffery that was not my intent; I intended to say that we need more time to demonstrate the benefits of our programs to the individual farmer. I apologize for the clumsy wording." Hostettler acknowledged the apology with a nod and said, "Are there other questions or comments regarding Williams' presentation? If not do I hear a motion to accept the financial report? Thank you Jason, do I have a second? Thank you Gloria, all in favor say aye. Are there any opposed? Thank you, I didn't think that the board would have any problem approving this report; it has been a long time since our company has been as profitable as it was this last quarter. I will call now on Mike Justin, Vice President for Legal Affairs."

"Thank you Jeffery, legal costs are up this quarter because we have, at the Boards direction, increased the number of patent infringement suits and the number of contract violation suits. It seems that there is some small percentage of farmers that believe that we cannot or will not follow up to catch and prosecute them when they attempt to cheat us by planting seed they harvested after signing a contract that forbids such action." Hostettler broke in again, "Sheila, pause again please. Mike you are a lawyer and I am sure you did not intend to imply that we have the power to or would prosecute anyone. If you will, re-phrase your statement. People, the proceedings of this meeting are being recorded and the record could someday be the subject of a legal subpoena; I ask that you be precise in your language!" "My apologies Jeffery, of course my intention was not to suggest that we have the power of prosecution, only that we can and will exercise our rights under the law. To date, we have won every suit we have filed and the word is out that trying to cheat us is not worth the cost. We have even won suits where the farmer claimed that windblown pollen from neighboring fields was the source of the DNA from our product that we found in his crop. I admit that I was worried whether we could counter this argument in court but Dr. Fredrick Hill from Genetic Progress Associates has proven to be an excellent expert witness with the ability to make juries understand the science in question. Many of these lawsuits are in appeal but we are confident that we will prevail in the end. I fully expect to work myself out of a job; when we began to be awarded big judgments, the attempts to defraud us will drop dramatically and our position as leader in every market we serve will be considerably strengthened. Ladies and Gentlemen as you know the function of the legal department here at GAI is not to produce revenue, but I can state with some certainty that the legal department will be significantly more than self funded as these suits are settled."

"Thank you Mike; are there questions or comments for Mike? Yes, Henry." "I would not presume to tell Mike how to run his shop but I would recount a mistake that

was made by another company on whose board I also sit. This company filed actions against a great many farmers throughout the mid west; the suits were valid but the company made the mistake of bringing in a large number of investigators and lawyers and bringing suit against multiple farmers in one area at the same time. The company won large judgments in the first two suits but in doing so antagonized the community; they lost the next five suits in a row. From then on, they would bring one suit in an area, try that and move to another location. Results were much better."
"Thank you Henry for the advice, I know Mike will keep it in mind. If there is nothing else, we will break for lunch and resume at 1:00 pm sharp."

Authors' note:
We interrupt our story to insert a complete reprint of an actual letter

An open letter to Secretary of Agriculture Vilasack from Dr. Don M. Huber Emeritus Professor Purdue University.
Dear Secretary Vilsack:

A team of senior plant and animal scientists have recently brought to my attention the discovery of an electron microscopic pathogen that appears to significantly impact the health of plants, animals, and probably human beings. Based on a review of the data, it is widespread, very serious, and is in much higher concentrations in Roundup Ready (RR) soybeans and corn—suggesting a link with the RR gene or more likely the presence of Roundup. This organism appears NEW to science! This is highly sensitive information that could result in a collapse of US soy and corn export markets and significant disruption of domestic food and feed supplies. On the other hand, this new organism may already be responsible for significant harm (see below). My colleagues and I are therefore moving our investigation forward with speed and discretion, and seek assistance from the USDA and other entities to identify the pathogen's source, prevalence, implications, and remedies.

We are informing the USDA of our findings at this early stage, specifically due to your pending decision regarding approval of RR alfalfa. Naturally, if either the RR gene or Roundup itself is a promoter or co-factor of this pathogen, then such approval could be a calamity. Based on the current evidence, the only reasonable action at this time would be to delay deregulation at least until sufficient data has exonerated the RR system, if it does.

For the past 40 years, I have been a scientist in the professional and military agencies that evaluate and prepare for natural and manmade biological threats, including germ warfare and disease outbreaks. Based on this experience, I believe the threat we are facing from this pathogen is unique and of a high risk status. In layman's terms, it should be treated as an emergency.

A diverse set of researchers working on this problem have contributed various pieces of the puzzle, which together presents the following disturbing scenario:

Unique Physical Properties
This previously unknown organism is only visible under an electron microscope (36,000X), with an approximate

size range equal to a medium size virus. It is able to reproduce and appears to be a micro-fungal-like organism. If so, it would be the first such micro-fungus ever identified. There is strong evidence that this infectious agent promotes diseases of both plants and mammals, which is very rare.

Pathogen Location and Concentration

It is found in high concentrations in Roundup Ready soybean meal and corn, distillers meal, fermentation feed products, pig stomach contents, and pig and cattle placentas.

Linked with Outbreaks of Plant Disease

The organism is prolific in plants infected with two pervasive diseases that are driving down yields and farmer income—sudden death syndrome (SDS) in soy, and Goss' wilt in corn. The pathogen is also found in the fungal causative agent of SDS (Fusarium solani fsp glycines).

Implicated in Animal Reproductive Failure

Laboratory tests have confirmed the presence of this organism in a wide variety of livestock that have experienced spontaneous abortions and infertility. Preliminary results from ongoing research have also been able to reproduce abortions in a clinical setting.

The pathogen may explain the escalating frequency of infertility and spontaneous abortions over the past few years in US cattle, dairy, swine, and horse operations. These include recent reports of infertility rates in dairy heifers of over 20%, and spontaneous abortions in cattle as high as 45%.

For example, 450 of 1,000 pregnant heifers fed wheatlege experienced spontaneous abortions. Over the same period, another 1,000 heifers from the same herd that were raised on hay had no abortions. High concentrations of the pathogen were confirmed on the wheatlege, which likely had been under weed management using glyphosate.

Recommendations

In summary, because of the high titer of this new animal pathogen in Roundup Ready crops, and its association with plant and animal diseases that are reaching epidemic proportions, we request USDA's participation in a multi-agency investigation, and an immediate moratorium on the deregulation of RR crops until the causal/predisposing relationship with glyphosate and/or RR plants can be ruled out as a threat to crop and animal production and human health. It is urgent to examine whether the side-effects of glyphosate use may have facilitated the growth of this pathogen, or allowed it to cause greater harm to weakened plant and animal hosts. It is well-documented that glyphosate promotes soil pathogens and is already implicated with the increase of more than 40 plant diseases; it dismantles plant defenses by chelating vital nutrients; and it reduces the bioavailability of nutrients in feed, which in turn can cause animal disorders. To properly evaluate these factors, we request access to the relevant USDA data.

I have studied plant pathogens for more than 50 years. We are now seeing an unprecedented trend of increasing plant and animal diseases and disorders. This pathogen may be instrumental to understanding and solving this problem. It deserves immediate attention with significant resources to avoid a general collapse of our critical agricultural infrastructure.

Sincerely,

COL (Ret.) Don M. Huber

Emeritus Professor, Purdue University

APS Coordinator, USDA National Plant Disease Recovery System (NPDRS)

Authors' note:

The USDA approved the release of RR alfalfa in 2005. A federal lawsuit was filed by the Center for Food Safety in 2006 citing Monsanto's failure to file the required Environmental Impact Statement (EIS). Federal District Court stopped all sale or planting of RR alfalfa until an EIS was approved. An EIS was approved by the USDA and sales and planting approved as of January 27, 2011.

For readers who would like to conduct their own research, a list of papers available on the internet is provided in the Appendix as a starting point. There is a great deal of information available – from sources both pro and con – on the effects of the industrialization of agriculture. We have included in the book a mere taste of this information; we invite the reader to investigate and form their own conclusions. You can read more about Dr. Don Huber and his credentials at http://action.fooddemocracynow. org?sign/dr_huber_ warning

CHAPTER THREE
The State of the World – Human

Authors' note:
Our story resumes.

North central Mexico

Antonio Lopez walked slowly up the mountain path leading to the small plateau were his family had lived and farmed for many years; it was not much of a farm; a few hectares of thin soil surrounded by barrancos (gullies) where the soil was long since washed completely away. It was not much but it belonged to his family and had supported them for many generations. Antonio had farmed the land just as his father and his father's father before him had farmed; they did not plow the land (it was too thin), they did all of their work with hoes. For as long as he could remember, Antonio and his whole family gathered every scrap of manure they came across – cow dung, horse dung, even sheep and goat dung was picked up and added to the dung pile under the thatched shed at the edge of the field. A scoop of dung would then be added to each hill of corn, beans, peppers or squash when the seeds were planted. Using manure for fertilizer was something that everyone in the area had always done; just like they saved the largest and healthiest ears of corn to be next year's seed corn. Many years of selecting the best of each year's harvest had resulted in a landrace of corn that was uniquely suited to the local conditions; the value of this harmony between their environment and their corn was demonstrated when a neighbor brought some corn up from far down the Yaqui Valley and planted it instead of the local variety. The foreign corn failed miserably even as the local corn around it did well. The experiment caused great hardship for the family who brought the new corn up into the hills and the people remarked on the wisdom of their fathers. Antonio was not aware of the fact, but there were (in the early 1940's) more than three hundred distinct varieties or landraces of corn in Mexico; each developed in and particularly suited to the conditions of a local area; many of these varieties had been in cultivation for hundreds of years.

Antonio still farmed as his father taught him even though most of his neighbors had long since dropped the traditional practices for the hybrid seed and fertilizers introduced by the proponents of what was being called "the green revolution." At first the results were little short of miraculous; the hybrid plants grew tall with the application of the new fertilizer and yielded three times what his crop produced. All was not sweetness and light, however, after a few years pests like the corn root worm, aphids and the corn ear worm began to take a serious toll on the corn grown in the new way. These insects had always been present in low numbers but their populations exploded in fields using the new practices. Strange new diseases began to appear with entire fields being killed or heavily damaged by leaf diseases and head smuts. The government people came and told the farmers what they must buy to spray on the plants or put in the ground but these things were expensive and people often felt ill after using them; two children died after playing where some of the powder had been spilled. Two years ago, the rains did not fall for sixty days in the summer and all of the new corn shriveled and died; in the few patches still being farmed in the old way, the corn leaves curled up tight in the hot sun but did not die. The local corn curled up its leaves during the hot day time and un-curled them to breathe only during the cooler parts of the day; the people joked that the corn, being true Mexican, had the sense to follow the custom and take a mid-day siesta. The new hybrids had no such abilities and died if they were not watered. When the rain finally fell, the local corn revived and made a crop; not a big crop but far more than the new corn made. The soil in the fields farmed in the new ways became hard and did not seem to be able to soak up and hold the rainfall; there were no earthworms in the soil and even the birds ceased to visit these fields. It took more of the expensive fertilizer each year just to maintain yields of the same amount. Many of the farmers who adopted the new methods, borrowed money to buy the seed and other things required and found themselves unable to repay the loans. Land that had been in the same family for generations was sold to pay the debts and the families moved away to try to find work. Even where the rains did not fail, farmers were having harder times pay-ing for all the things they must buy and still have enough to feed their families. With all of their problems, the new methods yielded more than the old ways and the extra production drove the price of corn down so that only a very good crop made enough to pay all the costs and still give the farmer a living.

Antonio had not deserted the ways of his father but the new methods still affected him and his family; the pollen from the hybrid corn blew into his field and contaminated his corn. His corn began to show the same problems that devastated the new corn and the price of corn fell so low that Antonio knew that he too would soon have to give up the land he loved and find other ways to feed his family.

New Delhi, India

Tom Corrigan sat waiting in the outer office of the Agricultural Attaché and used the time to review the notes he had taken over the last three weeks. Punjab State is known as the breadbasket of India and is where the "Green Revolution" flourished most strongly starting in the 1960's. Tom accompanied by Jajit Hara, an Indian agricultural economist working for the State of Punjab, had crisscrossed Punjab and the neighboring states as part of an orientation and fact finding tour. An employee of the agricultural consulting firm, Greystone and Larch, Tom had a B.S. degree in Agronomy and M.S. and PhD. degrees in Agricultural Economics. The Agronomy degree he earned right out of high school; he came back to the university to study economics after a five year stint of running his own farming operation turned into an economic disaster. Tom learned the hard way that his undergraduate education had prepared him well to produce bountiful crops but had not prepared him to produce profitable crops. He was in India as part of the team from Greystone and Larch fulfilling a contract with the United States Department of State to make a third party assessment of the state of Indian agriculture. A second part of the contract was to detail the effects on the Indian people of the recent joint initiative between the governments of India and the United States and a consortium of U.S. companies involved with agriculture. He was fairly sure that his report was not going to make any of the collaborators happy.

After seeing firsthand what the initiative was doing and the results of these actions, it was obvious to Tom that the purpose of the joint venture, known officially as the "U.S. - India Agricultural Knowledge Initiative" was primarily to sell more products for U.S. companies like Monsanto, Archer Daniels Midland and Wal-Mart. It was billed as "a second green revolution" and like the first Green Revolution it relied almost entirely on pouring more inputs into Indian agriculture. The plan called for: more nitrogen fertilizer, more insecticide, more fungicide, more herbicide, more agricultural mechanization and more "improved" crop seed. The main difference between the first and second green revolutions would be that this time most of the "improved" crop seeds would be the form of genetically modified organisms (GMOs). The purveyors of GMO seed have been having a bad time; in the U.S. the miracle plants were losing their luster as pests developed resistance to the poisons used and promised profits did not materialize. GMOs were banned in many parts of the world as well founded apprehensions over their role in various problems of plants, animals and humans continue to surface. Aside from agronomic questions, the last thing that the financially strapped farmers of India needed was to spend more money; they were already spending far more in operating expense than the potential for profit could justify. Though his report would not say it, it was plain that the well being of Indian farmers was not a high priority with the people running the initiative. The one point three billion consumers in India were the priority and they are a prize worth investing time and money to gain.

Much of the time Corrigan had spent in India was used in documenting the environmental changes brought about by some thirty years of "modern" agriculture. Heavy nitrogen use and mechanical tillage has burned the organic matter content out of the intensively managed soils leaving them with greatly reduced ability to take in and hold water. While he was in the northern Punjab, a two inch rain fell in three hours; on land farmed in the old way most of this rain soaked into the ground as it fell. On fields farmed with the modern techniques most of the water ran off – taking soil with it; water trapped in low spots still had not soaked in after three days. Corrigan pulled soil samples and took soil probe data wherever he could find side by side areas farmed differently. It was apparent even without seeing the test results that the areas farmed using the new techniques were in dramatically poorer condition than soil farmed in the old way. As the soil conditions worsened, farmers increased both fertilizer use and irrigation in a struggle to maintain yields. Yields could be maintained to some extent by these efforts but with the greater inputs profitability could not be maintained and what had been a trickle of farmer bankruptcies became a flood. Thousands of these bankrupt farmers committed suicide to gain the government death benefits to prevent their families from starving.

The increased irrigation was causing many areas to run short of water and much of what remained was contaminated with nitrogen compounds from the heavy fertilizer use and with various pesticides. The incidence of cancer and other diseases had increased dramatically in the people living in the areas farmed in the new way and "blue babies" born to women drinking water containing high levels of nitrates were common. The Green Revolution increased the amount of grain and other products produced by Indian farmers but this increase came at tremendous cost to the land and the people of India.

CHAPTER FOUR

Rebirth of a Farmer

Yoder Farm Ohio

Henry Weaver took a sip of the almost too cold to drink ice water with which his wife Anna had filled his water jug and looked out over the hay field he had just finished cutting. From where he stood on the highest point on the farm, the gently rolling acres of Yoder Farm stretched out in front of him like a patch work quilt, each patch being a little different shade of green and each with a little different texture, here the ripple of knee high corn, there the velvet of close cropped pasture and beyond the waves of heading wheat. Whatever the season, Henry never tired of gazing at this scene; even covered with snow in the dead of winter, Yoder Farm presented to the world a vision of well managed prosperity that pleased Henry to the heart of his being. Stout stone barns, well nourished animals and fertile fields all spoke of generations of Yoder's who had worked these acres and contributed to the prosperity. Though not a Yoder, except by marriage, Henry Weaver knew that this is where he should be and where the son that Anna had just delivered should grow into manhood. His life was good; much had changed since his boyhood as the ragged son of illiterate parents who eked out a meager livelihood as farm laborers on the windswept plains of northwest Texas. Henry and his five brothers and sisters worked in the fields from the time they were six years old pulling bolls from the cotton plants and stuffing them in the sacks they pulled along on the ground; the little ones with small sacks their mother made but from twelve or so years old, they dragged seven foot long sacks just like the adults. They worked in the fields because their earnings made it possible for their parents to feed and clothe the family. School was a hit and miss proposition; many of the little country schools turned out in the fall so the kids could help with harvest. Henry got a high school degree but it was debatable whether or not he got a high school education. Henry didn't know what he wanted to do with his life. He liked to farm; he was the one who put in a big family garden every year but he knew that he didn't want to work as a hand on someone else's farm. He knew that if he stayed in the panhandle he would wind up married to someone as ill prepared for life as he and with a house full of kids to boot. College wasn't an option so when he graduated from high school, he hitched a ride into Lubbock Texas and joined the Marine Corps.

Henry had heard all the horror tales about boot camp and was pleased to find that it was not as bad as he had feared. It wasn't fun but once the initial shock of being screamed at and publicly humiliated wore off, Henry enjoyed the challenges; he met and overcame each new challenge and with each success his confidence increased.

He made it through boot camp and graduated as a United States Marine with a 0311 (infantry) MOS (Military Occupational Specialty). Henry decided that he liked being a Marine; he liked the way he felt and he liked the way people looked at him when he wore his uniform off base for the first time. The war was raging in Viet Nam and recruit training was shortened from the peace time twelve weeks to eight weeks; the Marines needed fighting men. Henry and the eighty men left of the one hundred originally in his training platoon went straight from boot camp to the Infantry Training Regiment at camp Pendleton where they spent four weeks doing their best to pound flat, by running up and down them with full packs, the jumble of hills that make up the training area. After ITR they were granted thirty days leave; Henry spent all of it except travel time with his family and then back to Pendleton for staging and soon after on to Viet Nam.

Unlike boot camp and ITR, Viet Nam was much worse than he could possibly have imagined. The mind cannot conjure up the devils brew of terror, exhaustion, filth, rage, disgust and sorrow that was the normal condition of a Marine grunt out in the bush. Henry did his thirteen months with one thought on his mind – keeping himself and his buddies alive. He killed when he had to, he got very good at it, and saw friends mangled and killed dozens of times. He re-upped for six more months in country solely because doing so would get him back to the world for good with an early discharge.

With ten days left on his enlistment and just three days more on his deployment, Henry began to understand why "short timers" acted so strange; thoughts that he had not allowed to form were suddenly front and center and he couldn't get them off his mind, "Maybe I won't be going back into the bush; maybe I won't have to see anymore horrors; maybe I am going to get out of here alive." The prospect of living a normal life without people trying to kill you and you killing them was beginning to seem possible. Henry was especially looking forward to being with his family; it had been almost two years since he had seen them. His littlest sister, Roseanne, wrote to him every week and Henry had been racking his brain as to how he could get a better life for her and the rest of the family. From his first paycheck, he had been sending half of what he earned home; the money made life better for his family but didn't really change anything. When he got a promotion and an increase in pay, he kept sending the same amount home and started saving for a nest egg; that was three promotions ago and the nest egg was growing nicely. Henry was hoping to move the family closer to Lubbock and lease a piece of land where they could start a market garden. He and his two brothers could get jobs in Lubbock and help in the garden after work and on weekends. He had shared his plans with Roseanne and she wrote back to say that the whole family was excited about the possibility that they could work for themselves. The more Henry thought about it, the surer he was that it could be made to work; there was not a lazy bone in his entire family but none of them knew how to manage money. Lubbock was growing and they could sell a lot of fresh produce at good prices. If he could control the purse strings, they could start to build something for his parents' old age.

Henry and his platoon had just come in from an eight day patrol, moving all day and manning ambush positions all night, and they were all mentally and physically beat. They didn't have many amenities at this base camp, no hot showers, but they did have hot chow and a reasonably secure perimeter so you could sleep without keeping one eye open for VC infiltrators. Henry was looking forward to his first good nights' sleep in more than week when he was approached by a corporal from company headquarters telling him that the Captain wanted to see him. Henry announced himself to the clerk sitting at a desk under a fly cloth at the door of the Captains bunker and heard Captain Brownlee say, "Come in Sergeant Weaver." Henry stepped down into the half dugout half sand bag shelter and saw Captain Brownlee and a strange Captain wearing chaplains' insignia sitting on cots. "Sergeant Weaver, I am Chaplain Renault and I am afraid I have some very bad news for you. I am sorry to tell you but your entire family, parents, two brothers and three sisters, were found in their home dead of carbon monoxide poisoning." Henry went numb with shock and was unable to respond until Captain Brownlee spoke up, "Sergeant Weaver, your tour is up in a few days and under the circumstances they are cutting you loose early; there will be a chopper leaving here in one hour. Go get your gear and catch that flight back to Da Nang where arrangements will be made to get you stateside as quickly as possible. I am very sorry for your loss and I want you to know that I have never served with a better Marine."

Henry got off the bus at Hale Center Texas with everything he owned in the Marine Corps sea bag he carried on his shoulder and walked down to the Baptist

Church his family had attended for years. He had called the Pastor, Brother Ben Lee, as soon as he got stateside and learned that the congregation had raised enough money to bury his family in the church cemetery. Henry wanted to thank Brother Lee and the congregation and to give them four thousand dollars of his nest egg to be used when someone else needed help. The house was rented so Henry boxed up the personal possessions of his family and, except for a few keepsakes, arranged for the church ladies to give the belongings to whoever needed them. Henry didn't want to spend a night in the empty house so after a visit to the graves of his family, he caught the evening bus into Amarillo as a start towards Lima Ohio where the father of a Marine buddy, John Prentice, had offered him a job in his International Harvester tractor dealership.

Lima Ohio

Henry liked Gabe Prentice, who owned the dealership, and the work wasn't that hard but it wasn't that interesting either. He spent most of his time putting together implements that arrived at the dealership as a pile of parts and picking up and delivering tractors. He was returning from one such delivery when he saw a car off in the ditch and an older man and two women looking at the front of the car. Henry stopped the truck behind the car and walked forward, "Can I help you folks?" When he got closer, Henry could see that they had run off the road when a front tire blew out and both front wheels were buried in the muddy barrow ditch. "Sir, if you will steer the car, I think that I can pull it back up on the hard surface where I can change the tire." Henry pulled the car up on the road without trouble and as he got out of the truck the man stuck out his hand and said, "Forgive my manners, I am George Yoder and this is my wife Mildred and my daughter Anna." Henry shook his hand and tipped his hat to the ladies said, "I am Henry Weaver and am very glad to meet you." George Yoder, a big erect man in his sixties, was wearing an old fashioned black suit and the women were in dark dresses. "We were coming back from a funeral and I was afraid that I was going to have to walk to get a tractor and these town shoes are killing my feet." He opened the trunk of the car and started to drag the spare out when Henry intervened, "Sir you have your church clothes on; let me change the tire." Henry soon had the blown tire replaced and the Yoders ready to go. As he worked both George and his wife gently probed him for information starting with Mrs. Yoder, "I don't believe I have seen you around here before." "No mam, I have only been working for Mr. Prentice for a few months." By the time Henry had the tire changed and the blown tire in the trunk, the Yoder family knew that he was a single farm boy from Texas just out of the Marine Corps; in ten minutes they gained a pretty good knowledge of his history. George took out his wallet and asked, "What do I owe you?" "Not a thing Sir, I am glad I was able to help." Mrs. Yoder responded, "If you won't let us pay you, you must at least come to Sunday dinner tomorrow." Anna had been quiet the whole time but spoke up now to say, "You had best come; Mother is known far and wide as the best cook in this part of Ohio." "Thank you, I would like a home cooked meal. Where and what time do I come?" George pointed to a white two story house about a mile down the road and said, "Right down there at one o'clock."

Henry finished his drink of water and shook off his day dream; it did not seem possible but ten years had passed since a blown tire introduced him to the happiest period of his life. He went to work on Yoder Farm as a hired hand and loved everything about the new life; it got even better when he and Anna fell in love and married with the Yoders blessings. Henry progressed from hired hand to junior partner and as George began to slow down, to full partner. The only dark cloud was that for eight years Anna was unable to conceive the child that she and he so desperately wanted. They had began to talk about adoption when suddenly Anna was pregnant and before long Henry Weaver Junior, Hank, arrived to enrich the lives of his parents and his grandparents.

CHAPTER FIVE

The Way Things Were

Yoder Farm Ohio

Hank Weaver was in hog heaven. At age nine it didn't get much better than to be riding in the cab of the new International Harvester 806 tractor; hearing (and feeling) the roar of the powerful engine and listening to his Dad talk about farming. Hank had long ago decided that he would be, just like his father and his grandfather Umpa, a farmer when he grew up. Hank wasn't aware of the fact but that would make him the sixth generation of his family to farm the 396 acres that made up Yoder's' Farm. Otto Yoder moved to this valley from Pennsylvania in 1833 and settled his family on a forty acre tract that had come to his father as a bounty for service in the War of 1812; there had been Yoder's on this land ever since. Over the years the acreage grew steadily (with the exception of the time in 1861 when Otto's Great-grandson sold off 100 acres to get the money to buy his two sons out of the Union Army).

For all of this time Yoder's Farm was the illusive "family farm" that the politicians love to talk about; they usually had some hired help but most of the work was done by family members. They grew the crops common to the region: corn, wheat, oats, peas, alfalfa hay and mixtures of alfalfa, grass and clover for pasture; in 1950 Umpa added soybeans to the list and all of these crops were grown in a rotating sequence stretching over five to seven years. In the early years tobacco was grown as a cash crop and at times the fiber crops flax and hemp had been grown. In addition there was a five acre apple and peach orchard, at one time it had been over twenty acres, which also had several rows of grapes and was home to fourteen hives of honeybees. For many years the crops had been marketed primarily through livestock. Umpa was adamantly opposed to selling hay or grain as he believed that to do so was to export the fertility of their soil; it was much better to sell beef, pork, milk and eggs and keep their soil fertility at home in the form of manure. Hogs, beef cattle, sheep and dairy cows consumed much of the grain, hay and pasture along with (until 1936) work horses; chickens, turkeys, geese and ducks come in for lesser shares; Umpa did love his roast duck. There was always a big garden and the women of the family spent a lot of time canning, drying and freezing vegetables of all kinds. In the fall, hog butchering would add lard rendering, sausage making and pork smoking to the list of chores. Given the wide range of crops grown and the amount of livestock kept, the year was taken up by a never ending succession of soil preparation, planting, harvesting and processing with the day to day tending of livestock always taking precedence over all else. Winter time allowed for a more relaxed schedule but there were still chores to be done, meat to be processed and fire wood to be cut, hauled and split. Hank was sometimes envious of his friends that lived in town, such fits came on usually when he was hoeing weeds under a blazing August sun or hurrying in the cold dark of a January morning to finish his chores before the school bus came, but there were advantages to living on the farm. He had his own pony that he used to roam far and wide in the valley and there was time even when things were busy to fish in the creek and swim in the deep holes with his buddies that lived on neighboring farms; his Dad was teaching him to shoot and promised that this fall he would take Hank deer hunting.

Life was good but Hank was bothered, there was tension between two of the people that he loved best in the entire world. His father and his grandfather were in serious disagreement about the direction that the management of the farm should take. Neither ever said anything derogatory about the other to Hank but each made it a point to explain to Hank his point of view. Dad wanted to move more acreage into corn and soybeans while Umpa was determined to continue their program of livestock based production. Today his Dad was telling him, "It is the way things will be done in the future, Hank. In the same number of working hours, with machinery like this 806, I can farm at least twice as many acres of corn and beans as we are growing now and corn and beans are where we make our money. It is foolish for us to tie up so much land, time and effort in things like sheep and dairy cows that, most years, barely break even. We need to get rid of the animals and turn the whole farm into row crops." "Umpa says that we need the manure from the animals to keep our soil fertile." "Your grandfather grew up in a time when manure was the only fertilizer they had. Today we can buy the fertilizer we need spread on the land a lot cheaper than we can produce it through manure. Howard Bloom at the Coop showed me a study from Iowa State that said that cattle manure had only about eleven pounds of nitrogen in a whole ton of manure; in this study it only paid to haul the manure to fields that were very close to the barns. Aside from being cheaper, if we don't have to have pasture and hay for the livestock, we can triple our acreage of cash crops." This all made sense to Hank but then, when Umpa explained why he farmed the way his father had, that made sense too. Hank didn't say anything for a while but finally asked, "Will we have to sell my pony?" Henry Weaver reached out to hug his son around the shoulders and say, "We are not going to change over until Umpa agrees and that may never happen but if it does, I expect we can still afford to keep Chigger."

CHAPTER SIX

The Change

The tide of modern agriculture was rolling over the country and a very few years saw an unbelievable amount of change in the area; all up and down the valley farmers sold their cows and hogs and sheep, pulled up the fences and plowed up their pastures to put in more cash crops. With the ability to put fertilizer exactly where it could do the most good and with weeds and insect pests controlled with chemicals, the new high yield hybrids yielded corn crops almost twice as high as was common in the past. Umpa and some other old timers didn't like what was happening but even they began to come around when it became apparent that the new methods could be very profitable. New and bigger equipment and herbicides instead of hoes made it possible for one man to farm much more acreage and the advice coming from government agencies, and from the equipment and farm supply salesmen, was "Get big or get out." The amount of crops produced sky rocketed and exports of wheat, corn, rice and soybeans became a mainstay of the American economy. Prices for most crops fell with the new abundance but the government enacted price supports to supplement farm income; to go along with the

price guarantees, the government also set up acreage allotments telling how much of what crops each farmer could
grow. Being told what they could and could not plant didn't
sit well with most farmers but with guaranteed prices for
crops, the value of the land that had crop allotments soared
and cash rents got so high that many older farmers rented out their cropland and retired. Umpa rented the entire
farm except the orchard and ten acres around the house
to his son-in-law Henry and spent his time in the garden
and tending the orchard and his honeybees. Henry bought
bigger equipment, the equipment companies were glad to
finance it, and leased every patch of land that came open
anywhere around him; he paid higher rents than most and
was soon one of the biggest farmers in the valley. Hank
worked with his father after school and summers but the
work was different from what it was when he was younger.
In days past, they worked at one job for a few days or a
week; planting corn or cutting hay until a job was done
and then going on to something else; they also had the
livestock to tend so that they were constantly doing different things. Now work was long mind numbing hours on a
tractor doing the same thing day in and day out. One of
the biggest problems was timing; with so much acreage in
only two crops, it was hard to get things done in a timely
manner. When it was time to plant corn, you had to get it
done or see your potential for making a decent crop drop
like a rock. The same constraints applied to soybeans so it
seemed that life had become a series of rushing to meet
deadlines. When the push was heavy they ran at night with
lights on the equipment to get crops planted or harvested

and Henry told Hank, more than once, "We'll rest when the snow is on the ground."

The way that people farmed changed dramatically during this conversion to "modern agriculture". The amount of land farmed by one family increased greatly; bigger equipment and fewer products meant that one man could farm far more acres. The economic basis of farming switched from the production of many different products each with low volume but high profit margins to high volumes of a few crops with low profit margins. Young tigers like Henry Weaver had big equipment with big payments to meet and they bid up the price of leases to get the land they needed to increase their volume of production; increasing production became the focus of farmers, academics and producers of farm supplies. No one seemed to realize that with each new bit of production increasing technology they adopted, farmers increased the amount of money that they put at risk. Traditional farmers, like Umpa, did not have near the production of the young tigers but neither did they have anything like the expense. For the first time in memory, farmers in the well watered eastern part of the Nation began to go bankrupt.

Politicians responded with various "safety net" schemes designed to improve the financial condition of farmers; various combinations of price supports, low cost loans, direct support payments and crop acreage controls were implemented. No one seemed to understand that the economic basis of agriculture, as it was being practiced, was deeply flawed in several very fundamental ways. To acquire and use the recommended technology (the machinery and fuel, the fertilizers, the herbicides, the insecticides and the GMO seed) the farmer had to put more money at risk than could be justified by the potential for profit. Agriculture became more and more capital intensive with both high overhead costs and high operating costs. At one point the government did institute a pilot program, Low Input Sustainable Agriculture or LISA designed to help farmers reduce their dependence on purchased inputs but this didn't last long as the companies selling the inputs put pressure on the politicians to have it killed. The government programs did reduce the likelihood of catastrophic losses but at the same time limited the ability to make large profits. The new system of agriculture was born during a period of cheap energy prices, in some areas in the 1950's propane tractor fuel cost a penny and a half a gallon, little or no thought was given to reducing energy usage either directly in agriculture or in the materials: the fertilizer, the pesticides, the machinery, that quickly became essential to the industry. The American farmer got caught up in the go-go atmosphere of "modernize agriculture to feed the world." They even lost their ability to make production decisions based on the market tested principles of supply and demand; you planted what the government allowed you to plant, no more - no less. The results to their financial health, the health of their land and their independence have all been tragic. The farmer fared poorly but the politicians got two items of great value to them; cheap food to keep the voters happy and grain to export and improve our balance of trade. The American farmer quickly learned another version of the golden rule; "The one who doles out the gold, makes the rules."

CHAPTER SEVEN
Bristol Farms Inc.

S an Francisco California
Jacob Bristol sat in his office pondering what, if anything, Bristol Farms Inc. should do to mark its' one hundred and thirtieth year of existence. In June it would be one hundred and thirty years since his great-great-grandfather Thomas Bristol arrived in California and started a farm. For the first forty years of that century and a third, it was known simply as Thomas Bristol's farm. Jacob's great grandfather, Leon Bristol, formed Bristol Farms Inc. in 1890 when he began to get more involved in processing and distribution. Today the company owned: vegetable packing sheds, grain elevators, canneries, dairies, a small meat packing plant and a factory making several kinds of specialty food ingredients. The backbone of the company, though, was still the thousands of acres of certified organic farmlands that the company had put together since Thomas Bristol bought the first fifty acres in 1849. Building the company had been the life work of five generations of Bristol's and Jacob was hopeful that his daughter, Jennifer Elisabeth, would one day be the sixth generation to run the company. Jacob was waiting now for his daughter to arrive for their luncheon

date and he thought once again how fortunate they were to have Jen Beth; as her older brother Tom had named her when Jennifer Elisabeth proved to be too much for a three year old tongue to handle. Tom was gone now, he didn't return from his second combat tour as a Marine in Iraq; his death left gaping holes in the hearts and lives of Jacob, his wife Anne and Jen Beth. The family had always been close but the death of Tom made the three of them closer still; they of course loved each other but also they liked each other and liked being in each other's company. Jacob wondered how many parents could truthfully say that they liked their teenage children. He knew that he was biased but Jen Beth at eighteen was more mature and had a better grasp of business by far than most of the young people Bristol Farms hired fresh out of college. Jacob was saved from more soul searching by Jen Beth's arrival; she flew into the room like a breath of fresh air, kissed her father on the bald spot on top of his head (an action he pretended to hate) and said, "I have it Daddy; we endow a chair of organic agriculture at one of the big agriculture schools in the corn belt. You have always said that Bristol Farm's biggest accomplishment was proving that organic agriculture can be profitably practiced on a large scale; let's share the technology with the world!" "I like that Jen Beth, "The Bristol Farms Chair of Organic Agriculture"; it has a nice ring to it. Can you research what we are looking at in expense and write up a proposal for me to present to the Board of Directors? I would like to have all the facts in front of me before I broach the subject with the Board." "I can do that and I can also research which schools are most likely to do a good job with the program; some universities seem to think that organic agriculture is a joke or perhaps a communist plot. Maybe the information I dig up will help me decide where I want to go to school; right now, I don't know where I want to go but I do know that I don't want to go to school in California." "That is a decision for you to make Babe but you might better get started; even with your grades and achievements, you are going to have to go through the acceptance process. Your Mother called and she is not going to be able to have lunch with us; she had an emergency of some sort but said she would be home for supper."

Anne Bristol, Dr. Anne Bristol, was a pediatrician with a strong background in human nutrition and in the effects of chemical pollution. She met Jacob when, as a fourth year medical student, she visited Bristol Farms as part of a project to gather information on the toxic chemicals in such wide spread use in California agriculture. As part of her education, she was seeing patients in a rural clinic, under the supervision of an MD, and a steady stream of children and adults came through showing signs of chemical poisoning; she was delighted when Jacob told her that they used no poisons of any sort not even the "natural" poisons allowed by the organic standards. Jacob had taken over as CEO of Bristol Farms Inc. at the request of the board of directors and his father well before he had expected to have the job. His father, Philip, was CEO for ten years but he had neither liked nor wanted the job; his father was a scientist, a plant breeder, and he was not cut out to be chief executive of a company the size and complexity of Bristol Farms. Philip functioned best in the completely logical world of science where everything behaved according to well understood natural law; the illogical and often petty behavior of humans drove him to distraction. He tried to adapt but after a series of expensive mistakes on his part, he asked the board of directors to let him go back to his research and replace him as CEO with Jacob who had been acting as his understudy for two years. As was the tradition for family members entering the company, Jacob had spent several years working in lesser positions in various parts of the enterprise before being considered for a managerial position and he was still working hard, with long hours, to justify the trust in him shown by his dad and by the board. He had developed a reputation as a work-a-holic and he surprised his staff by spending an entire afternoon with the visiting scholar; even postponing some other meetings. The two young people were attracted to each other but both were so busy that it would be over a year before they met again. Jacob had been invited to speak on organic food production at a conference on food safety which Anne attended. They had dinner after Jacob's speech and both of them stayed at the conference a day longer than either had planned. They shared an appreciation for clean and nutritious food but they also shared an appreciation for each other and within the year, they were married. They were happy from day one but their early married life was frantic for both of them. Anne was finishing up her residency and was putting in extremely long hours; Jacob was equally busy attempting to straighten out problems in the Company that had developed during his Fathers' years as CEO. Philip was, by nature, a trusting person and several company executives had used his trusting nature to carve out private fiefdoms for themselves; Jacob had to establish his authority without driving away or alienating some valuable people.

The first years of their marriage were challenging but troubles of all kinds faded in importance with the birth first of Thomas and three years later of Jennifer Elisabeth. The impending birth of Thomas was the shove needed for Jacob to implement plans he had been working on for a couple of years and establish the Bristol Farms Organic Grassfed Dairy. All of the cows in the dairy would be tested to be certain that they produced only the A2 beta-casein protein. At one time all cows produced A2 milk but at some point a genetic mutation occurred and today many dairy cows produced the A1 variant of this protein. This A1 protein is the compound that causes some people to be unable to digest milk products properly; having only A2 producing cows would be a great marketing tool but also it meant that many more people would be able to enjoy the very real health benefits of their products. Jacob was determined to persuade the state to allow him to sell raw dairy products; the health benefits to the consumer of raw milk products are tremendous but gaining permission to sell them would be an uphill fight. The difficulty comes about, mainly, because the big industrial dairies fear the competition; they know that their milk, as they now produced it, cannot meet health standards without pasteurization and they spend money freely to buy political support and to demonize raw milk. Tommy had his own source of raw organic milk at the moment but the replacement would be ready when his Mother decided it was time for him to be weaned. Jacob and Anne agreed even before they were married that their children would be raised on a diet of organic food but also on grassfed ruminant meat and milk. Anne had spent years studying human nutrition and was a firm believer in the value of meats and animal fats (she was a long time member of the Weston A. Price Foundation); no wimpy vegan diet for her family. They ate very little sugar, very little flour and almost no processed foods; they ate some potatoes and some brown rice but their diet was heavy on animal products, fruits and fresh vegetables. Vegetable oils, except coconut oil and olive oil, were not allowed in her kitchen; most of her cooking was done with lard from pastured hogs, unless she could convince her brother the hunter to share his bear grease. Anne grew up in a family of hunters and starting to hunt again was one of the things that she promised herself that she would do; just as soon as her crazy schedule allowed.

CHAPTER EIGHT
The World Outside

Yoder Farm

Hank graduated from high school and was accepted at Ohio State where he planned to major in agronomy; money was tight right now; oil prices had gone way up and this meant that fertilizer and diesel and pesticides were all higher and they seemed to need more of each of these every year. Hank applied for and got a job on the university farm to help pay for his tuition and expenses. The job started June one so for the first time in years Hank would not be available to help his father farm; Henry assured Hank that when the crops were harvested finances would improve and that he could spend next summer at home. This would be the first time that Hank had been away from home for any prolonged period of time and he was excited and, though torture couldn't make him admit it, a little apprehensive. His roommate turned out to be a tall red headed farm boy from northern Kentucky named Jim Bledsoe; Jim had never met a stranger and he and Hank hit it off from their first meeting. Jim also had a job on the University farm; he would be working at the beef cattle center while Hank worked in horticulture. Given a choice between working at the Horticulture Center and the Row Crop Center, Hank chose horticulture; some of his fondest memories were working with Umpa in the orchard and in the little greenhouse where they started seedlings and grew tomatoes out of season. By the time he was seven, Umpa had taught him to graft fruit and nut trees and he thought he would burst with pride when Umpa told his friends at the feed store that, "Hank here can do orchard work as well as any grown man." Hank looked forward to sharing what he learned with Umpa but had barely gotten settled into the dorm and into his new job when his mother called for him to come home. Umpa had died.

On the bus going back to school, Hank had his first opportunity to reflect on his grandfathers' death; Umpa Yoder was found dead in the orchard. There had been an outbreak of army worms in his corn field south of the orchard and Henry hired a spray plane to apply insecticide to the field; no one thought to tell the pilot about the honey bees. He sprayed poison over the entire orchard where the bees were busy gathering nectar from the clover and alfalfa that Umpa planted between trees to supply nitrogen and act as living mulch. Umpa arrived to find all of his beloved bees dead; he had pulled the tops off of seven of the hives in a desperate search for live bees before suffering a massive heart attack and dying. All of the family was devastated by the death but Hank also felt something else. He felt an undefined but strong uneasiness that things were not right on even a more basic level; it didn't seem logical that so many of the tools they used to grow things, to promote life, should cause death on such a large scale. He wanted to talk to his dad about this feeling but Henry was overcome with grief over his father-in-laws death and carried a terrible weight of guilt over his part in the tragedy. Hank would not be home again until Thanksgiving but he felt a real need to discuss his doubts with his dad.

Back at school Hank was caught up in the rush every new college student feels; between class work, study and work on the farm, the days, and nights, seemed far too short. Most freshmen working at college jobs were limited to fifteen hours of work a week but both Hank and Jim Bledsoe talked their way into getting twenty hours. Jim tried for still more hours; even with classes and study time, he said, "After growing up on a hardscrabble Kentucky hill farm, I feel like I'm on vacation." Hank fretted through the courses required of all freshmen; he was anxious to get to the "important" stuff. Even though, he wasn't excited about English, chemistry or collage algebra, his pride and work ethic forced him to do well in all of his classes. The work in horticulture was a different story; it was fascinating and quickly became his passion. Hank asked for and was assigned to the sustainable agriculture section and it was almost like being back working with his Umpa. He worked under Mr. Scruggs who had been a technician in the horticulture center for many years; Mr. Scruggs and his student helpers were responsible for doing the hands on work required in setting up and carrying through the research projects and teaching demonstrations designed by various scientists. Hank quickly learned that Mr. Scruggs was every bit as demanding as Umpa; there was no "close enough" with Mr. Scruggs; you did it right or, as two students found in the first month, you went somewhere else. Mr. Scruggs didn't have a degree but he was self educated to a high degree and delighted in teaching both the art and the science of his craft to interested young people. Several of the research scientists Hank worked for had been student workers under Mr. Scruggs and the respect these people had for him was evident as they constantly asked for, and usually acted on, his advice. Hank's first year of college passed, it seemed, in the blink of an eye and after a brief visit home, Hank returned to the campus and a summer of full time work. He offered to stay at home and help but his father said that it was more important that he see to his education first.

The following year, Hank went home for Thanksgiving and again for Christmas and both times felt guilty as he would have preferred being back at work in the greenhouse. The atmosphere at home was not good; neither of his parents said anything but it was obvious to Hank that finances were still tight. His dad was drinking more than Hank remembered and, not at all in character for him, was extremely short tempered. Regardless of the topic of conversation, with his father present the subject soon changed to the high costs of farming inputs such as fuel and chemicals or the low prices for corn and soybeans. In one memorable rant after several drinks, Henry declared, "The damn chemical and fertilizer companies are cutting their products with water or sawdust or something so we have to buy more to get the results we've got to have. I used to make a good corn crop with a hundred pounds of actual nitrogen per acre and now it takes at least a hundred and fifty pounds. I think the soil test companies are in it too, I just got the results of the soil tests here on the home place and they say that we need a ton and a half of lime with two hundred pounds of potassium per acre and a bunch of other stuff. This ground has been growing corn for a hundred and fifty years and never needed lime, much less zinc and copper and all the other things that they say we need. If that weren't enough, the companies are saying that weeds are getting resistant to attrazine and 2-4-D and we will have to go to stronger and more expensive herbicides; I think they just want to wring the last dollar out of the farmer and are peddling us trash." Hank decided that this was not the time to talk to his father concerning his doubts about their reliance on herbicides, fungicides and insecticides.

When his dad took him to catch the bus back to school, he stammered as he asked Hank if he thought he could get more working hours. "Things are bound to turn around but right now, I am strapped. Buying bigger equipment has let me work more ground but until I get it paid down, money is going to be tight." Hank told his dad, not to worry; he could handle his school expenses and that he enjoyed his work. It was true that he enjoyed his work; between class work, Mr. Scruggs and his own intelligent curiosity he was learning why the type agriculture practiced by Umpa was so successful. The key was life in the soil; Mr. Scruggs explained how a healthy microbial population in the soil worked to make mineral nutrients available to plant life and at the same time protected plants from soil borne disease. In soils teeming with microbes of many different types, disease organisms did not build up to levels high enough to overwhelm plant immune systems. Well nourished plants growing in the low stress environment of a biologically active soil even resisted attacks from insects. He suggested a list of books for Hank to read and Hank started with *An Agricultural Testament* by Sir Albert Howard. This and other works from the sustainable agriculture section of the library explained why his dad and other conventional farmers were having such a hard time. The practices they were using; tillage, acid salt fertilizers, and pesticides of all kinds were killing off the life in the soil. These same practices were also destroying the organic matter content of the soil which reduced its water and air holding capacity and dramatically reduced productivity. It was widely admitted that the new technology had problems but it was believed by most farmers that, "The answer to the problems of technology is better technology."

Hank didn't go home at all in his junior year; he used the excuse of money being tight, which was true, but mainly he didn't want to be exposed to his fathers' rants. Every time Hank called home to talk to his Mom, he wound up listening to his father rave about the latest injustice that had been carried out against him. The even tempered, optimistic and sweet natured man that Hank knew from years past had become bitter and negative to an extreme. There was another reason Hank was not anxious to leave campus and her name was Jen Beth Bristol. They met as lab partners in a computerized accounting class and were soon spending as much time as possible together; Hank had never met a girl who could so completely captivate him. She was smart, funny and friendly while she radiated kindness and good humor; all of this and she was drop dead gorgeous besides. They spent a lot of time talking and he was surprised to find that she was a farm girl and that her Dad was an organic farmer. He told her about the changes that his Dad had made on the family farm and how the results, that had at first seemed so positive, were now going sour on all fronts. Jen Beth squeezed his hand, "Change is always hard; my grand dad came close to losing the company when he first took over from his father. I am sure that your Dad will get things figured out." Hank surprised himself by blurting out, "He won't get it figured out because he is wrong; farmers are supposed to promote life and he spends most of his time killing!" He immediately was ashamed of his outburst and was stricken at how disloyal it made him sound. Jen Beth didn't say anything; she just held his hand and arm tightly in both of her hands and leaned her head onto his shoulder.

Their senior year was half over and things were much better since Jen Beth was back; she had gone home for the summer and even with constant letters and phone calls, both she and Hank were miserable until she returned. They were both extremely busy; aside from her school work, she was involved as the company representative for the Bristol Farm Chair of Organic Agriculture and Hank was working as many hours as he could get to try to build up a little financial cushion. They plotted constantly on ways to spend time together. His folks had not offered any financial help in two years and Hank was afraid that things were going from bad to worse at home. He was dreading graduation when he would have to return home to help when his Mother called to tell him not to plan on returning to the farm but to look for a job. He tried to argue with her but she cut him off saying that she did not want him to come back that, "There is nothing here for you."

Christmas break was coming up and Jen Beth asked him to spend the time with her and her family in California. He desperately wanted to go but didn't want to tell Jen Beth that he couldn't afford to spend the money for air fare; he had to have enough to live on until he could find a job. She wormed the information out of him and blew it off with, "That is not a problem, Bristol Farms is always looking for bright young people and is happy to pay your way to California for a job interview; spending Christmas with me is just a bonus."

CHAPTER NINE
New Beginning

The plane banked into a sharp turn and dropped out of the low hanging cloud deck, lining up for a landing at San Francisco International, and giving Hank who Jen Beth had insisted take her window seat, a spectacular view of San Francisco Bay. They had been on the plane nearly five hours but Hank was far from bored; it was rare that he had Jen Beth to himself for more than a couple of hours and he was enjoying the opportunity. Very reluctantly Hank had broached the subject of whether Bristol Farms really needed a kid fresh out of college or if he was being given special treatment. He knew that Jen Beth came from big money, you don't endow a chair at a major university out of the butter and egg money, but they had never really talked about the scope of Bristol Farms business. "Hank, I haven't discussed Bristol Farms with you like I should have; I have tried to broach the subject a couple of times and it always comes out sounding like braggadocio. Bristol Farms is starting a major expansion and will probably hire between fifteen and twenty management trainees in the next six months. Dad has taken the company into just about every aspect of organic foods; the company produces a wide range of organic products and is growing rapidly in processing and distribution. We have our own marketing division, we are starting a division to manufacture vitamins and supplements and are expanding our research and development division; the company needs bright young people. Romancing the boss's daughter gains you points with her but you will have to earn a position in the company." Hank had a sudden moment of panic, "Lord, Jen Beth, have you told your folks about us?" Jen Beth patted the back of his hand, "No, Silly, but my mother has known almost from the start; she has always been able to read me like a book. Dad knows but doesn't want to know." Hank had been nervous about meeting Jen Beth's parents; now he was absolutely terrified!

Things went smoothly once they were on the ground; they collected their luggage and exited the secure portion of the terminal with no problems. Hank would have known Jen Beth's parents even without an introduction; her mother was a mature exact copy of Jen Beth and her fathers' face lit up like a neon sign when he saw his daughter coming toward him. Jen Beth hugged both her parents before turning to Hank; she took his hand and said, "Mother, Dad this is Hank Weaver and I hope you like him because I am crazy in love with him and am going to marry him if he will have me." Hanks jaw flew open and he stammered several meaningless syllables before managing; "Mr. Bristol, Dr. Bristol – I am very happy to meet you." Dr. Bristol looked on with an amused expression on her face and Jacob looked slightly stunned as Jen Beth recaptured Hank's hand and rose up on tiptoes to kiss him on the ear.

"I just thought I would get that out of the way so we could enjoy the holidays without playing guessing games."

Hank recovered quickly from his nervousness; the Bristol's could not have been more gracious or more anxious to put him at ease. They were gathered in the living room of the sprawling ranch style house where Jen Beth grew up; Jacob poured white wine for Anne and Jen Beth and asked Hank what he would like. Hank answered, "A beer would be good if you have it." Which produced an ice cold Tecate and a chilled mug. Jacob had been questioning Hank about his life on the farm and Hank surprised himself by responding to the questions freely and in depth. "My grandfather was very old fashioned in his farming philosophy and operated a much diversified farm. He had a few dairy cows, a few beef cows, a few sows and even a few ewes along with laying hens and poultry of all kinds. He did not believe in selling hay or grain; all of the hay and nearly all of the grain produced was marketed through the livestock. Even blemished fruit from the orchard and damaged or excess garden produce went to feed the livestock; one of my chores as a kid was to chop apples and turnips into pieces so the cows wouldn't swallow them whole and choke. Grand Dad followed a six year rotation plan on the whole farm; a plot would be in pasture (alfalfa plus grass and clover) for four years before being plowed down and seeded to corn for one year followed by winter wheat and then beans before being seeded once again to pasture. He saved seed from all his own crops and did not buy any fertilizer but he treasured the manure produced by his animals like misers hoard gold. The rotation and grazing reduced weed pressure to the point that one trip through a crop with a cultivator plus a little hoeing was usually all that was needed for weed control. Grand Dad didn't sell a lot of dollars worth of product but I can see now that he didn't spend but very little so the margin of return on what he did sell was good.

When my Dad took over and put everything into cash crops, we made a lot more production with more crop acres plus corn yields per acre went up with the added fertilizer and hybrid seed. Soybean yields went up as well with new varieties but input costs climbed even faster and we had financial problems almost from the start. At first we thought it was just the cost of new and bigger equipment but even when the equipment was paid down expenses just kept rising; Dad is working himself to death and getting in worse financial shape every year. I had always planned to go back to the farm but that is not going to be possible now." Jacob said, "Don't be too hard on your Dad; most of the farmers in the Country are having the exact same problems. The economics of farming in the industrial mode are basically flawed with way too much capital being put at risk given the potential for profit. This has a lot, maybe most, farmers in financial trouble. It is not widely recognized but damage that is even worse than the financial plight is being done by what is happening to our soils, to our people and to our rural communities. We can return our soils to a healthy state, if we start before they are eroded down to bed rock; we can produce food that is truly nutritious and so began to reverse some of the health problems of our people but one of the hardest things to reverse will be the loss of people and infrastructure from the farm areas. Small towns all over the U.S. are losing population and drying up; we are losing the schools and churches but also we are losing the little family run meat processors and the hatcheries and the Mom and Pop feed and seed stores. We have shown that organic farming can be successful on a large scale but it will be very difficult to reverse the concentration and centralization of processing, distribution and marketing. It would be a formidable task without active opposition but it will be even harder because of the collusion between government regulators and large corporations. Regulations have become one of the largest expense generators in both production and processing of foods; Bristol Farms is large enough that we have people that do nothing but monitor regulations and make certain that we are in compliance. It is expensive for us but for small operators it is an impossible burden. I have never been a fan of conspiracy theories but the level of inbreeding between some large agriculture related companies and the government agencies set to regulate them is frightening. Stories are all too common about how some bureaucrat or congressman forced through regulation favorable to a particular company and was soon thereafter named senior vice-president of the company. I apologize. You kids just got here and I spend our first evening together moaning about the state of the world; let's talk about more pleasant things." Hank interjected, "I don't know about Jen Beth and Dr. Bristol but I am very interested in this conservation. I have watched what has happened to my family and to our land; Dad has done what the experts recommended, worked his heart out doing it, and it has been disaster for the health of the land, for his financial health and for the well being of all of the people involved. Every day at the University we are bombarded with the concept that we must adopt all the new technology in order to "feed the world". I know that production is important but if the farmers can't make a living, who is going to feed the world when they all go bankrupt?"

Next morning Hank awoke early as usual and after a quick shower and a close shave, followed the smell of fresh coffee to the kitchen where he found Dr. Bristol and Jacob at the table drinking coffee and reading the morning newspapers. Dr. Bristol said, "Good morning Hank, sit down and I will get you some coffee." "Please Dr. Bristol, let me wait on myself." "OK, provided that you will call me Anne and old grumpy bear over there Jacob." Jacob looked at Hank over the top of his paper and winked, "I am only grumpy before my first cup of coffee and I don't know whether it is a blessing or a curse that both of the females in my life wake up disgustingly perky and cheerful." "It is a blessing like everything about your females", said Jen Beth as she swept into the room and proceeded to kiss her Mother, her Father and Hank in that order. "Well I am glad to have that question settled; your Mother and I both have to work today. What are you and Hank going to do?" "Hank has a three o'clock appointment with Mrs. Wilcox of the personnel department and I thought we might do a quick tour of the farms and other facilities that are close bye before we have lunch at Jin's; I haven't had really good sea food since last summer."

After breakfast, Hank and Jen Beth took her elderly Volkswagen Beetle and started up coast so Jen Beth could, "Show him where it all started." They crossed the Golden Gate Bridge and followed Highway 101 to its intersection with Highway 37 which they followed east until they crossed the Petaluma River; Jen Beth turned north on a gravel road and stopped where the road crossed a flowing creek. She pointed to a discrete metal sign that said, "Bristol Farms – Unit 1". "My great- great-great-grandfather founded Bristol Farms in 1849 when he bought this sixty acre tract. He partnered with the Jin family who, according to family legend, saved his life when he was attacked by thugs. Eventually both he and the Jin family outgrew this farm so he bought out their interest and both families moved to larger farms in the Petaluma and Napa valleys. The Jin family and Bristol Farms are the largest organic farmers in the area. They got a great start selling produce to the gold rushers; aside from a few people that found (and managed to keep) really big strikes, the people who made out best during the rush were the people selling what the miners had to have. A sack of dry beans sold for a small fortune and for fresh eggs or ripe tomatoes you could name your own price. The boom years didn't last long but when they did end, old Tom Bristol used the money he made during the gold rush to accumulate a lot of prime land."

They started back so as to have time for Jen Beth's seafood lunch before Hank was due for his interview. "Kevin Jin was several grades ahead of me in school and he turned out to be kind of the black sheep of his family; he majored in business in college and then went to chef school instead of into the family farming operation. Jin Farms loss was our gain though; Kevin serves the best food in this part of the world: wild caught seafood just hours out of the ocean, grassfed lamb and beef, pastured pork and chicken and fresh local vegetables. Everything he serves is organic and he does a lot of the cooking himself; you will like

Kevin but you will love his food!" Hank did like Kevin but was a little surprised that instead of the slightly built Chinese man he expected, Kevin turned out to be an NFL linebacker type at six feet three inches and two hundred and forty pounds; evidently organic food grows big kids. The food was just as good as Jen Beth promised and half way through the courses she ordered for them Hank began to worry that he would not be able to stay awake for his job interview. They made it to Bristol Farms Headquarters, where the interview was to take place, in time for Hank to walk around the block and he felt reasonably alert when he was ushered into Mrs. Wilcox's office. The interview was comprehensive and wide ranging; many of the questions obviously designed to see how well he could "think on his feet." Mrs. Wilcox questioned him about his life before college and seemed very interested as he described growing up on his grandfathers' "old fashioned" farm. She was impressed that he had worked his way through school and she complimented him on his grades. The position he was applying for was that of management trainee and Hank was pleasantly surprised when Mrs. Wilcox went over the starting salary and benefit package. She asked when he would be able to start and smiled when he said, "Just as soon as I can get back out here after graduation." Mrs. Wilcox gave him her office telephone number and said that if he would call between 2:00 and 3:00 pm tomorrow, she should be able to tell him whether or not he had a job.

Jen Beth was waiting for him in the outer office when he came out from the interview; Hank was ninety-nine percent sure that he would get the job but – just to be ornery – he put on a long face and a doleful attitude when he came through the door. Jen Beth looked up with a big smile that, when she saw his face, turned suddenly into a thin lipped mask of fierce resolve as she jumped up and headed for the inner offices. Hank caught her around the waist and pulled her back frantically telling her, "Whoa, whoa I was just teasing; everything is alright!" Jen Beth relaxed and stepped back and then reversing the motion, popped him solidly in the gut with a hard little fist. "Don't do things like that; you had me ready to snatch a senior vice president of the company bald-headed." She pulled his head down for a kiss and added, "Anybody that messes with my man will answer to me."

They spent the rest of the afternoon in the swimming pool at Jen Beth's' home where they learned that cold water does not necessarily cool ardor. They broke off the hedonistic interlude in time to shower, dress and, as a team, have supper almost ready when her folks came in from work. Around the dinner table the atmosphere was warm and the conversation was easy. Jacob asked what the kids had planned for tomorrow and when he learned that they had no solid plans, suggested that they attend the annual conference of the American Association for Sustainable Agriculture. "It kicks off in the morning at 10:00 o'clock in the old convention center and a close friend of mine will be delivering the keynote address; I think both of you will benefit by hearing Tony Hardeman. He was a died in the wool technology promoter for many years; sure that agriculture would never have another bad day just as soon as we figured out the right combinations of fertilizers, pesticides and hybrid crops for each farm. He was one of the strongest supporters of industrial agriculture, the whole

Green Revolution thing, until the scientist in him forced him to see that what is considered conventional agriculture today is built on a false premise; agriculture is not an industrial process and cannot be successfully operated as one. We can use technology to better understand nature and to better work with nature but it is a fool's game to attempt to use technology to control nature. Giving up old beliefs, things he not only believed but taught to thousands of students, was very hard for Tony; I had two courses under him in college and was very flattered when he came to me as one of the people to help him form his new beliefs. That was fifteen years or more ago and we have remained good friends ever since. This conference is a good opportunity for the two of you to hear Tony; I guarantee you will get a lot out of the experience. We buy a block of tickets to the conference every year for any of our people that want to attend and it is always worthwhile."

Next morning, Jen Beth and Hank left the house in plenty of time to stop by Bristol Farms headquarters for tickets and still be early for the start of the program. They wandered through the trade show where certified organic seeds and fertilizers and all kinds of products useful to organic farmers were on display; for the purists, there was even a section devoted to harness and horse drawn farm equipment. They had the good fortune to happen onto Dr. Hardeman as he too was surveying the goods on offer and Jen Beth took the opportunity to introduce herself and Hank. "My Dad had some things that he had to do this morning but said that he would do his best to see you before you go back; Hank and I are to take notes and report back." "Miss Bristol, with you growing up as the daughter of Anne and Jacob Bristol, I would be amazed if you could not give my speech at least as well as me. Your parents were, and still are, both tremendously helpful to me as I struggle to understand reality. I literally had to junk multitudes of things that "I knew" to be true and completely rebuild my belief system. Looking back, I wonder how I could have been so illogical but at the time it was hard to make the change." "Well, Dad says that you have one of the best minds involved in agriculture and that we should pay attention when you speak." Other people were stopping to speak with Dr. Hardeman so Jen Beth and Hank said their goodbyes and started back to get seats in the auditorium.

CHAPTER TEN

The Natural Way

"Ladies and Gentlemen welcome to the sixth annual conference of the American Association for Sustainable Agriculture; my name is Larry Hildebrandt and I am the current president of AASA. We have an outstanding program this year with thirty-two experts in various fields of sustainable agriculture presenting programs over the next three days. We also have the largest trade show in our history with sixty venders show casing their products; I urge you to visit the trade show and patronize the venders as it is their contributions that allow us to present conferences at what, I think you will agree, is a very affordable price.

We are fortunate this year to have as our keynote speaker Dr. Anthony Hardeman, Professor Emeritus at the University of Northern Missouri. Dr. Hardeman spent many years as head of the agronomy department at UNM and was an early day proponent of what is now called the "Green Revolution." After seeing some of the long term results of this industrialization of agriculture, Dr. Hardeman begin to question the science behind this program; the program that has brought more change to agriculture in a few years than had occurred in its' entire previous history. He now devotes full time to promoting and teaching methods of agriculture that are, in contrast to the industrial format, productive, profitable and sustainable. It is with great pleasure that I present to you Dr. Anthony Hardeman."

"Thank you, Mr. Hildebrandt and thank you also to AASA for inviting me to speak to your conference. I would like to start my remarks by giving a brief history of what has been called the "Green Revolution".

In the 1940's famine began to once again rear its ugly head in many parts of the world; there was an urgent need to increase food production worldwide. From the mid thirties to the mid forties agriculture in many places had been neglected due to the necessities of war; world food production was not keeping up with demand and people were suffering. The end of the Second World War brought about two other situations that radically changed the practice of agriculture: a surplus of manufacturing capacity in both the machinery and the chemical industries, and a severe shortage of rural workers. Many rural workers did not return to the farm after being in the military or working wartime factory jobs and the resulting farm labor shortage created demand for increased mechanization of agriculture. Manufacturing plants that had been engaged in building tanks and artillery pieces were converted to produce tractors and farm equipment of all types and farm production was mechanized at a rapid pace. With the war and its demand for large amounts of explosives ending, a surplus of ammonia and other nitrogen products was created; this excess was channeled into the production of nitrogen fertilizers which, for the first time in history, became cheap in relation to the prices of agricultural commodities. The availability of modern machinery and cheap fertilizer caused a boom in food production in those developed countries whose economies had not been destroyed by war; much of the world, however, was not economically in position to take advantage of the new technologies. The scientific community begin to study ways to increase food production in areas like Mexico and India where population had out grown the capacity to produce food but the local economies could not support heavy mechanization. They felt that the greatest need in making these areas more productive was for improved varieties of food crops that could utilize the newly available nitrogen fertilizer. The scientists concentrated on the breeding of such crops while adding other seemingly beneficial characteristics at the same time. One of the traits deemed important by the scientific team was the ability to utilize large amounts of nitrogen fertilizer without lodging, growing too tall and falling over, as many of the old varieties of food grains did in the presence of abundant fertilizer and water. To address this problem, they bred (using genetic mutations induced by chemicals and radiation) dwarf varieties of grain crops; as a part of this project they selected plants that devoted a larger percentage of the products of photosynthesis (the process that plants use to convert CO_2 into starches and sugars) to seed production and less to stem and below ground structures. We know now that this redistribution of energy also reduced the amount of nutrients supplied by the plants to the micro life in the soil by plant root exudates; this reduction decreased the amount and vigor of the soil biology reducing natural soil productivity and stability. A third trait emphasized was insensitivity to day length; most of the older food crop varieties were adapted to growth in a relatively narrow range of day length so that they could not be readily moved to areas with different lengths of daylight. Inserting this lack of sensitivity to length of day trait and the wide use of the dwarf genetics led to plants with very similar genetic makeup being produced over wide areas. We lost a lot of the genetic diversity that had in the past prevented disease out breaks from spreading over large regions. There were other modifications of plant characteristics as well with all of them designed to make plants more productive when ample water and high rates of fertilizer were applied. The initial results were little short of astounding; in a few years Mexico became self sufficient in grain production and India, while slower because they had farther to go, soon did the same.

For ten or fifteen years, the world saw tremendous growth in the production of food and fiber crops and the prices of these commodities fell as they became more abundant. This drop in commodity prices caused severe financial disruption in areas where small scale peasant farming made up a large part of food production. In most cases, the small scale farmer could not be profitable at the lower prices and many of them were forced out of agriculture and into city slums; this occurred in many different countries and while the human misery was regretted, replacing small farmers with larger more efficient operations was, on balance, considered a good thing.

Today, we are seeing very disturbing and unintended effects of the cultural practices that brought about the large increases in production. Soil organic matter content has plummeted everywhere acid-salt fertilizers have been used heavily; in far too many places the organic matter accumulations of thousands of years have been burned up in one generation. With the organic matter gone, soils lose tilth (the physical structure that allows them to take in both water and air). They also lose the ability to store large amounts of water and perhaps most important of all, they lose all soil life. It is soil life that is responsible for breaking down rock into plant available minerals; it is also soil life that holds mineral nutrients in organic forms that do not leach out into the ground water or tie up chemically. Soil life is the primary source of soil productivity; healthy and complex soil biology is also the first line of defense against both plant diseases and insect pests. With nitrogen fertilizer both abundant and cheap and chemical pesticides like DDT available, agriculture changed completely; in the eyes of many agriculture became an industrial instead of a biological endeavor. Problems occurred almost at once but the prevailing belief was "We need better technology." In less than a generation, agricultural scientists replaced centuries of accumulated knowledge with a totally new concept of what constitutes good agricultural practice. The results of this transition have been tragic. In the name of efficiency, farmers have been urged to specialize in one or two crops rather than using the synergistic mixture of crops and livestock that was traditional. Soil is too often treated as merely a medium useful to hold water and applied mineral nutrients rather than as the complex association of minerals, organic matter and living organisms that is capable of great productivity; such healthy and stable soil is vital to our very survival. Under continuous tillage, heavy chemical usage and no livestock presence, organic matter content is lost from soil. It is not only organic content that is lost under this management; several years ago the USDA estimated that for every bushel of corn produced in the United States, two bushels of soil is lost to erosion. For many years this loss was concealed by higher inputs of chemical fertilizers and by the development of more productive hybrid crops. Crop yields even increased under this regime which made its' menace even harder to recognize. We have been particularly poorly served by the scientific community that has "proven" the short term benefit of each new chemical, more expensive machine or entire new technology with little regard for their long term effects. It is absolutely imperative that we reverse the trend of the past forty years and re-shape agriculture into the biological endeavor that it was, at least for good farmers, for thousands of years. To do less is to threaten the very existence of our environment, our way of life and our people. Thank you for your attention; that concludes my prepared remarks but I understand we will have a question and answer session at this time. Is that the plan Mr. Hildebrandt?"

"That is correct Doctor. If you would like to ask Dr. Hardeman a question, hold up your hand and one of our volunteers will bring you a microphone. Yes down here to my left."

"Dr. Hardeman, I am a journalist not a farmer but I fail to see how changing from manure to chemical fertilizer could be as damaging as you have described. It is my understanding that minerals have to be in an inorganic form like the chemical fertilizers to be usable to plants."

"That is basically correct; but when they are in high concentration, these inorganic plant available forms are toxic to both plants and soil life; the problem is not the form of the material but the high salt concentrations of high analysis chemical fertilizers. Minerals held in organic compounds whether from manure, compost or soil humus are released in plant available forms slowly and uniformly by the actions of bacteria and other soil life. Nutrients are broken out of the organic compounds and re-mineralized (converted to the plant available form) at a rate that allows most of the material to be taken up by plants rather than building toxic concentrations or being lost to leaching. Elemental nitrogen for instance makes up seventy eight percent of our atmosphere but this form of nitrogen is totally inert; reactive forms (forms able to combine with other elements) of nitrogen are very rare in the natural world and in concentration are toxic to most life forms. When highly available nitrogen fertilizers are applied, they kill off the organisms nature utilizes to fix nitrogen from the air as well as the ones involved in releasing nitrogen from organic compounds. Researchers at Mississippi State University found that as little as sixteen pounds of actual nitrogen, applied as acid- salt fertilizer, will kill off all of the rhizobia (the bacteria that fix nitrogen in symbiosis with legumes) in an acre of sandy soil. These materials also burn up soil organic matter which is a prime source of mineral nutrients of all kinds in a healthy soil and is also largely responsible for the development and retention of favorable physical structure (tilth) in soil. By applying chemical nitrogen instead of manure or other organic material, we are both starving and poisoning the life in the soil that is critical to healthy productive soil. To give an extreme example of the effects of nitrogen fertilizers on soil, during the Second World War cement was in short supply in China, army engineers injected large amounts of anhydrous ammonia into clay soils and packed it to produce air field landing strips capable of handling the largest airplanes; they turned living soil into a lifeless substitute for concrete."

"Dr. Hardeman, I am a farmer and would like very much to get away from using chemicals of any sort; I don't like their effects on the environment but I cannot afford the cost of the organic materials used to replace them. How can I do away with chemicals and stay in business?"

"This is a great question because it goes straight to the heart of the conundrum. Let me answer your question with some more questions: How did the buffalo and other wild graziers survive the winter on frost killed grass without protein supplements? How did native grasslands thrive without fertilizer and with no one spreading poisons why did pests such as grasshoppers and weeds not take over the natural world?

The buffalo didn't need supplements because they adapted genetically so that their needs were fulfilled by what was available. Their young were not born until weeks after green pasture was available and the females had regained condition lost during a winter on poor quality forage. Milk production was limited in both amount and duration to an amount just sufficient to get the calves to the point that they were effective ruminants and able to flourish on a diet of forage. They also developed the ability to consume more forage than they needed when feed conditions were good and store the excess as body fat to be used when conditions were poor. Contrast this with what is considered good management today: big, heavy milking cows selected to have very little body fat are bred to calve in the winter so that they will wean big calves in the fall. To stay in decent body condition all winter while producing the desired amount of milk, the cows must be heavily supplemented with not only protein but also with energy. Aside from the expense, calving in the winter is hazardous to the health of both the cow and the calf. Did you ever see any baby animal born with a winter hair coat?

I know that it seems that I have wandered away from the topic of your question but in truth I have not. We will not be successful if we merely replace conventional fertilizers and pesticides with organic materials. We must design our programs to do away with the need for these inputs; we must replace money with management. To get away from buying fertilizers, we must encourage the conditions that build soil fertility; most important of which is high biological activity both in and on the soil. To build soil fertility we must: reduce tillage to an absolute minimum, bring animals back into the equation and reduce the loss of nutrients to soil erosion, to leaching and to exportation of nutrient dense products. If you sell 1000 pounds of beef, you sell 820 pounds of water, some carbon, hydrogen, oxygen and nitrogen that can all come free from the air but only small amounts of minerals like calcium, phosphorus and potassium; if you sell enough hay to produce 1000 pounds of beef, you ship off at least ten to twelve times as much of your mineral fertility. The Argentines for many years raised excellent grain crops by using a program where land would be planted to legume based pasture and grazed for four or five years before being plowed down and planted to crops for two seasons. This greatly reduced weed, insect and disease problems while producing fertile soil for crops and excellent – and very profitable – beef. The question should not be how to replace the chemical fertilizer and pesticide but rather how to change conditions on the land so that these things are not needed."

"Dr. Hardeman, I have read extension publications that state that the fertilizer value of manure is so low that it is not worth hauling to the field. Would you comment on this?"

"I would indeed; this is the perfect example of what I call "Mule blinder" science; you know the things they put on mules and horses so that they can only see what is straight in front of them. It is the inability of some people to see that, quite frequently, the whole is greater than the sum of its components. For many years we have operated on the theory that if we can reduce anything that we need to understand to its smallest components and then study each part, we can learn all there is to know. This is not unlike saying we can gain all the knowledge in the encyclopedia if we know all about the letters of the alphabet that make up the words in the articles. There is a great deal more to manure than just so many pounds of minerals; how those minerals are arranged in compounds and the relationships between these compounds and all of the life forms present determines the availability and the value of the minerals to the soil-plant-animal complex. The real value of manure is the life it contains along with the materials needed to sustain that life. Perhaps the greatest flaw of modern agriculture has been its failure to recognize the value of soil organic matter and the life that it promotes. The value of manure is one of those questions that would be very easy to answer; just put manure on one plot and the equivalent amounts of minerals, in inorganic forms, on another plot and see what happens over time. I rather doubt that any fertilizer company would want to sponsor that research but it is imperative that we find economically feasible ways to restore organic content to our soils. Today we find that, largely because of low organic matter content, many of our soils are dead and unable to perform their function as water reservoirs; crop production is severely limited but even worse, both floods and droughts are more common and more severe."

"I hate to break this up, it is fascinating but it is time for us to move into the various lecture rooms for the scheduled ten o'clock programs. Dr. Hardeman, thank you so much for your message and for your many contributions to sustainable agriculture."

As the applause slackened and people began moving out of the hall, Jen Beth and Hank left their seats and moved to intercept Dr. Hardeman as he left the podium and started toward the lobby. They waited in the aisle for him to approach and just as he acknowledged them with a smile, a young man stepped up to Dr. Hardeman and said, "Dr. Hardeman, my name is Roger Gordon and I write for The Sustainable Farmer magazine; would you be agreeable to spending a little time in an interview for an article?" "I've read your work Roger and I will make a deal with you. If my young friends here can join us and if you will get me a cup of coffee from the pot over there, I will take a minute to make a pit stop in the men's room and then meet you at that grouping of chairs right over there in the lobby." Roger Gordon introduced himself to Jen Beth and Hank and asked if they wanted anything from the refreshment bar. "Some coffee would be good." said Jen Beth "But let us go with you and carry our own." They got coffee and moved over to the chair grouping just as Dr. Hardeman arrived. "Thank you Roger, they make good coffee here and my caffeine level was getting low; what would you like to talk about?"

"Dr. what do you see as the biggest problem facing American agriculture today?"

"That is an easy one Rodger, for American agriculture and for agriculture worldwide the greatest threat is the widely accepted concept that we can industrialize agriculture and replace natural law and natural processes with technology. An example; a few years ago some soil testing labs quit measuring soil organic matter content on the premise that there was no feasible way to increase it and that the beneficial effects of soil organic content could be duplicated with technology. When our academics, our supposedly educated people, take such short sighted positions, we are in big trouble. I am afraid that we have produced an entire generation of scientists and farmers that no longer understand that agriculture is a biological endeavor; that we are dealing with life. Agriculture should be the art and science of promoting life so that we can use some of the energy that is surplus to the needs of the system for our own uses."

"I have heard you on other occasions say that technology has created more problems than it has solved. Can you give me an illustration of what you mean?"

"Again an easy one; we spend our resources on fighting what we don't want instead of on encouraging what we do want. In our zeal to eliminate pests; weeds, insects, and pathogens, we have killed off beneficial organisms along with the pests. We have lost much of the biological diversity that once held pest organisms in check; today, diseases of plants and animals, insect pests and weeds are all more prevalent than ever before. The use of pesticides has increased many fold while crop losses to pests have actually gone up; our water supplies, our soils and our foodstuffs, and yes our bodies, are now contaminated with these poisons. We could go on and on listing currently recommended practices that offer short term gains that must be paid for with long term costs. We must learn to look at the long term consequences of our actions."

"Do you see situations that could give rise to acute disruptions of our food supplies?

"Oh yes, the drive toward plant uniformity has brought about a reduction in the genetic diversity of major crops to the point that within a crop like corn, soy, wheat and rice all individual plants share a great many common genes and so are very vulnerable to catastrophic losses from outbreaks of mutant disease organisms. One malevolent mutant gene in any one of the four main food crops (like the southern corn blight that struck several years ago) could bring about famine on a scale that the world has never before seen. The southern corn blight affected only a portion of the national corn crop because at that time corn had a much wider genetic base; with the loss of that diversity, such a mutation could easily be catastrophic."

"Dr. what is your feeling about the practice of using genetic engineering to create new plants and animals?"

"The use of genetic engineering to create organisms resistant to particular pesticides is an excellent example of technology being utilized for short-term economic gain with very little understanding of the total and long term effects of these actions. For years we have been assured that genetic modified plants are completely safe and just as nutritious and that the pesticides in question break down completely in the soil and pose no dangers; it is obvious today that we have been badly misled. The scientific literature is full of examples of maladies ranging from more virulent forms of known diseases of both plants and animals to loss of soil fertility to totally new diseases; some of these new diseases are caused by pathogens that we have yet to identify but that are beyond doubt associated with the GMO pesticide resistant plant material/ pesticide combination. We do not know the long term effects of the chemicals that we use so freely much less the effects of the chemicals when combined with plants designed to be tolerant to these poisons. We are learning a little; we know now that glyphosate, the active ingredient in Roundup, does not break down in the soil as we have been told. The reason this poison does not appear in soil tests is that it binds to soil minerals which disguises its chemical signature. The minerals present in this combination are no longer available to plants. The so called Roundup Ready plants have had their genetic makeup tinkered with so that they can exist without certain minerals that are necessary for plant growth; hardly a trait likely to improve either nutritional value or plant well being. Reams of information are available in both academic publications and the popular press detailing serious problems for people, animals, plants and the soil caused by this technology. This information is available to anyone who can do a web search and yet the use of these materials increases every year.

Perhaps most disturbing of all, a new and virulent pathogen, that affects both plants and animals, has appeared where glyphosate has been used on genetically modified plants. We do not know what this organism is much less how to control it. The reaction of the chemical industry: "There is no proof that this pathogen has anything to do with us." The longer glyphosate has been used in an area, the more evidence of these and other maladies but Big Chem still screams, "No proof." While glyphosate is perhaps the most widely used chemical toxin, it is only one of a multitude of similar compounds in daily use worldwide.

The dangers of radical technology are made worse by the incestuous relationships common between the companies promoting technology and the agencies charged with protecting the common interests. Equally disturbing is the fact that much agricultural research is paid for by companies seeking approval of some product or technology; in 1961, the dean of agriculture of a major Midwest university made the statement, supposedly in jest, that "For two hundred and fifty thousand dollars, we can prove anything." In many cases, we literally have set the fox to guard the henhouse."

"Are there other practices of modern agriculture where you see a pressing need to change?"

"The last forty years or so has seen a development in agricultural practice that has never before been attempted on a large scale; we have taken animals out of agriculture. The concentration of livestock in factory style units has created waste disposal nightmares while robbing the soil of the nutrients and organic matter in the manures; the material that once formed the backbone of sustainable soil productivity by nurturing healthy populations of soil organisms has been turned into, at best, a waste product and more commonly pollution. These confinement units create hideous living conditions for the animals necessitating constant use of antibiotics to suppress disease to sub acute levels and give rise to health damaging working conditions for the human workers. This wide spread low level use of antibiotics is at least partially responsible for the explosion of pathogens resistant to antibiotics and the increase in hard to control diseases in humans. Bringing animals back to the farm is one of the most beneficial things that we could do for a number of reasons."

"Do you see any signs that main stream agriculture is ready to make the transition back to its biological roots?"

"Sadly, I do not; it will require a lot of education, and I am afraid some catastrophes, to convince people to change. In the new order, soil erosion, frequent drought and flood incidents and outbreaks of pests and diseases are seen as solely natural occurrences while the truth is that these phenomena are greatly influenced by the degradation of the soil and by the loss of biological diversity brought on by the practices of "modern agriculture". The cost, both financial and ecological, of the high input technology and its' inherent instability has reduced the farmer to second class economic status where at one time he was the number one generator of new wealth. The industrialization of agriculture has been a failure by any reasonable set of criteria that takes into account its' true cost to society. We must realize that biological capital, which I define as healthy soil supporting healthy and complex populations of plants and animals that are made up of healthy individuals, is at least as valuable as fiscal capital.

Dr. Hardeman, thank you; if I cannot turn these notes into a great article, I need to turn in my scribblers' license!

Gordon shook hands all around and left to write his article while the interview was fresh on his mind. Dr Hardeman invited Jen Beth and Hank to stay and visit awhile and after Jen Beth gathered up cups and brought more coffee, the three of them resumed the discussion. Hank led off with, "Dr. Hardeman, how would you go about restoring, in a financially viable way, a property that has been farmed conventionally for a number of years?" Dr Hardeman thought a moment, "Start by analyzing the conditions present on the property; these conditions should include the physical attributes: water availability, fencing, buildings and equipment and complete soil data but they must also include the condition of human resources. What is the financial picture of the operation? How capable and motivated is management? What labor is available and how good is it? Only by doing this inventory can you know what you have to work with; trying to force a particular program of production in a situation where it is unsuited will drastically reduce your chances of being successful. The purpose of this initial survey is to decide on a plan of action that makes the best uses of the available resources at the same time that it brings improvement to the weaknesses of the operation. Finally, what do you want to achieve with the operation? If I lay out a program designed to build long term ecological health, what I call biological capital, this is not likely to suit the desires of someone who is interested in maximizing short term gains. The logical way to approach any project is to decide what you want to accomplish and then decide how to best use the resources available to meet your goal." Jen Beth spoke up, "That sounds a lot like Holistic Management as put forth by Allan Savory." "That is exactly what it is; if you haven't, the first step should be to read Holistic Management by Savoy and Butterfield. One of the most powerful concepts put forth in Holistic Management is that success is greatly affected by how skillfully the resources of thought, labor and money are apportioned out to the various aspects of the operation. In contrast to the currently popular theory of "best management practices" where success is seen to be the result of having the best soil fertility program and the best weed control program, etc. etc. A more rational approach is to use resources at the place and time where they will yield the best results. To make this work, we must know what it is we are trying to achieve; we must have goals that we can measure results against. Everyone's goals will be different but terms like sustainable profitability and good quality of life and making the land healthier will come up a lot. Conventional agriculture practices driven by production and concentrating on bushels of corn per acre or pounds of calf weaned, without consideration of profitability and sustainability, are not apt to produce good long term results.

Like always, I get wound up and deliver lectures instead of advice; the short form is use the resources available in the ways that will produce the results you need to restore the farm. The biggest problem will usually be low soil organic content and low soil life. The fastest and most financially feasible way that I know to cure these maladies is pasture grazed at high stock densities. These corn belt soils developed when grasslands were grazed for thousands of years by herds of grazing animals; the animals stayed in herds for protection from predators and so had to move constantly so all members of the herd could get enough feed. These conditions produced grasslands with a wide diversity of plant species with high productivity and with healthy soil beneath them. If you can mimic the behavior of those herds, a large number of animals on a small area for a short period of time followed by a period of no grazing, you can produce beef- milk- lamb- whatever profitably and heal the soil at the same time. Jen Beth, Hank, I have thoroughly enjoyed this but I have a meeting in a few minutes and must leave you. Please give my best to your parents as I probably will not get a chance to see them this trip."

As Jen Beth and Hank started back to their car, he said, "I knew what he was going to say but had to ask. It will be over Dad's dead body that cattle ever return to Yoder Farm. I think it is fruitless but I am going to run some numbers and play "what if" and see if I can find a way to get Dad off the chemical treadmill."

At two fifteen, Hank called Mrs. Wilcox and found that he did indeed have a job starting a week after graduation.

CHAPTER ELEVEN
A Philosophy Forms

Petaluma River Delta 1850

Thomas Bristol straightened up rubbing his aching back and thought, "That is it; I am not going to use this damn tool of the devil another day!" The offending object was a heavy bladed weeding hoe with a fourteen inch handle that the Jins used one handed; stooping over all day didn't seem to bother them but it was about to kill Thomas. He promised himself that before starting work in the morning, he would find something to make a proper length handle for this hoe so that he could use it standing up. Thomas had asked Jin Li the reason for the short handles and was told, "It is the custom." That remark was one of the few from his new friends that seemed illogical to Thomas. Most of the things the Jins did made excellent sense; they were very good farmers but the short handle hoe was one custom he was going to break. With use, Thomas's Cantonese was improving; he and Jin Li were able to carry on a normal, if odd sounding, conversation in mixed English and Cantonese. It was harder for Thomas to converse with Jin Tan; the old man had almost no English but Thomas found him fascinating to talk with. Once, when they were eating their mid day meal at the edge of the field; Thomas commented that he wished they had some poison that they could spread and kill all of the squash bugs instead of having to pick them off one at a time to keep the little bastards from eating their squash plants. At a query from Jin Tan, Jin Li translated this remark into Cantonese. Jin Tan was silent a moment before giving a reply in Cantonese which Jin Li translated as: "A wise shepherd does not kill all the wolves. There should be balance in all things: life and death, hot and cold, sunlight and darkness. It is a rare man who has the wisdom and the balance to be trusted with the ability to deal out death on a large scale." Thomas listened intently before addressing Jin Tan, "Grandfather, I do not understand. Why would the shepherd not want to kill all of the wolves and why would we not want to kill all of the squash bugs?" "If wolves ate nothing but sheep and if the shepherd could kill only wolves, the answer might be different but neither is the case. The wolf eats mostly rabbits and rats; if you kill one wolf, to how many rabbits do you grant long life and many offspring and how will this abundance of rabbits affect the feed supply of the sheep? To kill the wolf that is eating your sheep is the action of a logical man but to use poison or traps to kill many wolves, and the other meat eating creatures that will come to the bait, will surely bring unfavorable and long lasting results. If we poison the squash bug, will we not also kill the lady bug that eats the plant aphid and the wasp that eats the cutworm and all of the other predator insects that feed on the pests that eat our plants? It is the law of nature that prey animals (rabbits, squash bugs, aphids) must reproduce much faster than do the predators that prey on them else prey animals would die out and the predators would starve. We disturb this balance at our peril; the wise man strives for balance in all things."

These were new thoughts for Thomas and he spent the rest of the afternoon weeding mechanically while his mind was otherwise occupied. He conjured up examples and then analyzed them to test the balance theory. Which was better, the big high yielding corn plant or the smaller plant that yielded less? That should be simple; you planted corn to make corn and more is better than less. However, large plants require more water and more fertility and more time to mature than do smaller plants; how do the additional costs balance with the additional yield? If you have to add more fertilizer and more irrigation and take the risk of losing everything to an early frost, which is truly the best choice? This was a new type of thought for Thomas; he had always been a very direct sort of man. You had a job to do; you did it in the quickest and easiest way but you didn't spend a lot of time thinking about it. Being around the Jins was causing him, for the first time, to examine his own thought processes. At first Thomas was sometimes exasperated with the amount of thought and discussion that the Jins put into making even the smallest decision. More than once he said to himself, "I could have had the job done in the time they spend deciding what to do." If he made a suggestion that did not meet with Grandfather Jins' approval, Jin would never tell Thomas no but would offer a parable from his seemingly in-exhaustible supply and wait for Thomas to figure out on his own what was wrong with his suggestion. Earlier in the week, Thomas had been in town when a ship loaded with Chilean nitrate made port;

the ship's captain was selling the nitrate as fertilizer and had a very convincing pitch. Thomas bought a small bag of the powder to show the Jins and started home; he wanted to borrow the donkey cart and go back for more. If what the captain said was true, just a few pounds of the material could replace many pounds of the dried fish they used as fertilizer. The Jins were in the fields when Thomas showed them the material and repeated the captains' sale pitch. Jin Li translated for his father and when he finished, Jin Tan asked if Thomas had tasted the material? Thomas replied, "No I did not taste it; why would I do that?" Jin Tan pantomimed taking some of the material and tasting it and with gestures made it clear that Thomas should taste the material. Thomas was still puzzled but put some of the material on his tongue and immediately spit out it grimacing at the bitter, salty taste. While Thomas was trying to get rid of the foul taste, Jin Tan dug into the soil and came up with one earthworm from the millions that lived in their fields; Jin Tan put the earthworm in the palm of his hand and gently lay some of the nitrate powder on the earthworm. The three men watched as the earthworm first squirmed fanatically and then died. Jin Tan made a comment and returned to hoeing weeds. Jin Li looked at Thomas and said, "Father asks if it would not be better to wait to salt the cabbage until after it is harvested." Thomas did not buy any of the nitrate.

True to his promise to himself, Thomas found a straight piece of hard driftwood on the beach – shaved it down to fit his hand and cut it to the right length to be a proper hoe handle. The difference between this handle and the stubby was tremendous; he covered ground much faster and was not half as tired at the end of the day. It was getting close to noon and he was looking forward to the lunch that one of Jin Li s' daughters would be bringing to the field. In the few short months that Thomas had been on the farm he had been totally accepted by the family Jin; he took most of his meals with them and was rapidly becoming fluent in Cantonese. Thomas had been exposed to the language when he spent several years on ships that plied between the Cantonese speaking ports of southern China and India but living with people who spoke only Cantonese was adding to his vocabulary in leaps and bounds. Once over the shock of having the huge hairy man in their lives, and finding that he liked kids, the children made a game of teaching him the language. Jin Tan and his wife had three married sons who between them had twelve children ranging from toddlers to teen agers so Thomas had no shortage of teachers.

With both willing labor and land available, Thomas and the Jins formed a partnership and put the entire sixty acres into cultivation; since English was his native language, it made sense that he be the merchant who dealt with the miners and ship pursers who purchased their produce. Twice a week Thomas would take a load of whatever was in season, the donkey cart had been replaced with a wagon pulled by a pair of mules, into town to sell. On most days, regardless of what he had to sell, he was sold out by noon. This worked well for a time but as more acreage came into production, the Jins were masters at intercropping so that each acre grew multiple crops during a year; they had to rent a building in town and hire a man to run a full time store and soon after another to haul produce in and fertilizers out. They hired people from the local Chinese community to gather and dry kelp and to dry and chop the trash fish purchased from the fishermen. Their little farm was expanding its' influence.

CHAPTER TWELVE
The New Generation

B ristol Farms Inc. headquarters California
For the first time in a long time, with the assurance that he was gainfully employed, Hank could look at the future with confidence. He never doubted his ability to make a living but he wanted more; he wanted to make a good life with Jen Beth and raise a family with her. He thought out exactly what to say and how to ask her to marry him but when the time came, he stammered and stuttered until finally, Jen Beth took his face in both her hands, kissed him, and said, "Of course I will marry you, silly; you never had a choice since that first day in Accounting 310." They decided to get married as soon as they graduated but since both would be starting new jobs, put off a honeymoon until they had earned some vacation time. They told her parents that night and when Jacob ventured that "Weren't they rushing things a little." Hank came close to having heart stoppage and Anne choked in strangled laughter when Jen Beth replied, "Daddy, I just want to be sure that you have a son-in-law before you have a grandbaby."

Christmas break was about over but on their last day in Frisco; they found a furnished apartment not far from

Bristol headquarters and signed a lease to start June 1. Back at school, Hank called his parents with all the news and asked if it would be convenient if he brought Jen Beth up to meet them the following weekend. Jen Beth borrowed a car from one of her sorority sisters and they left on the hundred mile drive as soon as they were out of class Friday afternoon. There had been several inches of snow the day before and the world was clean and fresh looking with a new coat of white but the landscape was bleak – mile on mile of stark open fields – no fences, no trees, no animals only homesteads with grain bins and a little timber on the banks of creeks to break the monotony. As they got closer, Hank began to point out areas that had been in pasture and in woodland when he was a boy. Crossing Limestone Creek, Hank was shocked to see that since he last saw it, all the trees lining its' banks had been bull dozed down – corn fields now came right down to the water's edge – and the banks were now raw gashes in the earth rather than the shaded green parks where he and his buddies used to fish and swim. When they topped the hill overlooking Yoder Farm, Hank could see the orchard that Umpa so loved; even from this distance it was obvious that it was over grown and badly in need of pruning. Henry and Anna Weaver met them on the front porch and after putting Jen Beths' bag in the spare bedroom and Hanks' in his old room, they gathered around the kitchen table for some of Anna s' famous, at least to Hank and his boyhood friends, hot chocolate. Henry was on his best behavior and nothing was said about Hank not coming back to the farm. Anna got up to start supper and Jen Beth fell in to help; they were immediately involved in friendly conversation that excluded the men. Henry was interested in what Hanks new job would entail and was surprised when Hank told him that at this point he would be going through a four month training program and would not know what he would be doing until he finished the course. In a low voice, Henry asked if he would make enough while he was in training to support a wife. "The pay is more than I expected to earn as a new hire and will be enough; besides Jen Beth has a good job in the marketing division, she went through the management training program the last two summers, so we should be fine." Henry rose from the table and said, "Let's put on a coat and walk down to the shop; there is something I want to show you." When they got outside, Henry said, "I told a fib to get out of the house; it is something I need to tell you not show you. It looks like we, they included your Mother in the letter, are going to be sued by Genesis Alchemy International for planting their pesticide resistant soybean seed without paying their patent fee. It is a lie, I never saved patented seed and haven't planted any of their seed for two years; it just got to be too expensive. Three years ago I bought enough old style beans to plant fifty acres and saved seed from that fifty to plant the rest of my bean acreage. Someone, I'm fairly sure it was Gary Doak from Doak Farm Supply, told GAI that I was saving and planting seed from their patented soybeans. Young Doak and the GAI sales rep for this area have gotten to be drinking buddies and spend a lot of time together. Gary got unhappy when I didn't buy herbicide resistant soybean seed and herbicide from him like I have in the past. He denied it when I bounced him but looked like an egg sucking dog when I asked him if he turned me in to GAI. It may have been someone else. Supposedly GAI is paying cash – cash like stacks of hundred dollar bills – to informers that turn in their neighbors. I don't know what I am going to do; they have sued several people in the community and even if the farmer wins the suit, they wind up with a hundred to two hundred thousand dollars in legal fees. I don't have and can't get that kind of money. I gave Jed Knuckle a thousand dollar retainer to try to head off the suit but I don't really think he will accomplish anything before the money runs out. I hate it that I had to spoil your visit with bad news. Your Mother and I are thrilled over your graduation, your job and your beautiful fiancé; you have done a fantastic job with no help from me. We could not be more proud of you. Let's go back to the house and try to enjoy your Mother's cooking."

They started back after lunch the next day and Hank told Jen Beth about the threatened lawsuit, "Dad didn't do what they claim but how do you prove a negative? They waited to make the claim until all of his soybeans except those he saved for seed were gone. They claim to have samples of beans from Dad's fields that carry the pesticide resistant gene. It might even be true; Dad planted their damn beans for years and it is possible that some shattered beans volunteered or some of their seed might have been left in a planter box. It could even come from beans blowing out of trucks going down the highway; it is common to see green soybeans growing on the roadsides where the grass and weeds have been killed with herbicide. This could be the final straw for Dad; even if he wins the suit, the legal expense will bankrupt him." "Is the farm mortgaged?" asked Jen Beth. "No, thank goodness, my grandfather put the farm into a trust after Grand Mother died. My mother gets the income from the farm for her lifetime but does not own the farm nor can she mortgage it. Do you suppose the courts would take any income she might receive from the farm if they lose the suit? That would leave her and Dad with nothing!" "I don't know the answer to that Hank but I think we need to ask the Bristol Farms legal department some questions; if this can happen to your folks and to other farmers, it could happen to Bristol Farms. I do know that contamination of organic products with genetic modified organisms is a big problem for organic growers, it is easy for pollen from GMO plants to blow into organic fields, but in your Dad's case it almost sounds as if the contamination was intentional or faked."

Their last semester of classes seemed to fly bye and the dreaded finals week was suddenly upon them. This final week was different for Jen Beth and Hank; as graduating seniors, both had grades high enough to be exempt from finals in every course they were taking. Instead of pressure and last minute cramming, they had time to relax and make plans. One decision was what to do with Hank's venerable International Harvester pickup truck that Umpa had left to him in his will; for the thirty year old truck to make the trip to the coast it would need new tires, at the very least, and then it was not certain it would get there. Selling it wouldn't bring anything but scrap iron price and Hank was agonizing over what to do when he remembered that Mr. Scruggs, who had recently retired, made a hobby of restoring old farm equipment. After one last job for the old truck, hauling their boxed up stuff to UPS to be shipped to California, Jen Beth followed Hank in a borrowed car and they delivered "Old Binder" as a gift to Mr. Scruggs on his little farm with a big shop outside of town.

The big day finally arrived; the graduation began with ruffles and flourishes from the school band and quickly deteriorated into a mind numbing series of speeches, interesting or important only to the politicians giving them, followed by the tedium of hundreds of graduates being called one at a time to file by and receive their diplomas. As soon as the ceremony was over and goodbyes were said to friends, Hanks parents drove them to the airport. Anna hugged both Hank and Jen Beth and apologized again that they would not be at the wedding; they had to get their bean crop planted and she was working in the fields with Henry. The lawsuit was not mentioned but Hank could not remember his father ever looking as haggard as he did on this day. After one last round of hugs, Hank and Jen Beth were on their way.

Jen Beth's parents offered her the choice of a big church wedding or the money that such a wedding would cost and Jen Beth said, "Give us the money and just enough wedding to make it legal." The ceremony was in her parent's home with just family and two of Jen Beth's closest girl friends present. They were married on Thursday morning; spent two nights in a beach resort on the coast and came home to their apartment on Saturday. They spent Sunday buying groceries and light bulbs and toilet paper at the local super market like old married folks and getting ready to go to work Monday morning. Jen Beth's Volkswagen bug was their only transportation, they would need another vehicle eventually, but the bug was enough for the moment since they were working out of the same location. Jen Beth had already spent time in the marketing division during the past two summers and was assigned to a section doing research on markets and buying trends; she would be working under a very sharp lady, Susan Andrews, trying to understand how people make decisions on what they buy. In addition, she would remain as liaison between the company and the Bristol Farms Chair of Organic Agriculture and as such would have to fly back to the University several times a year. Hank would spend a couple of weeks in orientation, becoming familiar with what the company does and how it is organized, before being assigned to short stints in several different divisions.

They quickly fell into a routine with Hank spending as much time in study as he ever did while in school; he had a lot of material from his trainee course to go over but most of his study was of subjects that interested him and that he felt the need to know more about. Hank still rolled out of bed at five o'clock just like he was still on the farm except now he spent the early morning studying and chasing information on the internet. Jen Beth didn't share what she called "his before dawn affliction" so he was quiet as a church mouse until it was time for her to start stirring; at six forty five, he would start the coffee maker and by seven Jen Beth would join him in their six by eight foot "kitchen" for coffee and conversation while she made breakfast. The one dark spot in their relationship came on Saturday mornings when Jen Beth was accustomed to sleeping in until nine or ten o'clock; there was no way Hank could do without coffee that long so he would take his laptop and walk down to the McDonalds in the next block. They didn't open until six o'clock but the coffee was fresh and hot when they finally did open and he could work without worrying about disturbing Jen Beth. Hanks' four month training period passed quickly and he was offered his choice of being assigned to the marketing division with Jen Beth or to the newly formed and relatively small research division. During his training rotation through the company, Hank met and briefly worked under the head of the research division, Dr. Tom Carthage; Dr. Carthage was engaged in researching ways to, as he put it, "Substitute management for money." The rationale for his work was that the future of Bristol Farms Inc would be in partnerships or joint ventures with individual organic farmers; the demand for their products was growing so rapidly that owning all of the land needed for production was no longer feasible. For these relationships to be valid long term they had to be beneficial to both parties; the surest way to assure Bristol Farms a steady supply of quality products was to make sure that their cooperating farmers benefited from the relationship and were consistently profitable. Dr. Tom was studying various methods of reducing the need for purchased inputs with the thought of increasing profitability and of reducing financial risk for their cooperators. Some of his ideas were unusual such as planting forbs that some would call weeds in clean tilled crops to hold down weed pressure and increase mineral uptake and some were simply increased use of crop rotations, pasture and crop combinations and more diverse mixtures of species for cover crops. Regardless of the practices used, his work was focused always on building the health of the whole farm; the whole soil- plant-animal-wealth-human complex as the way to create a type of agriculture that was productive, sustainable, profitable, and farmer friendly. After watching his father falling deeper and deeper in debt chasing higher production, Hank was fascinated by Dr. Carthage's common sense approach; instead of the conventional: "How do we reduce the cost of a practice?" Dr. Tom would ask, "How do we eliminate the need for the practice?" Hank spent time thinking about what was different about the way Dr. Tom reasoned and it came to him that the difference was in both the scope and the time frame that Dr. Tom considered. He weighed every tool by its effects, both short and long term, on every aspect of the soil-plant-animal-wealth-human complex we call a farm. Conventional agricultural management asked, "If I use this tool, will it increase production enough to increase gross profit this season? Will it cash flow?" Before Dr. Tom would sign off on a practice it had to demonstrate: that it was ecologically sound, it would improve rather than degrade the environment in the long term; that it was financially sound, it would create wealth in a sustainable manner; that it was sociologically sound, it was something that people could do (and just as important would do) to improve their lives. Any practice that failed anyone of these tests was not an option to be considered. A practice would of course be weighed also against other techniques intended to bring about similar results; a tool could pass all of the tests and still not be the best choice for the job. Tools A, B, and C could all pass the tests but there were always differences that would give one more value in a given situation. B might yield the highest monetary return while A gave the most soil improvement and C was best at reducing money at risk; the decision as to which of the tools to use would depend on what improvement was most needed at a point in time.

The work on profitability with its relevance to his family was what grabbed Hanks' interest but the research division had other studies going as well. One of these involved pesticides and how their use in conventional agriculture could affect organic growers and the general public. It was bad enough when an organic grower just had to worry about a neighbor spraying pesticide when the wind was too high or a spray plane treating the wrong field but the advent of GMO plants whose pollen floated in the wind to contaminate crops being cultivated under an organic regime could destroy the value of the crop and even threaten the organic certification of the farm. Companies were using genetic modification to insert foreign genes for a lot of different purposes and the use of these GMO plants was increasing rapidly and more cases of organic fields being polluted by drifting pollen were being reported. Analysts with the division combed news reports and court records worldwide to find instances of contamination and to try to find ways to reduce the likelihood of contamination. Some of the first work Hank did for Bristol Farms was following up cases of reported contamination with personal interviews with the affected farmers; he found a real need for more public awareness of the problem and for legislation giving more legal protection to farmers damaged by contamination.

CHAPTER THIRTEEN
A Death in the Cornfield

Yoder Farm

Henry Weaver sat in the cab of his pickup as the idling engine gave off fumes and the heater pushed back the seeped in cold. He sat and reflected back on the worst day of his life. It had started out pretty good.

He finished harvesting corn two weeks ago and the elevator called yesterday afternoon to tell him his last check was ready; it was not the best crop he ever raised but it was a good crop and since he had spent less than usual making it, it was the most profitable crop he had raised in years. He planted hybrid seed corn from one of the last of the small independent seed companies; it was about one third the price of the stacked trait GMO corn that he had used in the past and it yielded almost as well. His corn was not as clean as he would have liked; he skipped the pre-emergent herbicide again this year and had time for only one trip through with the cultivator to fight the weeds. His crop was pretty wooly, by the time the corn plants were in tassel, purslane and other low growing weeds covered the ground beneath them; he expected there were plenty of comments down at the Coop about "Henrys weed farm." He hadn't seen or thought about purslane in years, it was easy to kill with herbicides, seeing it again brought to mind his father-in-law saying years ago that a good stand of purslane would guarantee a good corn crop. From his farming days before herbicides he remembered the forb had strong roots that opened up tight ground and made plowing much easier; it made sense that corn roots could go deeper and spread wider where it grew. His father-in-law thought that by shading the ground it kept the soil cooler and made a rain go farther. Anna's mother used to gather purslane and use it in salads and as a cooked vegetable; he would have to gather a mess of it and see if Anna remembered how to cook it. His corn had dried down nicely despite the dire predictions on the effects of the weeds by some of his neighbors; he was not penalized for excess grain moisture and, miracle of miracles, corn prices held up all the way through harvest. He would have the money to retire another nice piece of the debt that hung over his head like the sword of Damocles and weighed on his every waking moment; it was a great feeling to see the debt figure go down instead of up. After all the hard years, they had put together two profitable years back to back and Henry was sure that they were at last on the right management track. Physically it had been a hard year; he had not hired any help this year. Both he and Anna had worked like slaves to get done everything that had to be done. Just as soon as he settled up with the bank, he was going to give Anna five one hundred dollar bills and tell her to go buy herself some new clothes and to not bring back any change; Lord knows it was time for her to spend a little on herself. As soon as she got rigged out, they would go out for a night on the town; dinner and then dancing at the supper club that she liked out on the lake.

Henry and Anna had a leisurely breakfast; for the first time in months Henry was still in the house when the sun came up. After a third cup of coffee, Henry drove into town. First stop was the Coop to pick up his check; he spent a few minutes shooting the bull with the farmers gathered there, who like him were enjoying a little post harvest rest and relaxation, as he had time to kill before the bank opened. He made his deposit and enjoyed the feeling of being rich for a moment before going to look for Jerry Sanders, his loan officer. Jerry was not in his office but his secretary said that he was in a meeting that was breaking up and would be here in just a minute. She offered Henry a seat and coffee; he took the seat but passed on more coffee; he still had half a caffeine jag on from breakfast. From where he was sitting, Henry could see Jerry and two other loan officers as they came out of a meeting room across the lobby; they stood heads together talking seriously for a minute before walking off to their respective offices. Jerry came in and greeted Henry with a smile and a hand shake but Henry could tell that something was not right; Jerry was way too subdued. Jerry opened the door into his office and said, "Henry, come in and have a seat." Jerry held the door until Henry came in and then shut the door after telling his secretary, "Lois, please hold all of my calls." Jerry sat down at his desk and said, "Henry there isn't any easy way to say this; the bank is calling your loan." Henry felt as if he had been kicked in the stomach; for a moment his body shut down and he was unable to even draw a breath, much less speak. The bank calling his loan was something that had not even entered his mind; two years ago, after Henry finally realized that further increasing production was not the way to profitability, he and Anna sat down with Jerry and laid out a plan to get their finances in order. They had to reduce expenses and since they had already cut their living expenses to the bone, the plan mostly involved cutting production expenses; Jerry was at first dubious but the first year was a success and Henry had already told him that this year would be better still. "Why, Jerry? Why, now? I thought you were pleased with the progress that we are making." "Henry, I am more than pleased and did everything I could to prevent this from happening. You and Anna are not the only ones affected; there are several other families in the same condition. It is those damn lawsuits! No suits have been filed as yet but GAI is going to file at least five that we know of; once a lawsuit is filed, it becomes a cloud on the Banks claim to the assets pledged as collateral for loans. Our lawyers tell us that since we feel certain that suits are going to be filed, we must call the loans to protect the Bank from a legal stand point." "Do your lawyers know that this will kill Anna and me financially and destroy any chance that we could pay off the loan in the future?" Jerry just shook his head and sat quietly as Henry got up and walked out of the bank. Henry got in his truck and in sort of a fog drove to Doak Farm Supply to tend the next item on his list of errands; he owed a small bill at the store and was scrupulous about paying his bills on time. Henry walked into the store and started back to the desk of the book keeper, Mrs. Williams; before he could get there Gary Doak, who had recently taken over the business that his father built, stepped out of his office and said in a voice just a trifle too loud, "Weaver, I want to talk to you." "What do you want Gary?" "We will no longer be able to sell to you on open account; anything you buy will have to be cash on delivery." "Gary I have traded with your father and this store for thirty years and have never been one day late in paying my bill. What is your problem?" "That was before you tried to gyp GAI and got your tail in a crack. I don't plan to have you sticking this store with a bad debt when they sell you out to pay off the lawsuit." Gary Doak was pudgy soft but he was four inches taller, forty pounds heavier and twenty years younger than Henry and was used to using his size and his position to intimidate people. He was still seething over Henry backing him down in front of people over the reward thing and with Henry not reacting, seeming almost cowed, Doak pushed harder, "In fact we don't want your business at all; we don't need to do business with cheats." Doak then made a mistake, he grabbed Henry by the arm and said loudly, "Come on bum, get out and don't come back." Actually the "back" was cut off when Henry wrenched his arm free and unleashed the frustrations of the day in one roundhouse punch that landed squarely on Doak's rather large and red nose. It was a two lick fight. Henry's work hardened fist hit Doak's' nose and Doak's' butt hit the floor. Suddenly Doak was flat on his back bleeding like a stuck hog from his flattened nose and screaming first for the police and then for a doctor as Henry walked back to Mrs. Williams to pay his bill and when that was done walked calmly out to his truck. Just as he reached it a police car slid to a stop blocking his truck and a young policeman jumped out shouting for Henry to get his hands up and lean spread eagle on the pickup. Henry knew most of the people on the police force but not this young man who had recently moved here and was a running buddy of Gary Doak. Doak appeared in the door screaming, "That's him, he tried to kill me Johnny! Arrest him!" The young policeman finished frisking Henry – taking his pocket knife – and without asking Henry a single question said, "Put your hands behind your back." He handcuffed Henry and read him his rights off of a card from his pocket. Henry answered yes when asked if he understood his rights and then seeing Bill Smyth, a friend and neighbor, standing in the gathering crowd said, "Bill, will you call Jed Knuckle and tell him what happened?" "I will Henry and I will also testify as to what really took place. I saw the whole thing." The policeman opened the rear door of his car and with a "watch your head" stuffed Henry into the rear seat. The police cruiser smelled faintly of vomit and Henry, with his stomach already rolling, had all he could do to keep from throwing up. For a man who had never had even a speeding ticket, being handcuffed and hauled off to jail with the whole town watching was almost as degrading as the scene at the bank. It was made even worse when a photographer from the Sentinel showed up just in time to get pictures of Henry being "perp walked" into the jail. Henry was booked in on a charge of assault and was sitting on the metal bunk in the drunk tank when Jed Knuckle arrived. Jed had been busy; he had an order signed by Judge Black releasing Henry on his own recognizance and had sent his paralegal to Doak Farm Supply to get statements from as many witnesses as possible. As they left the jail Sam Goode, a local farmer, stopped them and said, "Henry I just wanted to shake your hand, that slimy bastard has had more than a broke nose coming for a long time." Jed took Henry back to his truck and said for Henry to call him tomorrow when he should have more information about what was to happen.

Henry started his truck and drove slowly toward home. When he got to the turn off that would take him home, Henry turned instead the other way to one of his leased places; Henry pulled around behind the ramshackle old shed, all that was left of the Johnson homestead, and parked out of sight of the road. He sat there a long time listening to the faint ticking of his cooling engine and trying to understand how he had gone so wrong. He was not a stupid man; he was a frugal hard worker; he was not a drunk; he paid his bills and cheated no one; he was a good farmer who studied his craft. What the hell had gone wrong? When the bank called his loan, they would take everything: the equipment, the bank account, the seed beans and even the truck he was sitting in and Anna's car. Thank God that Yoder Farm was not on the note. As soon as that thought crossed his mind, he realized that he would be left with no way to defend Anna and him from the GAI lawsuit and if he lost, the bastards would find some way to take Anna's inheritance and only source of income. He had failed the most basic duty of a man. He had not only failed to provide for his family, he had squandered the resources Anna had brought to the marriage.

Maybe if he was not in the picture, Anna could find someone to make a life with, maybe if, maybe – it seemed to be getting dark awfully early tonight.

Jen Beth reached the door of her office just as the phone started ringing; her spirits lifted as a glance at caller ID told her it was Hank. The elation was short lived, however, as the tone of Hanks' voice told her something was very wrong. "Babe, my mother just called and I have to go to her; Dad killed himself last night." "Oh Hank, I am so sorry! I will get online and get us airline tickets and call Mother and Dad to let them know where we are going." "You don't have to go Jen Beth." "Oh yes I do; you are hurting and your Mother is hurting; at least I can cook for you and do what I can to make it easier for you." "Okay, I guess that is one of the many reasons I love you; I will tell my supervisor what is going on and come straight on to your office." For once, the airline schedule cooperated; Jen Beth booked them on a flight leaving at two o'clock. They would have just time enough to run by the apartment for clothes and toothbrushes and get to the airport the required hour early. Jen Beths' mother was with a patient so Jen left a message but she got right through to her Dad; she told him what was happening and asked him to call her supervisor who was out of the office. She promised to report in as soon as she knew something and hung up just as Hank walked in the door. Since both of their jobs required travel, they were old hands at getting ready and were packed and on the way to the airport fifteen minutes after they reached their apartment. They cleared security with no hold up and sat at their departure gate holding hands; neither of them felt like talking. Hank had called his mother from their apartment to let her know their plans and Mrs. Strickland, his mothers' neighbor and closest friend, answered the phone. His mother was resting so Hank gave Mrs. Strickland their itinerary to relay to his mother when she got up. Hank could hear a low mummer of voices in the background and knew that they belonged to friends of his parents rallying around. Hank loved Jen Beth for offering to cook and didn't say anything but by this time the house would have enough food to feed an army. His mothers' friends would set up a rotation with different ladies coming in to heat food, wash dishes and generally make themselves useful. Tragedy whether sickness, a death or a barn fire, brought out the best in these people.

While they waited for their flight to be called, Hank took the opportunity to call Dr. Fortner, their family doctor, to find what he could about his fathers' death. Dr. Fortner told him that Henry had run a piece of hose from the exhaust pipe of his truck through a partially open rear window of the truck, got back in the driver's seat and started the engine. Before he hung up, Dr. Fortner said, "Hank I hate this almost as much as you and Anna but at least Henry died without pain; he was a good man who was overwhelmed by circumstances – he deserved better." Hank then called one of his closest high school friends, Joe Hendricks, and got the whole sordid story from the foreclosure to Gary Doak's stunt to his father's arrest. He had been sad but now he was sick at heart thinking about the suffering this scenario would have caused his dad.

On the flight east, Hank and Jen Beth sat quietly holding hands with Jen Beths' head resting on his shoulder. Hank had been expecting bad news from home but it never entered his mind that the news would be that his father had killed himself. By the time their flight landed and they had gotten a rental car and driven to the farm it was close to midnight but the lights were still on and Anna was up to greet them.

Hank was carrying both of their bags so Jen Beth opened the door and let Hank enter first. He set the luggage down just inside the hall and reaching out to his Mother folded her into his arms. Hank had held it together up until now but hearing and feeling his Mothers soft weeping was too much and suddenly Hank was sobbing uncontrollably. He reached out to include Jen Beth in his embrace and the three of them stood crying; miserable but locked in the comfort of loving contact. After a moment, Anna pulled away and falling back on habit of a lifetime asked, "Are you hungry? There is food of all sorts." Both hank and Jen Beth refused food but accepted coffee and the three sat down at the kitchen table. Hank reached out to cover his Mother's hand with his own and asked, "What in the world happened?" "Hank, they just wore him out; wore him down to nothing. He put everything he had into making the farm work; he was physically exhausted from working unbelievable hours and he was mentally fragile from too much stress. The combination of the bank calling our loan after being so pleased with our progress, the threat of an unjustified GAI lawsuit and being humiliated by being arrested like a common criminal was more than he could stand. I keep thinking that there must have been something more that I could have done to help him but I didn't help enough and he is gone. Oh God, I miss him so much!" Hank held his mother for a moment and then he and Jen Beth helped Anna, still weeping softly, to bed. Hank carried their luggage up to his old room and sat on the edge of the bed where he slept for so many years and suffered pangs of guilt interspaced with flashes of sheer fury. He was at fault in that he should have seen that his father was in danger but there were people out there who, solely for personal benefit, had actively plotted to harm his Father. Hank knew that neither his mother nor his father would approve but he felt a burning desire for revenge on the people who had destroyed his father.

Hank awoke in his old room on the second floor to the smell of coffee and frying bacon and for a moment expected to hear his Dad call out, "Rise and shine, times a wasting" just as he had heard so many times in the past. For the first time in their marriage, Jen Beth was up before him and he had not even known when she got out of bed. He hurried through his morning routine and started downstairs where he could hear Jen Beth and his mother talking softly. Jen Beth was dressed and standing at the stove cooking while his mother, still in her robe, sat at the kitchen table drinking coffee. Hank leaned over to kiss his mother on top of her head and she squeezed his hand and said, "I believe we had best keep this beautiful girl; she had coffee made before I woke up and won't let me do a thing toward breakfast." "She does have her uses", said Hank as he bent to kiss his wife. Jen Beth served up plates first to Anna and Hank and then one for herself and they sat down to eat. As they finished breakfast, Anna said, "Hank, I would appreciate it if you would make the arrangements for your father's funeral; his body is at Brown's Funeral Home and I would like for him to be buried next to my parents in the old Yoder burial ground by the orchard." "I will tend to that this morning. When do you want the service held?" "Pastor Longmire was here yesterday and said that he could hold it in the morning at eleven o'clock. I have a list here of men I would like for you to ask to be pall bearers." Henry read over the list and when he came to the name asked, "Jerry Sanders?" "Jerry has always been a friend to us and he did what he could to prevent the bank from calling our loan; your father would want us to ask him." Hank knew that his mother was right but thought to himself, "Mother and Dad are better people than I am; I won't do it but I would like to spit in Jerry Sanders eye and dare him to do something about it."

Hank and Jen Beth went first to the funeral home to pick out a casket; Mr. Brown was relieved but tried not to let it show when Hank told him that his father had burial insurance through his lodge membership. Hank told Jen Beth, "There were many good things about living in a small town but they came at the cost of everyone in town knowing all of your business." Some of the good was demonstrated when, on the short walk they took around town to see some of the men on the pall bearers list, they were stopped repeatedly by people offering condolences and good wishes. Hank left the bank and Jerry Sanders as their last stop. When Hank and Jen Beth entered the bank, Sanders looked up from his desk and came out to greet them and usher them into his office. Hank spoke first, "Mr. Sanders, I would like you to meet my wife, Jen Beth." "Mrs. Weaver, I am pleased to meet you; I only wish the circumstances were different. Please, come in and sit down; can I get you something to drink?" When both Hank and Jen Beth declined, Sanders sat down behind his desk and said, "Hank, I can't tell you at this time what is going to happen with your parents loan; obviously the situation has changed." "Yes, I would say the situation has changed and I do need to sit down and talk with you but now, at my Mothers' request, I am here to ask you to be a pall bearer at my Fathers' funeral." Sanders covered his eyes for a moment with his hand before swallowing hard and saying, "I would be honored Hank; please thank your mother and tell her she is in our prayers."

With Jerry Sanders, they had contacted four of the six men on the list; two were farmers that didn't live in town and Hank would try to reach them by telephone. On the way home, Hank told Jen Beth that he would need to hook up the snow plow to his Dads' four wheel drive tractor and plow a trail from the road up to the burial plot but as they pulled into the farm they met two of the neighbors coming out. They had brought tractors and plowed out a path and then packed the snow on an area around the plot where people could park.

The church was full and Pastor Longmire set the tone when he said, "We are here to celebrate the life of Henry Weaver." He went on to tell of several instances where Henry had gone out of his way to help someone who needed it. Some of these stories Hank knew but several he had not heard and he wished he could tell his Dad how proud of him the stories made his son. As Pastor Longmire finished his eulogy, a man stood up in the back of the church and said, "Pastor, I need to say something." There were several gasps as people turned to see who had spoken; it was George Doak the father of Gary Doak. He was obviously ill and weak, he swayed slightly and grasped the back of the pew in front of him for support, but his voice was strong. "As you all know, my family played a shameful role in this tragedy and the record has got to be set straight. In my sixty four years I have never known a more honest man than Henry Weaver. Anyone who would believe that he would cheat anyone or take anything that was not his did not know Henry Weaver. He was the most scrupulously honest man I have ever known; twice when we under charged him, he called it to our attention and paid the correct amount even though he was having financial problems at the time."

The obviously distressed man paused as if calling upon his last reserves and continued, "I had suspicions that I did not want to believe when my son Gary began spending money that he should not have had but it was not until this morning when I braced Gary, after I found thirteen thousand dollars in one hundred dollar bills in his desk, that I got the truth. Gary and Jim Turner, the GAI rep, cooked up a scheme where Gary would make secret accusations against people, Turner would convince GAI that the accusations were valid and the two would split the reward. Gary has given a full statement to the district attorney and is now in jail. Anna, Hank all of you my friends, I am so sorry and I only hope that I live long enough to repair some small part of the damage done." George turned and started toward the door but made only two steps before collapsing face first on the floor. Pandemonium broke out in the church with everyone speaking at once while attempting to see what was happening until Pastor Longmire said loudly, "Friends, Dr. Jonas and Dr. Fortner are with George and will take care of him. Please be seated and let us finish our tribute to the life of Henry Weaver. Let us pray." Anna was seated between Hank and Jen Beth and she seemed to shrink before their eyes as she sat crying softly and shaking her head in disbelief.

After the grave was closed and people had paid their respects to Anna and to Hank, Mrs. Strickland took charge of Anna. She sat her down with a plate of food and a glass of red wine, into which Hank saw her slip a shot of vodka, and cajoled Anna to eat and drink; when a little of the food and all of the wine was gone she took Anna to her bedroom. Marge Strickland came back from settling Anna and said, "Hank if you would fix me a really stiff bourbon and water, perhaps I could clear my mind of the loathing that I feel for Gary Doak and the immense sorrow that I feel for his parents." Hank fixed the drink and brought it to her and after thanking him Mrs. Strickland said, "Now is not a good time but I have a story that I need to tell you and Jen Beth. I would not bring it up at this time except that I know that you will be talking to the bank and you need to know that not everyone in that bank was a friend to Henry and Anna. Please be on your guard and don't trust Albert Horning the bank President or Howard Peoples the lawyer. You probably remember my Uncle Tom Sample and his wife Rose, the bank called their note two years ago in a very similar manner to the way they threatened Henry and Anna. It ruined Tom and Rose, they lost their farm and now he is working in town as a building janitor. He would not talk to me about what was going on at the time but finally confided in me when he heard that Henry and Anna were in trouble. Tom saved and planted some patented seed in violation of his contract with GAI and young Doak and his GAI thug buddy came to him and told him that they knew what he had done. Doak told Tom that he could use store records to prove how much herbicide and how much herbicide resistant seed Tom bought and that the only way that Tom could keep from being sued into the poor house by GAI would be to sell his farm, at about two thirds of its worth, to something named Property Management Inc. Tom didn't know who owned this company but I found out later, through a niece who works in state government, that Albert Horning, Howard Peoples and George Henning, another lawyer in town, are all shareholders. They have been buying up farmland all through the area and it looks like they were using the bank and the GAI threat to force people to sell out cheap." Hank sat absolutely still for a moment before saying, "Thank you Marge, that is information that I very definitely did need to know."

Anna was back with them after a short rest and that night, after going over the farm books, the three of them discussed the financial problem. Earlier in the day, before they left the grave site, Jerry Sanders asked Hank if he and Anna could meet with him and Albert Horning, the bank president, at ten o'clock the day after tomorrow morning. "We need to sort out the situation and understand what options we have."

Anna was adamant that she did not want to wait until the bank called their note and sold them out. "I don't know what the equipment will bring at auction but people know that Henry kept his equipment in good shape and it should sell well. I would like to hold an auction just as soon as possible and also see about getting the money back that Henry had already paid on cash leased ground; that amounts to fifty-three thousand dollars. Your father made great strides the last two years in improving the profitability of his operation; with what is in the bank and by cashing in everything except my car we can probably get the debt down to a figure that I can retire over a number of years by leasing out the farm." Hank knew what the thought of someone else working Yoder Farm did to his mother and reached across the table to squeeze her hand. Hank did not mention to Anna what Marge had told him; at this point, Anna didn't need the pain that knowing that her husband's death was caused by the criminal greed of a grubby little small town Mafia.

Hank and Jen Beth arrived a few minutes early for their appointment at the bank; Jerry Sanders came out to greet them and enquired about Anna. Hank replied that Anna wanted him and his wife to represent her interests. Sanders did not look happy but took them to one of the meeting rooms off of the bank lobby. "Albert will be here directly and I see Howard Peoples from our legal department coming now." Sanders had just introduced Hank and Jen Beth to the lawyer when Albert Horning arrived. "Hank and Jen Beth Weaver this is our bank president, Albert Horning." After hands were shaken and everyone was seated, Sanders opened the discussion with, "What we would like to accomplish today is to review the situation and see if we can't come to a course of action that will benefit all parties." Before he could continue, Horning spoke up, "Excuse me Jerry but, Young Lady, this will probably be rather boring; are you sure that you would not rather wait out in the lobby?" Hank could see the color rising on Jen Beths' neck like lava in a volcano flowing toward the surface and he would have sworn that her ears flattened against her head like an angry cat as he watched. He put a hand on her arm and turned to Horning, "My wife has a double degree in economics and business administration; she has the best grasp of business principles of anyone I know and I can say without fear of contradiction that she is the smartest person in this room. I doubt that she will be bored." "Ah - ah yes, I see." Jen Beth visibly relaxed from her crouching tiger attitude and smiled sweetly at Horning, who looked decidedly uncomfortable. Sanders quickly took back the floor, "Henrys' death of course changes everything as does the revelation that fraud may have been committed by young Doak and Turner, the GAI representative. I feel quite certain and Howard tells me our legal department agrees that it is highly unlikely that GAI will file any lawsuits involving any of our customers. The bank will not be calling your parents loan and will work with your mother toward an equitable solution." "Mr. Sanders, we talked this out last night. Mother is going to auction all of her and Dads' assets and apply the proceeds to the note; the sale will, in all probability, not bring enough to retire the note and it was Mothers' intention to ask you to give her several years to pay the remainder. On the way in this morning, my wife and I decided that we will make arrangements to pay off the remaining balance so that Mother is under no obligation to this bank." Horning spoke for the first time, "Young man there is no need for all that; we have told you that we are not going to call the loan." "Mr. Horning, why did you tell my father that you were calling his loan and now tell me that you are not calling it?" "Circumstances have changed; GAI will not be filing a lawsuit so the danger to the bank is much less." "Mr. Horning, my family has done business with this bank for many years; we have made you quite a lot of money as have other families you were ready to throw under the bus with us over threats of lawsuits. You knew my father to be an honest, hard working farmer who had finally gotten his operation running in the black; he was making money, and making you money, while many others were losing money. Did you make any attempt to see if there was a shred of evidence that he had cheated GAI? Did you do anything to try to help any of your customers who were under attack or did you simply wash your hands of the whole affair and fold before GAI like Pontius Pilate before the mob? We will pay off the note in full; we no longer want to have any association with this bank. You killed my father just as surely as if you had put a gun to his head and pulled the trigger!" Horning rose red faced and sputtering from his chair and leaned over the table toward Hank almost shouting, "Young man, you can't talk to me like that; we did nothing wrong. You can't hold us responsible for the foolish actions of your father!" Hank stared to rise with his right fist already cocked but Jen Beth pulled him back and spoke, "Mr. Horning, I suggest that you not antagonize my husband; I believe, and feel your attorney will agree, that there is a strong possibility that a jury might find your bank liable in Mr. Weavers' death." Hank rose and turning to Sanders, said "Here is my card, Mother asks that any contact with her be through me or her attorney Mr. Knuckle. Good day." Hank pulled Jen Beths' chair back and they walked out, feeling the almost physical intensity of the stares that followed them.

CHAPTER FOURTEEN
Backwards toward the Future

Yoder Farm

That evening after they went over the day's events with Anna, including telling her that they were going to assume any balance remaining on the note after the assets were sold, Jen Beth called her parents to report; they listened attentively as she told all that had occurred. When the report was complete, Jacob said, "Honey put Hank on the phone, I have an idea trying to form." "Yes sir?" "Hank, how much acreage is in your Mothers farm and what kind of land is it?" "There are three hundred and ninety six acres total in Yoder Farm with about three hundred eighty five acres in cultivation. There is an adjoining one hundred and sixty acres in cultivation that belongs to an aged aunt – Mother has a lifetime lease on this property and will inherit it in time. It is mostly class one soil with some roll to it; most of the farm is deep silty clay loam over a calcareous gravelly clay sub soil." "Hank, do you think that your Mother would be interested in leasing the farm to Bristol Farms to be converted into a demonstration organic farm?" "Sir, I can almost guarantee that she would be very interested." "Next question then, is running such a project something that you and Jen Beth would be interested in doing? I think this could grow far beyond just running Yoder Farm; if it is successful, it can be the way that Bristol Farms attracts good farmers to become our suppliers. The way we find the farmers we will have to have to supply the production we are going to need." "Jacob, I can answer that question right now because it is something that Jen Beth and I have talked about even before we married; we would love to turn Yoder Farm into a profitable organic operation, your daughter is very vigorously shaking her head yes so I guess I answered that right." "Hank, you and Jen Beth stay there and help your Mother get her affairs in order. Let me know how much you need to clear the note; Anne and I personally will loan you the money. I will call both of your supervisors and tell them that you are on assignment for me; what I would like you to do is to start thinking about how you can turn Yoder Farm into a profitable organic operation and write a report to be presented to the Board of Directors. If we get this done, Bristol Farms can be your bank, supply information and technology and buy your produce but your plan needs to be something that a farmer can sell to a hard headed country banker. Eventually, a big part of your jobs will be to hold field days and schools for prospective client farmers so you will need to document everything you do, and the results, both good and bad, as if it were a university research project. To succeed it will have to be profitable, sustainable and family friendly; you can call on anyone in the company for advice; legal, agronomic, whatever. Check with your Mother and if she is agreeable, find out what acreage like yours is cash leasing for and plan to spend, maybe a twenty percent premium. We need to go with real world figures from the start. To be viable, we would need to have, at the least, a five year lease with a five year option. Send me a draft of your report as soon as it is ready and we will go over it together before we go to the Board. This is your and Jen Beths project but I would suggest that you start with comprehensive soil reports, chemical, microbial, physical, and any other that you and Dr. Carthage think could be useful. Let me know if your Mother agrees and at what price and I will have the legal department send a lease and a check for the first years lease."

"Are you sure, Babe, it is a long way to Jin's seafood?" "Hank, you have talked about what you would like to do since I first met you and this is the opportunity. I am a little short in the hands on experience department but I learn quickly; let's make this work!" "OK, let's find Mother and see what she thinks." Anna was at her desk going over the farm books. "Mother, what would you think of Bristol Farms leasing Yoder Farm and turning it back into an organic farm? We have been talking to Jen Beth's folks and they would like for Jen Beth and I to take a farm that has been in conventional agriculture and turn it into a productive and profitable organic operation. Bristol Farms is going to need a lot more organic produce in the near future and is very interested in setting up several demonstration farms to show farmers that it can be very much in their interest to become organic farmers. Bristol Farms would cash rent the farm for a twenty percent premium over what similar land is renting for in the area." "You and Jen Beth would be running the farm?"

"That is the plan if it is something that you would like to do." "Oh Hank, I can't think of anything that would make me happier than to have you two here working my Daddy's farm."

Hank had made arrangements with Teel Auction Company to hold their sale on Saturday ten days from now. His Dad, or more correctly his Mother, kept meticulous records, right down to the date and the number of hours on each engine at oil changes. Hank made up a list of all of his parents' equipment detailing all pertinent information: make, model, serial number, age, purchase price and date, date and engine hours at last service, and any repairs and Jen Beth transferred all of this information to a spreadsheet on her laptop. All of the information for each piece of equipment would be posted on it on sale day.

Hanks' parents had also kept complete income and expense records for each parcel of land that they were farming; there were thirteen years of these records and Jen Beth pointed out what a treasure trove of information they could be in pointing out the contrast between a conventional and an organic regime on the same acreage. "Do you think your Mother would be comfortable with us using these records for demonstration?" When asked, Anna said, "If it will help keep one family from falling into the trap that we got into, use the records in any way they are useful." Jen Beth spent several days transferring data to her computer before working her mathematical magic on the numbers and starting to churn out tables and graphs showing all sorts of relationships. The first graph that she showed Hank was a thirteen year summary of total income plotted against total expense; this was interesting but not really informative. It showed both income and expense rising at a fairly uniform rate until the last two years when both fell off dramatically but with expense falling much more than income. More useful information began to appear when she plotted profitability per acre by crop and by year. On the same sheet she plotted yield in bushels per acre and expense of production per bushel. For corn this chart showed that while production rose more or less steadily, costs did the same and the overall effect was that profitable years and unprofitable years tended to alternate in occurrence. Jin Beth, the economist, said this was a classic situation that denoted that too much money was being put at risk given the potential for profit. "You will see this situation when markets, driven by either product supply disruption or price artificially influenced by outside pressure, fluctuate wildly. The more common reason is that the business is just running too close to the edge; there is not enough margin between the cost of production and the sale price of the product. The last two years your Dad cut his expenses dramatically and broke out of this pattern, yields fell but expenses fell even faster and profitability increased; he sold fewer bushels but got to keep a much larger percentage of the sale proceeds. This same, too much money at risk for the potential for profit, scenario can and often does affect organic farms; if we are going to make a financial success of this, we will have to come up with ways to hold purchased inputs to a minimum." "Babe, we need to get you with Dr. Carthage; a big part of his work is aimed at doing just that, coming up with ways to substitute management for money."

Expense vs. Production

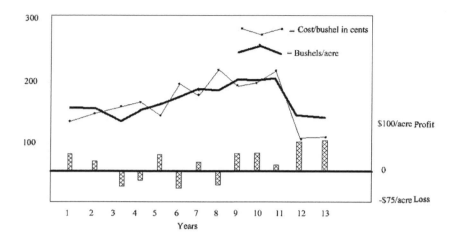

The picture became even clearer when she broke out and plotted expenses by category: land rent, fertilizer, seed, pesticide, fuel, hired labor, hired machinery, trucking and engine hours in the same way. The problem was not in the amount of production; it was that the cost of production was too high. Looking over the charts of the expenses, Hank asked Jen Beth to chart the average annual sale price of corn against the expenses. Hank scanned this new chart, "Well well, who would have thought it? Every time the price of corn goes up, the cost of pesticides, seed, fertilizer and land rent goes up by about the same percentage. For all those years, Dad was playing against a stacked deck. Everybody supplying inputs to him set their prices high enough to insure themselves a profit; the farmer can't do that, he can only take what is offered" "Hank, I want to spend some time with this; I am not sure how to use it yet but your parents recorded a wealth of information that deserves to be analyzed." Hank nodded, "The first thing I would like to see is what herbicides were used and in what amounts on the home farm and Aunt Ella's hundred and sixty in the last five years; some of those things can persist in the soil and, aside from destroying soil life, kill germinating plants for years. I think I had better take soil samples from all over the farm and do grow out tests with a lot of different plants; if we have herbicide hang over, we need to know it before we plant a bunch of expensive seed. We need to get soil samples in to Dr. Carthage so I might as well get soil for those when I get soil for grow out tests. In fact, since this snow fell before the ground was frozen, with a pentameter and a bulk density sampler, I could start collecting data on the physical condition of the soil at the same time. I will check in the barn for soil probes and sample bags and then get online to order what other equipment I need." Hank found his Dads' soil test equipment with two sampling probes and plenty of sample bags and then stopped by the old greenhouse where he and Umpa had spent so many happy hours; it had not been used since Umpa died but everything was still there right down to a stack of firewood for the little cast iron stove used to provide extra heat. There was even a carton of transplant cups that would do just fine for his herbicide tests. He would get the equipment he needed coming and then start thinking about dividing the farm into similar areas for the soil sampling.

Hank found a meticulously drawn and dimensioned map of the farm in his Dads' files and scanned it into his computer so that he could access it with his mapping software; he then went online to the USDA Soil Survey website and located maps showing the boundaries of the various soil sites on Yoder Farm. He made an over lay of this map and added it as a removable layer to his fathers' map; he would use the USDA soil sites to determine the area to be included in each soil sample.

Hank heard the house phone ring and heard his mother speak briefly with someone before calling up the stairway, "Hank, would you come down and talk with this man? Please." Hank took the phone, "This is Hank Weaver." "Mr. Weaver, my name is Joe Meyers; I am an attorney with the Consumer and Producer Legal Defense Coalition. The Coalition is a non-profit organization whose purpose is to defend the legal rights of both food producers and consumers that have been damaged by the actions of cor- porations or other entities. I know that this is a very diffi- cult time for you but I would really like to sit down and talk with you and your Mother; we feel that there is a strong possibility that you were damaged by overtly illegal actions of GAI." "Mr. Meyers, we are not a family that is inclined to file lawsuits; I doubt very much that my Mother would be interested in bringing suit against GAI." "I understand, Mr. Weaver but if our information is correct, you may have no choice; we have reason to suspect that GAI is planning to bring suit against all of the parties that were accused by Jim Turner of having violated the patent laws. Evidently, they feel that not pursuing the suits would amount to an admission that unethical and illegal acts were committed by their employees; such a perception would be extremely damaging to their reputation. They feel that the best way to contain the damage is to win at least some of these lawsuits and thus tarnish the believability of the witnesses against Jim Turner and Gary Doak." "Mr. Meyers, I believe we had better meet with you; when and where did you have in mind?" "I will come to you; I plan to meet with several other farmers in your area next week. When next week would work for you and your mother?" "We have an auction scheduled for Saturday so for us the earlier in the week, the better." Anna and Jen Beth had been listening to Hanks' part of the conversation and were obviously anxious to hear what was happening; Hank filled them in on what Meyers had told him. "Do you mean after Gary Doak confessed that he and Turner made up the charges out of thin air, GAI still has the gall to file the suits?" "That seems to be the case, Mother." Jen Beth spoke up with, "It may just be a bluff to get the criminal charges dropped against their man Turner. I know a little about the Consumer and Producer Legal Defense Coalition; they have done some good work defending organic growers that have gotten cross wise with some of the agri-business giants. Let's not get too depressed until we meet with Mr. Meyers." "I agree Babe, but we do need to contact your Dad; this puts a new perspective on the situation and he may want to re-think his offer." "Hank, I agree we need to call him but I can guarantee that Dad will not let a threat like this change his mind; it is more likely that it will make him want to double down and expand his position." "Why don't you call him now; he may want to have someone from the legal department sit in on our meeting with Meyers."

Jacob listened to Jen Beths' account of what had transpired without interruption until she finished. "Jen Beth have you determined a fair lease price for Yoder Farm?" "I think so Dad, we have the figures on what Henry was paying, one place he leased joins Yoder Farm and the others

are close by, and Hank talked to several other land owners and farmers in the area." "Good, take an average of
what the nearby farms leased for, add twenty percent and
call me back with the figure; I will have a lease drawn up,
sign it and fax it to you; give me routing instructions to
a bank account and I will wire the first years rent. I want
Bristol Farms tied to Yoder Farm and Hanks' mother just
as soon as we can get it done. I know Joe Meyers of the
Coalition, he is a good lawyer, by the way, and I will have
someone from our legal department contact him and be
at the meeting. I need to think it through a little more but
you two and Mrs. Weaver think about the pros and cons of
Yoder Farm and/or Mrs. Weaver forming a limited liability
partnership with Bristol Farms. It might make a difference
if GAI knows that Mrs. Weaver has allies beyond her local
attorney. Get me the lease figures, the routing instructions
and a fax number and you two go on with your project."

"You called that right Babe, your Dad sounds as if he
is looking forward to tangling with GAI." "It goes beyond
just business Hank, he truly believes that GAI and others
like them are poisoning our people and our planet. Dad is
a true believer in the capitalist system, politically he makes
Rush Limbaugh look a little pink around the edges but he
also believes that no one has the right to harm other people in pursuit of profit or ideology or anything else for that
matter. He believes in the benefits of organic agriculture
to people and to the environment and wants to see the area
devoted to organic production increased in the Midwest
and other areas. He is convinced that between the tax
and spend welfare state promoters and the moon struck
pseudo environmentalists, California, the most productive

agricultural area in the world, will soon be forced out of agricultural production. The companies like GAI that promote dangerous products and policies play into the hands of the radical anti-agriculture bunch and give them real ammunition by failing to police their own selves when it comes to harming others. Every time a batch of E. coli contaminated meat makes people sick or a bunch of produce has to be re-called from the market because of pesticide contamination, the calls for more government regulations grow louder. Dad believes that the way to prevent these things is to hold companies, and individuals, accountable for their actions. It makes a lot more sense to set standards as to what is wholesome and what is not and let people figure out ways to meet the standards rather than to set up rigid procedures that everyone must follow. This approach is logical and would work but the government bureaucracies and the big food companies fight this concept at every opportunity. The bureaucracies don't want to give up the control and the people that it takes to draw up regulations and enforce them and the companies do not want to have to self-certify that their products are wholesome. To do that would put the responsibility on them rather than on the government and would require slowing down the production lines in slaughter plants and doing a more thorough job of keeping processing equipment clean and maybe even using higher quality ingredients. It is cheaper for them to pay for the government inspectors and fill out all the forms so as to be able to say, "We followed all the rules; it is not our fault." The large companies can spread the costs of regulation over large quantities of product and keep their prices competitive. These costs, however, make it harder and harder for individual farmers or even small companies to market food products directly to the public, not because their products are sub-standard, just because' with limited amounts of production, they cannot afford to jump through all the regulatory hoops. It is easier for the small producer to produce clean wholesome food than it is for the big company but it is almost impossible for them to compete when the question is not "Is this good food?" but rather "Did you fill out all three hundred pages of this week's report?" Sorry, but I get mad when I think of how things could and should be done. If all of the regulations that are in place today had been present when America was young, we would have an economy half the size of Albania's and my ancestor Thomas would never have started Bristol Farms."

CHAPTER FIFTEEN
Beginning the Dynasty

Upper California coast 1850

Thomas was on his way to town with a load of produce; Henry Gable, their usual teamster, didn't show up for work so Thomas had to put aside his plans for the day and make the trip to town and back. This was the second time for Gable to miss work and Thomas was through with him; when he came dragging in, three hours late, Thomas told him to leave and not come back. Thomas awoke this morning in a grand mood; the weather was beautiful, the crops were growing, they were making money and life was good — except for that damn drunken teamster. Thomas had never before had employees; he had crewmen under his orders when he was first mate on the Jenny Hardin but that was a different situation. Shipboard everybody followed orders and did their job, slackers were not tolerated, the mere mention of the possibility of stranding in a foreign port was a strong incentive to performance. They really needed to hire more people but Thomas dreaded having to put up with the problems that came with employees. As he rounded a slight curve, Thomas saw a wagon by the side of the road and two women digging what, from the blanket wrapped bundle beside the hole, had to be a grave. Thomas stopped his team where he could tie them to a tree and walked up to the women. When he got closer he could see that there was one older women and one younger and both were thin and worn looking. Two mules were grazing on tether ropes and they too were thin. Thomas approached the women and removing his hat said, "Ladies, may I help you?" The older woman said, "Thank you sir; I am Mrs. Leon Channing and this is my daughter Emma, we are burying our husband and father." Mrs. Channing let the shovel she was holding slide to the ground and she would have followed it had not her daughter put an arm around her waist. They had evidently been camped here for several days; there was a fire pit with a blackened coffee pot and two straight back chairs by the fire. Emma helped her mother to one of the chairs and brought her a cup of what Thomas could see was plain water. "Ladies, if you will permit me, I will finish digging the grave. While I do that Miss Emma, would you fix us something to eat? There are vegetables of all kinds on my wagon and there is coffee and a side of bacon in the chop box under the seat. Emma started back to his wagon and as she passed him, looked up shyly and said, "Thank you." "Miss Emma there is a basket of ripe peaches in the front of the wagon, why don't you and your mother have some of those while the food is cooking?

Thomas went to work on the grave while the two women started coffee and a big pot of stew. When Thomas finished, the two women watched as he carried Leon Channing to the side of the grave and lowered him into it. Mrs. Channing read the 23rd Psalm and started a prayer before breaking down in sobs. Emma helped her mother back to her chair and helped Thomas fill in the grave. "I come this way often, Miss Emma; I will make a grave marker and put it up the next time I come." Mrs. Channing had regained her composure and brought a third chair out of their wagon for Thomas; she brought him a cup of coffee and urged him to sit. Emma brought him a bowl of stew and one for her mother before getting her own. The stew was mostly vegetables and needed salt but it was hot and filling and both women finished one bowl and went back for more. "As you must have guessed Mr. Bristol, we have been dire straits since my husband got sick two weeks ago; I cannot thank you enough for your kindness." "If I might ask Mrs. Channing, where are you going?" "We lost our little farm and Leon heard that there was work to be had a mining camp farther up the Petaluma River. Now that he is gone, I don't know where we will go." "Mrs. Channing, I have a farm about five miles north; why don't you and Miss Emma come there? You can camp on the farm and get rested up; you can decide what you want to do later. We don't have much but we have plenty to eat and you are more than welcome. I need to take this load of vegetables into town and then I will be going back to the farm. I will be back here in about four hours and if you wish, we will hitch your team and you can follow me."

Thomas rolled into the farm leading the Channing's in their wagon just as people were coming in from the fields; normally he would have had to stop and take on a whole wagon load of little Jin's but the presence of strangers made the kids shy. He showed Emma, who was driving, where

139

to park their wagon and then unhitched both teams and turned them into the corral with a feed of hay. He brought Mrs. Channing the box of staples he had put together from their store in town and showed her the wood pile and the well. The Channing wagon was parked just a few yards from his open bedroom window and he fell asleep that night hearing the soft mummer of women's voices for the first time in a very long time.

Next morning, Thomas started down to the barn to do chores just as it was getting light enough to see; he was surprised to find Miss Emma using a twist of hay to brush the, soon to calve, Jersey heifer. Emma had evidently already started chores as the heifer was eating hay from her bunk and the chickens were scratching busily for scattered grain. "Good morning Mr. Bristol, this is a beautiful heifer. What is her name?" "I've only had her a little while and haven't gotten around to naming her; why don't you do the honors and name her? "Oh may I? She looks so very much like a cow that we once owned. I will name her Velvet in remembrance of that fine cow. My Mother sent me to ask if you would take breakfast with us. She has biscuits baking and bacon and oat porridge cooked." "Well thank you, I would like that; let me feed the mules and I will be over directly." Thomas fed the mules and the Jin's donkey and gathered the dozen or so eggs that were in the laying boxes to take along to the Channing's. He seldom cooked, it was easier to eat with the Jin's even if breakfast was only tea and rice cake, the anticipation of a proper hot breakfast had his mouth drooling as he hurried through his chores. He presented the eggs to Mrs. Channing and she quickly added scrambled eggs to the mornings' menu.

The three chairs were aligned on the up wind side of the small cooking fire and Emma motioned him to a seat and brought him a cup of strong coffee. Mrs. Channing lifted the lid off a Dutch oven and the aroma of fresh baked bread flooded the area; hot bread was not in the diet of the Jin's and that and blood rare beef were the things Thomas missed most. The biscuits were excellent though Thomas agreed with Emma that they would be even better with butter instead of bacon grease. "Can you churn butter, Miss Emma?" "Oh yes, that was one of my jobs when we had our farm; Dad kept eight to ten cows and sold sweet milk along with butter, butter milk and cheese. Mother is a master cheese maker and was teaching me." Thomas worked his way through the feast, at the moment he was savoring the oat porridge, when he tried to make it, the stuff turned out with the consistency and taste of wallpaper paste; this had the delightful nutty taste and chewy texture that Thomas remembered from long ago at his Mother's table in England. When the last crumb of Thomas' third biscuit was gone, he broached a subject that he had been mulling since he saw Emma brushing the heifer. "If we could come to mutually agreeable terms, would you ladies be interested in running a small dairy herd, maybe five or six cows, and making cheese? We could fix up the little house next to the barn for your quarters; I or one of the Li boys would do any needed heavy work if you can handle the milking and make the butter and cheese. Would this be something that would like to do?" Emma was smiling broadly but turned to her mother to give their answer. "Mr. Bristol That is something that Emma and I would like very much. Thank you for the offer and we will do our best to make it a success." "Very good, be thinking about what we will need besides cows and I will start gathering things. I would also like part of the deal to be that you cook for me at least part of the time." "That is no problem, Sir. It is no harder to cook for three than for two." By this time the sun was high and Thomas was sure that the Li's would be wondering where he was but he left the Channing's in a very good mood – though more than a little bit too full.

Miss Emma and her mother started that afternoon cleaning on the little house that had once housed a couple employed by Don Pablo as gardener and cook; by night fall they started to move their meager possessions out of the wagon and into the house. After many anxious days, they now felt safe and were looking forward to sleeping under a roof for the first time since they lost their farm.

Thomas sat easy as the mules clopped along at an easy pace on their way back from town; he got fidgety with the forced inactivity of riding back and forth to town but it was a good time to think and plan. At first the farm was just a way to make a living but it was rapidly becoming something that he wanted to build. He liked working with the soil but had found lately that he also liked the business side of the enterprise; he seemed to find new opportunities to make money everywhere he looked. Between the gold hunters and the ships there was a great market for foodstuffs of all kinds. The Spanish ranches in the interior had thousands of head of cattle but until the gold hunters came, practically no markets but the hide and tallow trade. Cattle were beginning to be driven to the mining camps and killed to sell meat to the miners but the hide and tallow killing was done on the coast and without ways to keep it from spoiling, the meat was basically a waste product. From his years at sea, Thomas knew firsthand how bad most salt cured beef, the infamous "salt horse", was when it got to the sailors. He also knew that there were ways to preserve beef that would produce a quality product that could move in international trade. He had seen canned salmon from Scotland and had eaten canned tomatoes in English ports; he needed to find out what it would take to set up a cannery. Even with their excellent markets, during peak harvest times they had tomatoes go bad before they could be sold. If the same machinery could be used for multiple foods, they could can tomatoes when they were in season and things like fish, beef and even butter at other times. He would explore the canning option but in the mean time there were ways to preserve food that they could use immediately. He had fallen in love with sun dried tomatoes when his ship was in dry dock in Italy and beef jerky and even salted beef could be very good if care was taken during its' preparation.

As he approached the farm and home, Thomas was snatched from his day dreams by a woman's piercing scream and raucous male laughter; the mules had already quickened their pace in anticipation of getting out of harness and being fed and they broke into a rapid trot when Thomas slapped their rumps with the reins and urged them to a faster pace. When the team turned into the barnyard, Thomas could see three men standing over someone lying in the road and, from the corner of his eye, Miss Emma running full tilt from the barn toward the group. He hauled his team to a stop and hit the ground running toward the three men. One of them held up what Thomas recognized as the pant portion of the black pajamas worn by all the Jin's while another dropped his trousers and was bending over what Thomas could now see was Jin Tan's oldest granddaughter. He snatched his hoe from the road side storage shed without breaking stride and looked up just in time to see Emma swing the pitchfork she was carrying and jab the four tines of it into the would be rapist's butt like it was a mound of hay. The man screamed and tried to scuttle off on all fours; he was doing his damnest to get away from Miss Emma and her pitchfork but she kept pace with him leaning on the fork handle to drive the tines even deeper. The thug holding the girls' pants tried to grab the pitchfork away from Emma but Thomas arrived at that moment and, with a full swing, slammed the back side of his hoe into the man's head. The last of the three abandoned his friends and ran, as hard as someone as drunk as he could, away from Emma and Thomas and the rapidly approaching angry mob of black clad, hoe wielding Jin's. Thomas managed to get the pitchfork away from Emma and pull it out of the speared thug; who fell flat on his belly blubbering, "Don't kill me. Don't kill me" while trying to pull up his pants and cover his head with his arms at the same time. The family Jin arrived in mass and the women took charge of granddaughter while the men surrounded the two thugs (the one Thomas tried to brain was coming more or less awake) banishing their heavy bladed hoes and muttering dire threats in Cantonese. Emma started to shake violently and would have gone to the ground had Thomas not put his arms around her and held her close; even with his pulse racing from an adrenalin high, Thomas was amazed how soft and warm and right Emma felt in his arms. With a guilty start, Thomas gently disengaged from Emma and asked Jin Li if Jin Soo, his daughter, was harmed, "Frightened and humiliated but not harmed which is good; had she been harmed, I would have been honor bound to kill these two foul creatures." Thomas turned to the two thugs, "Get up and get out of here before I kill you myself. If you ever come back, I will feed you to my hogs – one live piece at a time." He had moved away from Emma to read the riot act to the thugs but they came together again in what seemed to be a completely normal move. They stood there not quite touching as all of the Jin's from Jin Tan to the smallest child came forward to bow and offer them their thanks. It was a solemn moment until Jin Chan, who was six years old, bowed to Thomas and Emma, said a polite "Thank you" and then, grabbing his bottom with both hands, went prancing off in a high stepping run squealing, "Ow, Ow, Ow". Jin Tan swatted at his grandson as he ran by but was chuckling when he did so while everyone else roared with laughter. Thomas and Emma started back to the barn; after just a few steps, Emma stopped and said, "Oh Thomas, in the excitement, I forgot; Velvet has the most beautiful heifer calf! It looks as if our dairy will start sooner than we thought." When they resumed their walk to the barn – she with her pitchfork and he with his hoe – it seemed perfectly natural that they walk hand in hand.

CHAPTER SIXTEEN
The Specter Fades

Yoder Farm

Joe Meyers knocked on the front door at Yoder Farm right at the agreed upon time of nine o'clock on Friday morning. Hank took his coat and ushered him into the kitchen where Jen Beth and Anna sat at a table spread with Anna's ledger books and stacks of print out from Jen Beth's computer. Meyers accepted a cup of coffee just as another knock at the front door announced the arrival of the Bristol Farms lawyer, Wallace Crown, who had been with Bristol Farms for fifteen years and had worked with Joe Meyers in the past. After introductions all around, Meyers opened the discussion, "Wallace and I talked on the phone for a while last night; we have gone over the situation and have an approach that we would like to discuss with the three of you. We both feel that GAI is using the threat of law-suits to attempt to get you and the other farmers to bring pressure on the district attorney to drop the fraud charges filed against their employee, Joe Turner. I have watched for a number of years as GAI, and other companies, have used the threat of financial ruin through legal action to bully farmers into settlements that were not justified by the

147

facts. Rather than just defending their rights, the companies have allowed these suits to become extortion, income generators for the companies and the law firms they hire. At the Coalition, we have compiled ten years of data on these types of cases and a clear pattern has developed. In the early days of patented seed, there were instances of farmers violating their agreement not to plant patented seed that they grew and the companies sued and won a number of these cases. Some of these early suits involved large farming companies, many of which were guilty, but as time went on nearly all of the new patent infringement suits have been filed against small farmers with limited resources. When faced with years of legal expense, many of these small farmers will agree to pay some amount just to make the threat stop. I have talked with a number of these people that were completely innocent of any wrong doing but paid up just to remove the threat of financial ruin. At the Coalition, we feel that these suits will continue to be filed against innocent people so long as it is profitable to do so." Anna said, "Do you mean that GAI has filed suit against farmers that they knew were innocent in other places; that it was not just the Doak boy and some thug acting on their own?" "Mrs. Weaver that is exactly what I mean and for the first time we have the where with all to prove it. The law firms handling these cases have teams of so called "investigators" that travel the country gathering "evidence" against farmers. We have suspected for a long time that much of this "evidence" is manufactured out of thin air and fraud but since these cases seldom go to trial, much of the evidence is never examined; if a case does go to trial, they simply do not introduce any suspect evidence.

We have known what was going on for a long time but have had no way to verify our suspicions; that changed about a month ago when we learned that Joe Turner is actually named Jesse Thompson and is a felon with multiple convictions for fraud and extortion. Our informant and that is what he is, a paid informant – a felon and a disgusting excuse for a human being who would be useless as a witness in a trial – worked with Turner-Thompson on one of these teams and has given us a world of information that we are in the process of verifying. We take nothing that he tells us as fact but use his leads to find the truth. We will have more than enough evidence to completely discredit Turner-Thompson and force GAI to drop any thought of bringing suit against anyone who he accused." Hank was the one to express what all of the Weavers felt, "That is fantastic! It will take a tremendous load off of us and off all of the other families they have targeted in the valley." "You are correct Hank and if you wish we can leave it at that but the Coalition and now Bristol Farms has a proposition for you that you may or may not want to consider. We can destroy Turner and Doak but GAI will merely put out a press release apologizing that a rouge employee did such a horrible thing; they will get some bad press but no real damage. What we would like for you to consider is filing a wrongful death suit against GAI and their lawyers; we believe that we can win such a suit but even if all we achieve is to get evidence of serious and repeated wrong doing by the company and their law firms into the record the state will be strongly pressured to consider criminal charges against the company." The room grew quiet as Anna sat and twisted a dish towel around and around between her hands. "If we do this, what is the likelihood that it will prevent GAI or someone else from doing to other people what they did to us?" "Mrs. Weaver, if we manage to get evidence of fraud and extortion that was performed repeatedly over several years into the legal record, I can almost guarantee you that it will put a halt to any future such activity by GAI and would have a chilling effect on other companies who might be considering similar actions. I would expect, at the very least, that everyone in GAI who was directly involved would be terminated and most likely sued by the company. It would be a public relations disaster and would severely affect the value of the company." "What sort of cost are we looking at?" "There would be no cost to you Mrs. Weaver, the Coalition has been looking for such an opening to rein in these kinds of abuses and would stand all legal fees and all expenses of any kind; I might add that Bristol Farms just made a quite generous contribution to our legal defense fund." "Hank, what do you and Jen Beth think? Is this something we should do?" "Mother this is your decision and we will support whatever you decide; I admit that I would like to see GAI punished for what they did to Dad." "Mr. Meyers, we will do what you ask but I do not want us to take one dime from any settlement; I would like to see any money recovered put to use helping farm family's get away from the use of the poisons these companies are promoting."

"Mrs. Weaver, you are doing a brave thing that will bring you pain as you have to relive painful events but I truly believe that you are doing something very good that only you can do. We will start preparing the suit and get it filed just as soon as possible. When we file, I would expect GAI to drop all thought of pursuing action against any of the local farmers; I would like to get that threat off their minds as quickly as we can. I see that you have been going over records; are these the records of Mr. Weavers farming activity?" Jen Beth answered, "They are and they are unbelievably complete. Henry and Anna recorded every expense; not only what was purchased but when and where it was used. There is a day by day history here of the last thirteen years. There are records of the production of every crop by year and by field. Look here, for instance, Henry purchased fifty bushels of certified Sandusky variety soybean seed from Mayfield Seed Company on March 3rd three years ago for nine dollars and seventy-five cents a bushel and used them to plant the north fifty acres in the west half of the northwest quarter of section 16 on June 10th. Those fifty acres yielded twenty five hundred forty bushels when he combined them on October 14th and 15th. There are receipts from the seed cleaner where he had the soybeans cleaned and bagged to be saved for seed. You can follow through to the next season and see that Henry used seven hundred and forty bushels of this seed to plant seven hundred and eight acres of soybeans in six fields. The remaining eighteen hundred bushels Henry sold as seed beans to three different farmers; names of purchasers, bushels purchased, price per bushel and dates of sales are all listed right here. Over here are Henry and Anna's bank records for the same thirteen years and copies of their income tax returns for the same period. What I am doing right now is seeing how much of the information in the ledger entries I can verify from other sources; I have been able to find supporting information, bank statements, loan payments, invoices, etc, for every entry I have examined so far. We expected to have to prove that Henry did not buy any glyphosate in the past three years and when and where he used what he bought in the years before. I think we can convince a fair jury in any court that Henry was innocent of the charges made against him by GAI with nothing more than the information recorded here." "Mrs. Weaver, I was going to ask if I could have one of our accountants go over these records but I can see that will not be necessary; you have given us far more ammunition than I could have hoped for to convince a court of Henry's innocence. With this information, we can show that there was nothing but malice behind the charges and that will go far toward us winning the suit."

As the meeting was breaking up, both lawyers pleading time constraints in refusing the offer of lunch, Anna said, "Mr. Meyers, I don't think that I want to add the bank to our suit but I would very much like to know how Albert Horning knew that GAI was going to file lawsuits against the five families and I would like for the public to know just how ready the bank was to sacrifice those families." Joe Meyers put down his briefcase and taking a note pad from his pocket recorded a brief note; he started to put away the pad but stopped as another though came to him and wrote a longer note. "Mrs. Weaver that is an excellent suggestion; I will include Mr. Horning in our list of subpoenaed witnesses and I will know the correct answers to the questions he will be asked. Young Doak has retracted his confession, claims he was coerced even though his father was present when he confessed, but I don't think that will present much of a problem for us and may cause Doak to be charged with perjury. The elder Mr. Doak has said publicly that he plans to testify against his son which would make any claim of coercion rather hard to sell to the court. Mr. Crown and I are going back to town and get started on this; we will be in touch but if you have other thoughts or ideas, please contact one of us." Hank had still not told his Mother about Marge Strickland's uncle and the role of Horning, et al in his troubles but began composing, in his head, a letter giving Meyers and Crown all he knew or suspected of the situation.

With the decision to file suit made, there was a noticeable reduction of tension on Yoder Farm; people slept better and smiled more often. Jen Beth spent the time when Hank was busy taking soil samples designing a method of tabulating and analyzing the years of data. She was not yet satisfied with her methods but it soon became clear that the greatest problem with the way Henry operated for years, and many farmers still operated, was too high a level of input (expense) given the potential for profit and the degree of uncertainty (risk) present in factors beyond the control of the farmer. Yields increased tremendously under the all out high input program but margins, the difference between cost per unit of production and income per unit of production shrank to a level that was insufficient to cover any unexpected drop in income. Bad weather, a disease outbreak or a fairly small drop in the market and the farmer was faced with a net loss for the year even though he produced a large crop. With a serious setback such as flood or drought, the farmer could easily lose an amount of money equal to the profit expected in five or more years. There had to be a way to determine when increasing production by increasing inputs made financial sense and when the risk of increasing inputs was too high. Jen Beth could see that such a judgment could only be valid if it considered the entire situation but she would have to devote some serious thought to designing the needed tools. She did not have the answer but it was very obvious that analyzing production practices in isolation with the prime question being "will it cash flow" was a recipe for disaster. Certainly a practice must generate enough extra income to pay for itself (cash flow) but just because it will cash flow does not mean that it is a good use of money, even if it is a good use of money, is it the most advantageous way to use the money at that point in time? Jen Beth remembered reading that farmers made something like eighty five percent of their financial decisions based on information they got from people who were trying to sell them something. She was going to try to come up with ways to help make better decisions and she thought again about the book *Holistic Management* by Alan Savory and Jody Butterfield. In this classic the authors give some very logical ways to test whether or not a decision is correct; the first thing she should do is read *Holistic Management* again.

One decision that they all approved as correct was to sell all of the big equipment; the auction company had been advertizing the sale for several weeks, with snow on the ground farmers were not busy and the auctioneer assured the family that they would have a good crowd for the sale. The day before the auction, the auction crew arrived early and with, Hank helping got all of the equipment that was to sell lined up and ready to go. They would sell everything that was on the bank note which meant that they would be left with only the equipment and tools that had belonged to Umpa. Their only tractor, aside from a little lawn mower/garden tractor, would be the thirty five horse power Farmall that Umpa had once farmed with but then used only to tend his orchard and to till his garden. They would not have the big equipment but they would have a wide range of smaller farm equipment, going back to horse drawn versions, and all kinds of tools, both power and hand, to work wood, metal and leather. When six generations of people live in the same location, they accumulate things; especially when they are self sufficient farmers and craftsmen like the Yoder's. As a boy, Hank was amazed at all that Umpa could do; when Chigger got tender footed from too many miles on gravel roads, Umpa fired up the old coke forge, took a bar of iron and made him a set of perfectly fitted shoes. He could fix most anything that broke, from harness to plows, and he made his wife a beautiful cherry wood china cabinet from a tree from their woodlot that he felled, sawed into lumber, cured and planed. Hank spent many happy hours with his grandfather and by the time he was ten or so could correctly use and care for all of Umpa's hand tools and, with supervision, most of the power tools.

The day of the sale dawned bright, clear and not too cold; people came out in droves and the equipment sold even better than the auctioneer had estimated. Hank had sold all of the cash land leases Henry had purchased and when this money and Henry and Anna's cash on hand was added to the sale proceeds, the remainder left on the bank note, including interest to date, was thirty six thousand and forty dollars. Jen Beth's parents wired this amount to the bank, Hank and Jen Beth signed an interest bearing note to her parents and the Weaver family was free of all association with the First State Bank of Cayuga.

Hank and Jen Beth had been discussing how they were going to develop a profitable farm but the realization that they owed thirty six thousand dollars before they started put a new sense of urgency to their planning. It was no longer an academic exercise; it was real life and the interest clock was ticking.

Hank finished with the soil samples and decided that before he did anything else, he would prune Umpa's orchard; the broken limbs and raggedy appearance seemed an affront to his memory of his Granddad. That night at supper when he told Jen Beth and his mother what he planned for the next morning, Jen Beth asked if she could come along, "I need some exercise." Anna spoke up, "If you are going to prune the orchard, save me some apple wood and some pear wood for the smokehouse; we haven't had home smoked ham or bacon since Umpa died." As Hank got ready for bed, he came back from the bathroom to find Jen Beth, looking quite fetching in her favorite nightwear, one of his tee shirts, intently studying something on her computer, "Hank did you know that people sell all kinds of fruit wood to be used in home smokers and barbeques?" "I hadn't thought about it; when I was a kid, a lot of people had smokehouses but most of them had fruit trees so they had their own source of fruit wood. What does fruit wood sell for on the internet?" "I have looked at a half dozen sites and the price varies from about a dollar and a half per pound to five dollars a pound depending on the amount in a package; ten pound bags of chunks average about two dollars and fifty cents per pound." "Is that freight paid?" "No freight is extra." "Missy, I think you have just found our first alternative product if we can figure a way to cut it into chunks and bag it without spending a bunch of money."

The day was cold but clear with no wind as Hank and Jen Beth loaded up the saws and pruning hooks that Hank had used so many times with his Grandfather. Hank hitched Umpa's log sled behind the Farmall and with Jen Beth driving the pickup, they drove across the snow covered fields to the orchard. Up close the trees were not in as bad shape as Hank had feared but they did need pruning. Hank pulled the sled up alongside the first apple tree and started the pruning as Umpa had taught him; first the dead wood and then the crossed limbs and limbs growing too low and finally the thinning and shaping to provide sunlight penetration and air flow. He cut several limbs and then showed Jen Beth how to drag and stack them, butt end forward, on the sled; since they might want to cut up and bag the wood, Hank took binder twine and tied each eight or ten limbs into a bundle so that they could handle it easier and also keep the different kinds of wood separate. They worked steadily through the morning and started back to the house when they ran out of room on the sled about the same time their breakfast wore off. It would take several days to finish the job but they would have a lot of wood and Hank was already thinking about how to cut it into chunks. They pulled the sled into the now empty drive through hay shed and unloaded before going in for dinner; Jen Beth still had trouble with eating dinner at noon but whatever it was called, Anna's food was always good. After they ate and lay down for a short nap, they went back and cut another load; they would be sore tomorrow but both of them enjoyed the physical activity and working together.

After supper, Hank went down to the shop and began building the contraption that he had been designing in his head all afternoon. He found a replacement blade for a potato digger – just a rectangular piece of flat hard steel twenty four inches long with bolt holes and one sharp edge – and bolted it sharp edge down to a piece of heavy angle iron. He cut two eight inch pieces of two and a half inch pipe and welded one on each end of the knife assembly. He then cut two pieces of two inch pipe five feet long and stuck one pipe through the piece of two and a half inch pipe on each end of the knife assembly; when he welded a piece of the angle iron to each end of the two five foot pipes, he had a frame that would allow the knife to be raised and lowered like a Guillotine. He added brackets to fasten a tractor powered hydraulic cylinder to the top of the frame and to the knife assembly and he had his power wood chopper. He would have to add a table like frame to rest the bundles of branches on as they were fed into the chopper and a stop plate to regulate the length of branch cut and a remote hydraulic valve so one person could both feed the branches and operate the knife but he knew that he could find everything he needed either in the parts storage or the scrap pile. Nothing that might possibly be of use someday was ever thrown away on Yoder Farm. They were not going to get rich selling fruitwood from their small orchard but it could be another product to offer customers in what Hank hoped would someday be their retail farm products store here on the farm and also on the internet. As Joel Salatin says, "It is a lot easier to sell one customer three different items than it is to sell one item to three different customers."

The more Hank thought about how to make a go of their project, the more respect he gained for his grandfather. The beauty of the way Umpa farmed was that everything fit together and each piece supported other pieces. The small flock of sheep produced wool and lambs to be sold as well as meat for the family but they had other value as well. Ten days or so after the corn was laid bye, cultivated for the last time, lambs and sometimes geese would be released in the corn to eat weeds and grass that escaped the cultivator or sprouted after lay bye. They might prune a few low corn leaves but much preferred the weeds and tender new grass. Through this simple technique Umpa turned a negative (weeds in the corn) into a positive (lamb chops). Umpa's hogs didn't race through life on a concrete floor stuffed with purchased feed to be killed at five months of age as was the case with "modern" hogs – they received a full feed of corn for only the last few weeks after spending eight to ten months of grazing green pasture and being the designated cleanup crew for excess or blemished fruits and vegetables; you have never seen true satisfaction until you see a bunch of pigs with a trough full of chopped turnips. The handful of dairy cows didn't bring in a lot of money, mostly just sales of butter when the spring grass was flush and cheese later in the year, but they provided all sorts of dairy products to the family and the skim milk and whey provided a source of animal protein to the hogs and to the poultry. They utilized and gave value to products like blemished or damaged vegetables and provided manure to be composted and used on the orchard and garden where it was hard to graze larger herds of animals. They gave added value to the cover crops that Umpa planted to build fertility and even provided feed for the poultry in the form of insect larva in their cow pats. The same sort of analysis could be done for each crop that Umpa raised; the pasture fed the cattle and the sheep and the horses; it even provided a good portion of the feed for hogs and poultry. Keeping land in mixed species pasture for several years greatly reduced weed, insect and disease pests in the crops that followed and when plowed down, provided the nutrients to grow two or more years of row crops without the need to purchase fertilizer. Umpa's farm was like a big troupe of singers and dancers supported by a full orchestra, each player came in at just the right time to do his bit, so long as Umpa provided the direction.

CHAPTER SEVENTEEN
The Foundation

Petaluma Valley 1856

Thomas Bristol was a happy man; nearly everything that he had put his hand to in the last seven years had succeeded. It was good that his farm had grown tremendously and that his various businesses; the dairy, the cannery, the meat processing plant, the flour mill and the winery were doing well. The best news, however, was that his wife Emma had finally conceived their second child. After their son Leon was born, Emma had been unable to conceive – the one dark spot in their life as both of them wanted more children.

Shorty after he and Emma married, Thomas moved them to the Petaluma Valley where they had the opportunity to farm on a much larger scale. The Jins moved as well and located just down river from Thomas and Emma; the two families still cooperated closely. Thomas did much of the marketing for the Jins' crops and as both families increased the amount of land they farmed, the Jins brought in Chinese families to supply the needed labor.

Even with the additional labor, the expanded scale of their operations required that they develop new methods of production; using seaweed and dried fish to maintain fertility was not feasible on a large scale. Both families used some bat guano and Thomas briefly used some of the Chilean nitrate that Jin Tan had ruled out as "salt." After seeing the damage to his soil in two seasons of use, Thomas admitted that Jin Tan was correct and halted all use of the mined product. Thomas was not an educated man but he was a thinking man with strong powers of observation. He was experimenting with the use of fish cannery waste but the ways to build fertility that showed the most promise for large acreages were green manure crops plowed down and manure from his dairy herd and from his chicken and hog farms. After a brief period of hauling feed in to the cows and manure out to the cropland, Thomas woke up and had the cows herded out to graze the areas he wanted to fertilize. After the cows learned the routine, a boy and a dog easily handled this chore. Cover crops with mixed species of grasses and legumes would be grazed off one small plot at a time and when Thomas saw that they were wasting manure, and labor, by having the cattle come back to the barn at night, he designed a mobile milking shed that allowed the cattle to stay in the fields full time. Depending on the season and how long a plot had been in pasture, the cover crop might be allowed to re-grow to be grazed again or it might be plowed and put into crops to be harvested. Even with the cow herd expanding as they sold more cheese, they did not have enough cattle to graze as many acres as Thomas would like; much of their crop acreage was prepared by simply plowing down a season's growth of cover crop. Keeping track of where each parcel of land was in the rotation required good records and advance planning. It was necessary work but not a chore Thomas relished; he was at the kitchen table struggling with laying out the sequence of use for each parcel when Emma asked if she could help. She had attended school in Missouri before her father moved the family to California and she had a much better head for numbers than did Thomas. Also everyone could read her precise and neat hand writing and soon she was the designated secretary- treasurer- book keeper for the operation.

After the failure of the Chilean nitrate, Thomas made it a point to discuss any new practice with Jin Tan; the old man had no formal education but he was a treasure house of practical knowledge of the natural world. Jin Tan firmly believed that the secret to productive agriculture with few pest problems was to mimic nature as closely as possible: Jin Tan did not plow the soil. As one crop was harvested, the residue was cut down and laid on the soil to act as water retaining and weed suppressing mulch; the next crop would be planted by parting the mulch to uncover and plant in mineral soil. Unlike soil plowed regularly, soil farmed in this manner gained organic matter content and became more productive every passing year. There was no doubt that this method worked but it required a great deal of hand labor. In an effort to reduce the amount of hand labor, Thomas tried to analyze just what the factors were that made Jin Tans' fields different:

- The soil was always covered with plant material alive and dead so water infiltration was good and evaporation was reduced
- Before one crop was harvested, Jin Tan planted another crop in the same area so there was always something green and growing allowing sunlight to be harvested everyday and giving the lady bugs and green lacewings and other beneficial creatures a steady source of food and shelter
- The soil was never plowed so that earthworms and other soil life were protected and this kept the soil friable and receptive to root growth.

He might not be able to use the exact same techniques but Thomas made a conscious effort to use only practices that could duplicate the results of Jin Tan's management on the land. After much thought, it dawned on Thomas that the key to success was to Manage so as to favor those things that he wanted, healthy soil and healthy plants, rather than to manage against those things, weeds and pests, that he did not want. He needed to take every opportunity to promote life.

Watching how Jin Tan dealt with the immigrants he brought in for labor, Thomas observed that aside from being a good farmer; Jin Tan was a very good man. Southern China was in the midst of a terrible famine and people were desperate to get out; fathers were selling sons and daughters into slavery to save the rest of their families. People would agree to almost anything that would get them out of China and there were plenty of degenerates, both Chinese and American, ready to take full advantage of the frantic people. Jin Tan could have secured the needed labor for little more than a bowl of rice a day but he dealt fairly with the families; giving them the means to live in dignity and even helping to buy back children left behind in China. Thomas remarked to Jin Tan, "You could have had all of the labor we need for a fraction of what you spent but I think it was money wisely invested; these people love you and will do all in their power to repay your kindness." Jin Tan replied, "A man who would profit by heaping misfortune on helpless people is wicked but also he is a fool. A man creates his own destiny one action at a time; honorable actions bring about good fortune and happiness. Dishonorable behavior may gain unearned gold but it draws sorrow like rotten meat draws flies." Thomas told Emma about this conservation and they discussed the concept at length; they agreed that this would be the way they would run their business, indeed their lives, by judging every decision not as to whether it was legal or illegal but rather was it honorable or dishonorable. Just as Jin Tan managed his farm to favor those things that he valued, healthy soil and healthy plants, they would manage their business affairs to create satisfied customers and contented employees.

CHAPTER EIGHTEEN
The Road Back

Hank held a prolonged discussion by e-mail with both Jacob Bristol and Dr. Carthage on how to start rebuilding the health, ecological and financial, of Yoder Farm. The three family members also talked long and late at the kitchen table about what to do and how to go about it. The consensus was that all or most all of the land should go into pasture as the fastest and most economical way to rebuild the health of their soils. Hank was dismayed when the results of his soil tests came in; only a few spots on the farm had as much as three percent organic matter content and most areas were well below two percent. The land had become more acid in the last few years and the amount of soil life was lower than was considered to be healthy and was very out of balance with valuable organisms like beneficial fungi and carnivorous nematodes being in short supply. Hank already knew that earthworm populations were way down from his childhood when two or three shovelfuls of soil from any field would yield enough worms for a long summer's afternoon of fishing. The only really healthy soils on the farm were in the orchard and in

Umpa's garden; the orchard had not been plowed in years and Umpa had put manure composted with straw on the garden each spring. Henry was a believer in soil testing so they had records going back to the point when Henry took over management. At that time, most fields on the farm had around five percent organic matter with a range of four point five to six percent. Jen Beth with her passion for charting data showed them that the drop in organic content correlated exactly with the length of time that an area had been out of pasture and in cultivation. For thirteen years Henry had, as was recommended practice, kept the fields clean tilled; when it was possible, he plowed in the fall or early winter and when snow prevented this, he plowed as early as possible in the spring. This meant that he was often plowing wet soil, which greatly reduces soil tilth (the porous physical structure that allows water and air to penetrate and be held in the soil). In taking soil samples Hank discovered corn cobs and pieces of corn stalks at all depths down to twelve inches; many of these pieces showed little or no signs of rotting. People tend to think of decay as a bad thing but it is the process of decomposition that keeps mineral nutrients in a constant cycle of life – growth – death – decay – life. With the low oxygen levels brought on by the loss of soil tilth, soil life could not break down this plant material into humus; such a conversion would have converted the raw organic matter into mineral nutrients bound in stable organic compounds that soil life could slowly release in plant available forms. This conversion would also greatly increase the ability of the soil to hold water and air in a balanced manner. Hank found as well a two to three inch thick compacted layer of soil, a plow pan, starting at about twelve inches deep; this layer was present everywhere Hank probed and was the result of the repeated plowing to the same depth. This compaction would both restrict the depth to which plant roots could grow and greatly reduce the amount of water that the soil could take in and make available for plant growth. "Hank, your Father knew that the plow pan was limiting his yields, we talked about getting a subsoil plow but between what the plow would cost and the fuel it would take to rip the whole farm, we just didn't think that we could afford it do it." "I think you were right Mom; from what I have read and from talking to Dr. Carthage, subsoiling is very expensive and its' effects don't last; unless the structure of the soil is changed, the soil will run back together like concrete and the compaction will be reestablished. Dr. Carthage suggests that we use a combination of deep tap rooted plants and soil drenches of compost tea to alleviate the compaction. The tap roots of plants like sweet clover and tillage radishes can penetrate hard pan and the microorganisms in properly made compost tea can establish self perpetuating populations that can colonize the spaces between clay platelets; pushing them apart to allow air and water to get between them and restoring good soil structure. He has had great results using these practices to break up hard pans in the central valley of California; even on lands that continue to be plowed.

Since we don't plan to plow except perhaps every five or six years to rotate pasture into row crop and we will be building organic matter content and soil life, he assures me that the compaction problem will disappear over the course of a few years and soil tilth will began to improve quickly. We are limited on equipment, time and money, we don't have land prepared for our little conventional grain drill and we don't have a no-till drill, I think we should get ready to broadcast a mixture of legume and grass seeds as soon as the snow cover begins to dwindle. The fields are not rough and Dad had gotten all of the corn stalks shredded before snow fell; I think that I can get a decent stand of forage by spreading the seed and letting the alternating freeze and thaw of the soil surface plant the seed. I remember Umpa doing this one year to plant alfalfa when the weather kept him from having his land ready for spring planting. I mentioned this planting technique to Dr. Carthage and he agreed that it was worth trying; it wouldn't work in coastal California with its' mild climate but he too has seen it work very well where the seed can reach mineral soil and the ground surface thaws during the day and then refreezes at night. Dr Carthage is putting together a mixture of seeds for us; alfalfa with red clover, sweet clover, white clover and grasses like perennial ryegrass, timothy, smooth brome and orchard grass but he is adding things like chicory, tillage radishes and some other beneficial forbs. The idea is to have a widely diverse forage sward with a lot of different forage plants represented so that all or most all ecological niches are filled with plants adapted to that particular niche set of conditions. Evidence is emerging that an excellent way to improve soil health is to fill the soil profile with living roots of many different kinds of plants for as much of the year as possible. I can use the Farmall and Umpa's three point broadcast spreader and get over a lot of ground in a hurry; the surface will be very wet when it thaws so I will only run when the surface is frozen. To drive on that muddy ground would destroy soil structure. I may have to run mostly at night so I had better make sure the lights on the tractor are in working condition."

After looking at their options and what they needed to accomplish Hank and Jen Beth decided that finding some stocker cattle to graze on a gain basis made more sense than borrowing enough money to buy cattle of their own; they were looking at the expense of fencing and setting up a water system. They would also need an electric fence charger and temporary fencing material so that they could closely control where and for how long the animals grazed. They would have to re-fence the perimeter of the place, when Henry and Hank took out the original fence, they rolled up the wire and saved nearly all of the fence posts and stacked it all in a shed. They left the corner braces in place as boundary markers. It would be a lot of work to put the perimeter fence back but not as expensive or as time consuming as if they had to start from scratch. At one time, every fence on Yoder Farm was pig tight, net wire with one barbed wire below and three above, they would have all the wire and posts they would need. Hank remembered griping about having to roll up the miles of wire but once again the Yoder principle of "waste not, want not" came through. When Jen Beth asked where they would find cattle, Hank told her that his college roommate, Jim Bledsoe, had taken a job with a cattleman in Tennessee who ran a lot of stocker cattle; Hank then had to explain to her that stocker cattle were animals that had been weaned off the cows and were being grown on grass before going to a feedlot. "I thought that you wanted to produce grass finished slaughter beeves." "That is one of our goals but I don't think that we are ready to get into finishing cattle just yet; we need to be in something that will bring in money sooner and to be honest; I need some experience managing grazing animals. I know the theory but I also know that there is a lot that I don't know. Let's see if we can get Jim to send us some cattle that are straight; that have been weaned and had all the needed immunizations; to graze from late spring to mid fall. We will have very high quality forage that is capable of giving young cattle what they need to make excellent gains. I have run some numbers, using what I hope are realistic figures for stocking rate, death loss and rate of gain, and I believe that three hundred seventy to three hundred and eighty pounds of gain per acre of pasture is a reasonable expectation. I think that we could actually carry more cattle than I figured but I want to be conservative starting out. At a cattleman's meeting, I heard Bud Williams, a very good stockman, make a simple but very profound statement, "It is a lot better to have more grass than cattle than to have more cattle than grass." I think that this land, with the right management and some improvement in soil health, has the capacity to produce at least five or six hundred pounds of beef per acre a year but it will take us a few years to get the land and the forage base in shape and our management refined. We will be looking at something like sixty nine dollars an acre seed cost but the pasture should last at least five years. If we can get fifty cents per pound of gain and make three hundred and seventy pounds gain per acre, we are looking at a gross income from five hundred forty acres of one hundred thousand dollars or one hundred eighty five dollars an acre for the season. If we amortize the seeding cost over five years, the gross return to land, management and labor would be twenty eight thousand dollars. One hundred eighty five dollars an acre income doesn't sound like much compared to six hundred dollars an acre for a good corn crop but the fifty two dollars an acre gross profit that we would be expecting is more than most corn farmers make and will look a lot better when we get some debt paid down and the fencing and water development is paid off so that the interest bill is reduced. I like a statement Walt Davis made in *How to Not go Broke Ranching,* "The amount of money coming in is not nearly as important as the difference between what is coming in and what is going out." I think we should make up a sign with that statement and nail it over the office desk. I have made up a chart showing the figures I just quoted and where they came from; my data presentation is not as slick as what Jen Beth can do on her computer but I think you can make sense of it.

Anna had been quiet during the discussion but spoke up now, "Hank, not to be a wet blanket but you have not budgeted any money for harvesting costs or fertilizer." "That is the beauty of this program Mom; the cattle will do all the harvesting and at the same time fertilize the soil. At least ninety five percent of all the minerals in the forage eaten by cattle come right back to the soil in dung and urine. In low organic content soil with low soil life and a lot of bare ground, much of this mineral will be lost to the system but with healthy soil with good ground cover they are taken up by soil life and later become available to plants. This recycling combined with nitrogen fixed by the legume plants and more minerals broken out of rock by the increased biological activity will allow us to gain fertility rather than have to add additional minerals. These soils, some of the best in the world in their original state, developed over eons of grazing at high stock density by herds of bison and elk. We need to create the same conditions; a lot of animals on a small area for a short time and then rest from grazing until the manure and trampled forage have been reincorporated into the soil by microorganisms and the plants have recovered from the effects of grazing. I don't expect that we will ever have to buy another pound of fertilizer."

Financial analysis of grazing program
Expense

Land lease 556 acres @ $90/acre = <u>$50,040/year</u>
Seeding 540 acres @ $69/acre amortized over
five years=$37,260 /5 = <u>$7,452/year</u>
Permanent fencing =$975
Temporary fencing= 280
Water system   <u>11,616</u>
Total improvement expense $12,871/5 = <u>$2,575/year</u>
amortized
Interest on $136,141 @ 8% = <u>$10,891/year</u>

Total annual cash expense
$50,040 land lease
7,452 seeding
2,575 water and fencing
<u>10,891 interest</u>
$70,958 total cash expense

Debt

$36,000 holdover on bank note
50,040 land lease
37,260 seeding
1,225 fencing
<u>11,616 water system</u>
$136,141

Income

540 acres X 1.2 head/acre = 648 head
180 days X 1.75#/day gain = 315# gain per head
648 head X 315# = 204,120# minus 3% death loss =
204,120 minus 4,082.40 =200,037.60 # of gain X
$.50/pound = $100,018.80 gross income
$100,018 minus 70,958 =$ 29,060 return to management/
labor and debt retirement
$29,060 / 540 acres = $53.82 / acre gross profit

This is a lot tighter than I would like – we need to come up with a way to either extend the grazing season or increase the amount of beef produced per acre and it needs to happen without increasing expenses." Anna had been quiet but after looking over the chart said, "I see $36,000 that will come out of the debt load. There is no way you are going to assume Henry's and my debt at the bank and not take it out of the lease payments! In all our years of marriage, we never had fifty thousand dollars net income."

Hank and Jen Beth were unloading the last of the orchard trimmings, "Hank, where did your grandfather sell his fruit?" "At one time there were people who brokered fruit; they would contract with farmers to buy their crop and then sell it to grocery stores in the cities. This market disappeared when the little Mom and Pop stores were pushed out by super markets; the super markets wanted to deal with companies big enough to supply dozens of stores with tons of fruit. With the brokers out of business, farmers pretty well went out of the orchard business in this area; at onetime Grandfather had over twenty acres in orchard producing several varieties' each of apples, apricots, cherries, peaches, grapes and pears. Umpa loved his orchard but when he lost his market, it didn't make sense to continue on a large scale. This is a good area for fruit production but no market." "What are the chances to develop a local market? There are a lot of people within fifty miles of here and who wouldn't love to have just off the tree organically grown fruit? You can grow fruit organically, can't you?" "We can grow organic fruit; it is mainly a question of having healthy soil and lots of biodiversity. Umpa used cover crops under his trees and grazed them with sheep and chickens, when a wormy apple fell off the tree, there would be two sheep and four chickens fighting to see who got the apple, not many worms got a chance to mature. The beneficial insects hatched out in the cover crops and then when Granddad grazed off an area, the beneficials went up into the trees to prey on insect pests. Most insect pests spend at least part of their life cycle in the ground so in a healthy environment with robust soil life, the predator organisms, from nematodes to moles underground and from lady bugs and spiders to bats and birds above ground, keep pest numbers under control. Disease pests can be handled in much the same way; keep stress off the trees by promoting: good air flow, a good water cycle, a robust mineral cycle and good energy flow. Much of conventional orchard practice: clean tilled ground, routine spraying of insecticides and fungicides, acid salt fertilizers and crowding of the trees, actually promotes stress and disease. One of the most damaging traits of the "poison the pests" programs is that the beneficial organisms that prey on pests are killed off with the pests, predator species always have a slower rate of reproduction than do their prey species, otherwise the predators would run out of food, so reducing predator numbers allows pest populations to explode.

The biggest difficulty that I see in us getting back into the fruit business would be in finding labor to harvest the fruit, picking apples and peaches used to be a great way for kids to make money in the summer but since the farms have been consolidated into larger units; the rural population has dropped and we no longer have the kids. Your Dad put his finger on it when he said that one of the biggest faults of industrialized agriculture was the loss of people on the land. To make it work, we have to figure out how to operate with less hand labor." "Hank, what if we let the customer do the hand labor? Why couldn't we set up a program where people pick, not only fruit, but sweet corn and green beans and tomatoes and pumpkins? We could set up a farm store and have products already harvested or people could harvest their own for a lower price. It would take a lot of organization and we probably would lose some produce by not getting it harvested on time but we could start small and learn as we go. If we had our own store, we could sell everything from produce to eggs and chicken; we could sell other peoples products; I bet Anna has friends that would love to have a place to sell baked goods and I guarantee there are farm wives close by that would like to work a few hours a week tending a store. We could even get a few cows and sell raw milk and butter; what would it take to put your grandfathers' milk barn back in shape? Anything that we can sell at retail price here on the farm should have a higher profit margin than if we sold the same item wholesale; we just have to make sure that we don't spend more making the sale than we have margin. What if we started out with just an open air fruit stand in one of your Dads' equipment sheds? Some tables for produce and a couple of used coolers for perishables is all we really need so long as the weather is nice. The orchard is right here close and we could plant the U-Pick vegetables close by so one person could tend the store and oversee the people picking produce." Hank had been following intently, "I like it; we could plant an area with a mixture of rye, vetch and crimson clover sowed at a heavy rate and then roll it down and plant in the mulch. The heavy mulch will hold back weeds and also provide nutrients to the soil as it decays; it would also give people a clean surface as they pick. Rodale Institute has developed a roll down crimper that mounts on the front of a tractor so that with a rear mounted planter, in one pass you can roll down the cover crop and plant at the same time. It will be slower but I bet I can do a fair job using Umpa's old rolling stalk chopper to roll down the mulch – I can modify one of the old two row planters to handle the heavy mulch and we will be in business. In years to come we can use cattle at high stock density to build soil productivity but for now, I can put down chicken litter compost and plant the cover crop. We already have the orchard and one way or another we can grow crops like sweet corn, green beans and tomatoes that people can pick easily; I think your U-Pick idea can work. Let's try to come up with some realistic numbers and include it in the report for the Board of Directors. Long term, mixed species pasture and grazing animals, mainly cattle under high stock density, will be our primary tool to improve and maintain soil productivity and also to add value to crops like grain and legumes. Aside from building soil health, land kept in pasture, in a mixed sward of grasses, forbs and legumes, for four to six years will develop a high degree of biodiversity so that the cultivated crops that follow should have much less pressure from weeds, insects and diseases. We need to do all we can to increase that diversity above ground as well as in the soil; I will start building bat houses and bluebird houses and see if we can't attract some help with insect control. We may have to sell some grain for cash flow but I would like to see most of the grain we produce used for poultry and hogs while the dairy cows and beef cattle remain strictly grass fed. The benefits to humans consuming meat and milk from grass fed ruminant animals are very real and, if managed properly, the animals are healthier. Having grass fed products can give us a marketing edge even before we get certified organic.

We need to draw up a multiyear plan complete with maps showing how each area of the farm will be used each year. I have drawn up a map showing how I think we should put in water lines and fences; except for a single high tensile electric wire running basically down the centerline of the farm, all paddocks for grazing will be made daily with temporary fencing. The water line will be buried under the electric fence with frost free faucets spaced so that we can locate drink tanks pretty well where ever we need them. By making all of our paddock breaks with temporary electric fence we have tremendous flexibility and can determine exactly what percentage of the forage is eaten by varying the size of the areas we put on offer. I want to move the animals at least once a day and at times we may want to move several times in one day. For livestock, we can make a gate through the high tensile wire by just raising it on an insulated pole – equipment will have to go through gates on the end of each stretch of wire. Our fields will be small but that is a good thing; crops like corn or wheat will be surrounded by pasture and biodiversity, from birds to beneficial insects will be high along these borders. Every acre of our crop land will get the benefits of this biodiversity and Granddads' two row and four row equipment will be just right to work these small fields.

We need to develop a business plan showing projected income and expense for each enterprise as well as a labor budget in man hours by season and enterprise. We will have to make a lot of assumptions and are sure to be wrong at times but there is no way we could make this work without detailed planning. We will gather all the information we can and make the best plan we can but we will be watching and ready to change the plan soon as we see a flaw."

Yoder Farm

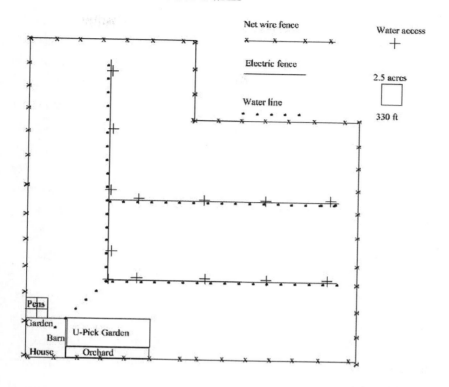

Net wire fence

Electric fence

Water line

Water access

2.5 acres

330 ft

Pens

Garden

Barn

House

U-Pick Garden

Orchard

Hank came in at noon to find that Joe Meyers, the Coalition lawyer, had called and asked that he call him back as soon as possible. They had not been in contact with Meyers since he and the Bristol Farms attorney, Wallace Crown, filed the lawsuit against GAI for the wrongful death of Henry Weaver. Hank was a little surprised at the call; Meyers told them that he expected to hear nothing from GAI until the deadline for them to respond to the suit was eminent. He called Meyers' office and the lawyer answered on the second ring. "Hank, thank you for getting back to me; there have been some startling developments that will affect our case. First, following up on your letter regarding

Property Management Inc, my investigators have gone over the last ten years of real estate transactions involving these people and I will be amazed if we don't see multiple criminal indictments of all of the principals and some of the hired help. It is pretty clear that Property Management Inc has used the threat of criminal prosecution, the threat of lawsuits by GAI and financial pressure from the Bank of Cayuga to buy up farms at discounted prices. When they first started out, they were very careful but as time went by with no repercussions they got sloppy. I think that we will have a strong suit of fraud and criminal conspiracy against Property Management Inc. and all of its' principals but in the meantime, I intend to submit some of what our investigators found as evidence that GAI, through its employees, engaged in criminal activities going back at least seven years. I would normally caution you to not speak of this with anyone but an incident occurred last night that will probably bring this entire situation out to the public in the next few days. Gary Doak and Jim Turner were found dead in Doak's' wrecked pickup in the bed of Limestone Creek. There has been no ruling as to cause of death for either man but my investigator has friends in the Sheriff Department who tell him that the wounds both suffered were too severe to have occurred in a wreck that did so little damage to the truck. The Sheriff believes that the two were beaten to death and the wreck was staged to explain their wounds. If this is correct, I feel certain that the Sheriff will find the perpetrators in short order. This whole mess may collapse before we get the chance to get to court."

Joe Meyers' prediction that the truth would come out became fact even sooner than he expected. Monday afternoon Sheriff Hayward arrested George and Luke Grimes, a pair of small time crooks, for the murder of Doak and Turner and within three hours both confessed; they claimed that they were hired by Howard Peoples and only intended to scare the two but were pretty drunk and hit them too hard. Each asserted that it was his brother that hit too hard with a club while he only slapped the two around. The Sheriff caught wind of the Grimes brothers when Calvin Griggs, a farm manager for Property Management Inc. came to Sheriff Doyt Hayward with the story that George Henning, a partner in the management firm, had come to him four days before and tried to get him to hire someone to put the fear of the devil in Gary Doak and Jim Turner; he suggested two brothers, ex-cons named Grimes. Henning told Griggs that Doak and Turner were trying to blackmail more money out of the partners. According to Griggs, he refused to get involved and when Doak and Turner turned up dead, came to Sheriff Hayward. Griggs admitted to knowing that the partners were stealing farms and how they were doing it; even admitting that he had played a part in some of the schemes. "I guess I am a thief Sheriff but I ain't no murderer." The Sentinel, the local newspaper, put out a special four page edition covering the whole sordid mess. There were two full pages of photographs of the partners; Albert Horning, Howard Peoples, George Henning and Stanley Cross and four Property Management Inc employees being taken to jail in handcuffs. The lead story in the special edition was that the Bank of Cayuga was closed indefinitely while the banking authorities conducted a complete audit.

CHAPTER NINETEEN
Progress

Yoder Farm

The rest of the winter seemed to fly bye; Hank and Jen Beth spent weeks putting together a month by month five year projection detailing everything they hoped to accomplish with the farm. Both income and expense were predicted by crop enterprise and date and then each crop was subjected to a gross margin analysis to determine how much it contributed toward covering the overhead of the farm. Particular attention was paid to a calendar of labor requirements; it did no good to grow a crop if you could not get it harvested on time. What they were looking for was a mix of enterprises that were individually profitable with low inputs but that also complimented; or at least did not compete strongly for labor and other resources with the other enterprises. They soon realized that there really is "no free lunch"; crops that offered high returns per acre like tomatoes and asparagus offset this bounty with high requirements for establishment costs and especially for labor. It was obvious that to manage many acres of these crops would require bringing in outside labor. They decided that Jen Beth's suggestion of offering fruit and vegetables on a "U-Pick" basis was worth a try. They had the orchard with apples, peaches, pears, apricots and grapes and could add several kinds of berries; this plus a large garden featuring tomatoes, green beans, peppers, and a large patch of each of sweet corn and pumpkins. They had a big advantage in that generations of Yoders had saved seed from the vegetable varieties that were the most reliable and best tasting. The corn varieties might be contaminated with pollen from the GMO corn grown all around them but the vegetables would breed true; one bite of a ripe tomato from one of Umpa's family heirloom varieties and they would have a customer for life. Grazing would still be the focus of their efforts but the U-Pick feature would provide a diversified source of income and the opportunity to start building a clientele of retail customers that would be valuable when and if they pursued grass finished meats or other direct marketed products. Anna was just as interested as Hank and Jen Beth in seeing the plan succeed and listened intently as they discussed options. They were talking about how to handle the shortages and surpluses of produce that were sure to happen if they relied solely on customers to do the harvesting when Anna said, "What you need is the ability to can and freeze surplus produce and offer customers the preserved as well as the fresh. It used to be that everyone had a big garden and put up lots of canned goods for the winter. Now people, even most farmers, don't have gardens and fewer still do any preserving. I bet we could find several farm wives that would like to work a few hours a week picking and preserving fruits and vegetables. It would be a little backhanded but we could do the canning and freezing right here in the kitchen. When

I was a girl, there would sometimes be five or six women working here and on the screened in porch putting up food of all kinds. It was work but it was also a social event and a lot of fun."

The time to seed the pasture mixture was fast approaching; Dr. Carthage called to say that he was shipping the seed already blended and with the legumes inoculated with their proper strains of rhizobia. He went one step further and inoculated all of the seed with mycorrhizal fungi, a very beneficial native soil dwelling life form that is severely damaged by modern farming practices. His own experiments and research work at several universities indicated that forages supporting colonies of this fungus were healthier and much more productive and drought tolerant than plants lacking these organisms. They were fast approaching the "mud" season when the soil surface would thaw during the day while the subsurface stayed frozen. If Hank could get the seed spread on frozen surface, the alternating freeze and thaw should plant the seed in the top one quarter to one half inch of the soil. The old Farmall didn't have a cab much less a heater but Hank found and mounted the Plexiglas wind screen and the canvas panels that directed engine heat back to the driver's seat and, with enough clothes on, the cold was bearable. The seed arrived at the freight depot and Hank borrowed his friend Joe Hendricks' bobtail truck to pick up the bagged seed and arranged to leave it on the truck until he got it planted. They lucked out in that a cold snap blew in and the ground didn't thaw for four days. With Jen Beth bringing the seed truck to him to fill the spreader and to keep his coffee thermos full, Hank finished seeding the five hundred and forty acres without having to run at night. Joe Hendricks got a pained expression on his face when Hank told him that they were seeding the whole place to pasture; the expression turned to one of total disbelief when he learned that Hank was not going to plow and prepare a seed bed but rather he intended to simply broadcast the seed on top of the ground.

With the pasture seeding done, Hank planted fifteen acres next to the orchard with a double rate mixture of cereal rye, vetch and crimson clover as a cover crop to be rolled down as mulch for the U-Pick garden. He then turned to the fencing and water lines; he had four miles of exterior fence to replace plus a little over two miles of high tensile electric fence and two and a quarter miles of water line to install. He was going to need some help in order to get everything done by the time the pasture was ready and the cattle arrived. Hank went to see Jonas Miller, an Amish friend of his father, who farmed six miles south and who supplemented his farm income by doing construction work. Jonas came to the farm and he and Hank agreed on a price per mile for which Jonas and his sons would use the saved fencing materials to re-fence the perimeter just as it was in Umpa's day. Jonas was obviously curious about what Hank and Jen Beth were doing so Hank explained what they hoped to accomplish; show farmers that they could prosper using organic techniques. He became very interested when Hank explained that Bristol Farms needed organic produce of all kinds and hoped to gain a steady supply by forming mutually beneficial long term relationships with farmers. That night,

Hank told Jen Beth that the Millers just might be their first recruits.

As the weather warmed, their broadcast seed germinated to an excellent stand; Hank was pleased but he was also apprehensive. There was a very real danger that a hard freeze, one that caused the soil surface to heave as the cold expanded it, could pull the little plants up enough to break off their roots and kill them. The danger of this would lessen as their soil gained organic content and became healthy but Hank didn't breathe truly easy until the danger of severe temperatures was past.

The ground thawed under a weak spring sun and Hank was able to start laying water line with a rented ditching machine; instead of frost free faucets he decided to install plug in fittings in access cans made from pieces of twelve inch polypropylene drainage pipe with plate steel covers. With one of these installed five hundred feet in from the perimeter and then every one thousand feet underneath the electric fence he could locate drink tanks in each of his temporary paddocks without having to drag about a lot of water hose. Hank was reading everything he could find on time controlled grazing; he happened on to *The StockmanGrassFarmer* magazine on line and it turned out to be a great source of information. Not all academics are convinced but there are a lot of people practicing time controlled planned grazing with very good results both financial and agronomic. The practice allows producers to present forage to the animals at precisely the right stage of maturity to best meet their nutritional needs. By keeping the graze periods short and using recovery periods based upon the growth rate of the plants, the diet of the animals is uniform from day to day; this helps prevent digestive or metabolic upsets in the animals and prevents animals from re-grazing plants before they have fully recovered. Hank spent some time talking with the Holt family who run a grass based dairy in the hills to the north; they routinely gave the cows a fresh break of grass after each milking and considered it to be one of the most profitable practices that they used. From their experience, short graze periods mean more forage intake which translates to lower feed costs and more milk in the tank. They told Hank that they liked to keep good quality dry hay available to the cows, especially in the early spring, and showed him the hay rack on a trailer that they pulled into each new break. On green forage, the cows eat very little of the hay unless the protein content of the forage they are grazing gets too high; when this happens, due to sudden spurts in growth or management error, the cows will consume hay to gain energy with which to balance the additional protein.

Hank got the water line and electric fence finished and Jonas Miller and his sons were making good progress on the perimeter fence. The pasture mix was six inches tall and growing and Hank began to think that they just might be ready for the cattle that Jim Bledsoe wanted to send on April 15. The cattle were not trained to electric fence so Hank put a single strand of electrified poly wire around the inside of Umpa's large fenced garden spot to act as a training pen; the cattle would recognize the net wire fence and not run through it even when startled by a shock from the electric fence. People may think that cattle are not very smart but they are smart enough to not touch a hot wire twice. He had planted the garden to the rye, vetch and clover cover crop mixture and there was a lot of forage present. His thought was to hold the cattle in the training pen long enough for each of them to learn not to push against the electric fence, and also long enough for them to eat and trample down the cover crop, and get them out on pasture as soon as possible. He bought some good quality grass hay from the Holts and modified two of Umpa's farm wagons into mobile hay racks. The early season forage was going to have very high moisture content and also be high in protein; Hank knew that the cattle would need the energy supplied by the hay until the pasture forage matured enough to have a good balance between protein and energy. In future years they could plan to have a mixture of young and older forage available but for now they would have to use hay.

Hank had been working nights in the shop to convert an old two row planter to be suitable for use as a no-till planter; this project went so well that he decided to attempt to build a roll down crimper that would mount on the front of the tractor so that rolling down the cover crop into mulch and planting the crop could be done in one pass. Once again having access to years of accumulation of scrap iron, old equipment and other "good stuff" came to his rescue. The finished machine looked a lot like something made by a little boys' "transformer" toy but Hank was pretty sure it would work; as Umpa was fond of saying, "Pretty is as pretty does." The rye and vetch cover crop on the U-Pick garden spot was thick and beginning to make rapid growth; Hank and Jen Beth were not ready to start advertizing for customers just yet but they were hopeful.

CHAPTER TWENTY
It Comes Together

The cattle came in right on time; Jim Bledsoe came with them and the cattle's condition was just as agreed. The steer calves weighed four hundred sixty three pounds average, were uniform in age and condition, had been weaned twenty six days before and had received all of the needed immunizations. They came off the trucks quietly and began grazing and examining their new home with interest; every once in a while there would be a small commotion as some calf touched his nose to the electric fence and jumped back but that soon ceased as calves quit being shocked. Evidently many of these calves had some experience with electric fence or else were smart enough to learn by watching others.

Hank and Jim walked out into the rapidly growing pasture and Jim agreed with Hank that the forage would be "washy" and low in energy for the first week or ten days. The mixture seemed to be about forty percent legume sixty percent non-legume, mostly grasses, and the maturity level was less than Jim would have preferred. He liked Hanks idea of keeping dry hay available to the calves and suggested that Hank make the move to a fresh break of forage in the afternoon after the plants had received several hours of sunlight. This would give the plants more time to convert carbon dioxide into sugars through photosynthesis and thus raise the energy levels in their leaves. He also suggested that Hank get two other pieces of equipment; a refractometer to measure the brix or sugar level in forage and a packet of pH testing strips to test the pH of the cattle's urine. If the urine tests much above a pH of 7, the animals are getting too much protein and not enough energy and they will not perform as well as they should. Low energy to protein ratios like those found in very immature forage can cause digestive and metabolic upsets like scouring and bloat. Young growing animals need a lot of protein but a lush fast growing forage sward such Hank was about to turn out on can be too rich in protein even for young cattle. Jim also warned that there is the occasional animal that simply cannot tolerate a ration as high in legumes as Hank had. "If you get a chronic bloater, pull it off the legume pasture and we will put it somewhere on a grass only diet."

Hank was pleased with how the cattle were performing; they went through about ten days of the expected poor performance before the energy level of the forage rose but the cattle were now doing well. Their manure had lost the looseness that had made it dangerous to walk too close behind them and they were filling up early and spending more time ruminating and resting than they were grazing. Allowing the forage to develop height and density before presenting it to the animals allowed them to fill up with less work and less energy used in the work of grazing meant more energy available for growth.

Hank fenced in an area of forage for the days' grazing allotment with temporary electric fence each afternoon and was now giving the cattle enough area in each break so that they were just taking the tops off the plants and leaving a lot of leaf ungrazed. He needed to get back around to the areas first grazed before the forage remaining ungrazed ahead of the cattle became overly mature and tough. The principle "fast growth = fast moves" that he had read so often finally became clear. When growing conditions: moisture, temperature, hours of sunlight, amount of leaf on the plants and soil fertility are good forage grows and matures more quickly. During these periods of rapid growth the time period between grazing periods needs to be shorter so that plants don't become too mature. As growing conditions declined with the arrival of heat and dry weather, Hank would reduce the amount of area in each grazing break so as to give the forage in front of the cattle the longer amounts of growing time (smaller breaks = more breaks = more days of recovery) that it would need to recover from the previous grazing. He was able to put the animals on the smaller areas because of the large amounts of forage he had left in the paddocks in earlier graze periods. The ability to do this was dependent upon having the proper stocking rate (pounds of animal per acre) so that during the growing season, no more than about forty percent of the available forage was consumed in one grazing period on any one area. It was a finely tuned ballet of matching growth rate, the amount of forage grown, with the amount of forage consumed while keeping the forage in a narrow range of physiological maturity. The beauty part was that the practices that most benefited the animals were also very beneficial to the plants and to the soil. Grazing is often portrayed as being harmful to the vegetation and to the soil; abusive grazing is indeed harmful but properly managed grazing is the most powerful tool available to improve the health (the stability and productivity) of both forage vegetation and the soil in which it grows. Hank knew that he was a long way from being an expert grazier (one who manages grazing animals) but this only made him more conscious of the need to constantly monitor what was actually happening on the ground. He needed to monitor forage growth, animal performance and forage disappearance and fine tune his management so that the actual results closely resembled the results called for in his grazing plan. Jim Bledsoe had impressed on him the need to be aware of the conditions over the entire pasture: in the break he was grazing at the moment but also in the areas he would be grazing tomorrow and next week and next month. If forage was not growing as fast as the plan had assumed, he needed to slow down (make smaller breaks in his case) to give the forage more time to recover. If this caused the animals to consistently consume too large a percentage of the forage in a break; he was over stocked and needed to remove animals. The opposite scenario, animals not consuming as much of the forage as the plan assumed, was not as much of a problem. He could add animals or not depending on circumstances; forage not eaten would form mulch on the ground stimulating soil life and eventually be taken back into the nutrient cycle. This year's "wasted" forage would be next year's fertilizer.

Hank liked working with the cattle though as he told his friend Joe Hendricks, "There is not much work to it; I go out in the morning to make sure the cattle are all right and the water is ok and then I go back after lunch to move them to a fresh break of pasture. I built a roofed salt and mineral feeder on a sled that moves with the cattle so that they always have access to minerals and the area around the feeder doesn't get trampled into a mud hole. While they start grazing the new break, I roll up the back fence of the break that we just came out of and move it forward to form a new break for tomorrow. I bought a used golf cart so that I wouldn't have to drive a truck or tractor on wet ground and I can move the cattle, take up the old fence, build the new fence and be back at the barn in twenty minutes; a little longer if I have to move the water trough. If I know that I am going to be tied up with something, I can build a break or even several breaks ahead of time so that Jen Beth or Mother can run down and move the cattle in a few minutes."

As soon as the ground was warm enough, Hank pulled his Rube Goldberg roller- planter into the area they planned to use as a U-Pick garden to plant what he hoped would be the first of several crops, planted six days apart, of sweet corn for roasting ears. Dr. Carthage had found them seed of an old variety of open pollinated sweet corn that has outstanding taste. The corn was a short season variety so it would be safely self-pollinated before the long season industrial corn surrounding them flooded the air with pollen. Aside from roasting ears, Hank hoped to save and sell seed from this corn and also from a mid season flour corn that Dr. Carthage liked. They would not be able to sell it as organic but they would have the process down and be ready to go into organic production as soon as their certification process was complete. He had to do quite a bit of adjusting and tinkering but he soon had his odd looking contraption running and he planted four acres without a hitch. He was working close enough to be seen from the county road and several trucks came close to running off the road as he came through rolling down four foot tall rye and dragging a planter. He grinned to himself as he envisioned the scene when they got to the coffee shop and reported, "You will not believe what that damn fool kid is doing now." Anna and Jen Beth had come down to see the début of Hanks "Transformer" as they called it and they were suitably impressed. When they walked out on the planted ground, they found the soil covered with a six inch thick mulch of rye, vetch and clover that had been neatly laid down, still rooted in the ground, with the stems crimped every eight inches along their entire lengths. The corn was planted in a narrow slot that the planter cut through the mulch and as they dug into the furrow, they found the seed two inches below ground level and nicely covered. The mulch was not dead but the crimped stems would prevent the plants from growing. The shade of the thick mulch should prevent weeds from germinating anywhere with the possible exception of in the planting slot where hopefully the corn would soon shade these out. Hank planted two acres of the flour corn and two more acres of sweet corn on the opposite side of the U-Pick patch; this was to be seed corn for a larger planting next year. He would stagger plantings of sweet corn so as to have roasting ears over a longer period of time but intended to save seed only from plants that were pollinated before the surrounding corn released pollen. On the next batch he planted, after it warmed up a little, he planned to plant pole beans with the corn so that the beans could climb up the corn stalks. Jen Beth and Anna had compiled a list of what and how much they wanted planted in the U-Pick area; part of these would be transplants: tomatoes, peppers and onions which he had growing in the greenhouse, and part would have to be hand planted but the Transformer could make short work of anything that had large seeds and could be planted in a row. Hank also thought that he could use the machine to prepare a furrow in the mulch where small seeded plants like carrots or spinach could be hand planted.

That night the mood at the supper table was decidedly upbeat; it had been a lot of work and more was to come but they were well on their way to achieving what they had laid out in their plans to have accomplished by midsummer. The mood was dampened considerably when Joe Meyers called to tell them that the judge had set a trial date of October tenth for their wrongful death lawsuit against GAI and the group doing business as Property Management Inc.

Bristol Farms Headquarters

"Jacob, have you got a minute? Something just came in that you should see." Jacob Bristol looked up from his computer screen to find his chief legal officer, Henry McCoy, standing in the doorway to his office holding a sheave of papers, "Come in Henry, what do you have?" "A notice of intent to sue from something called The Committee for Truth in Food Advertising. It claims that our labels on Bristol Farms dairy products stating that our dairy cows are not treated with bovine growth hormone infers that milk from other cows that may have been treated with BGH is substandard or unsafe and they demand that we remove the labels immediately. They claim that since the FDA has approved the use of BGH in dairy cattle, our use of labels stating that we do not use the material is in fact a claim that our product is more wholesome than that from treated cattle and as such amounts to false advertising." "That is quite a stretch – we don't make any claims – just a statement that we don't use BGH." "I know but they claim that even mentioning BGH creates, and I quote, "An atmosphere of confusion and doubt in the minds of consumers as to the safety and wholesomeness of dairy products in general." "Is there any possibility that they could win the suit?" "You know as well as I do that it is impossible to predict what a jury, or even a judge, will do but I would feel very comfortable about defending against this suit." "Unless you see some reason to do otherwise, I would just ignore it" "If you don't object Jacob, I think that we should respond, giving the reasons we think that such a suit would be without merit; if for no other reason than to prevent them representing us to some judge as unresponsive to their "legitimate" concerns. I also think that we should find out just who this Committee is and who is funding them; I have been around food law for a long time and I have never heard of them." "I will leave it in your capable hands, Henry; you might mention that the use of BGH is prohibited by the USDA Organic Standards and that ours is a certified organic dairy that must abide by these standards."

The conversation with Henry broke his concentration on the Bristol Farms budget problems he had been pondering and Jacob found himself thinking instead about how the quality and safety of the world food supply had been affected by the growth of corporate agriculture. Large farms were nothing new, ambitious people had long built empires by being smarter and willing to work harder, sometimes by being more ruthless, than most people. The last forty or fifty years however had seen the growth of companies that concentrated not on controlling the means of production, the land, so much as brokering farm commodities and controlling the processing, distribution and marketing of farm products. Some of the most successful of these companies also supplied the ever increasing amount of inputs: from credit, to seed, to chemicals that industrial agriculture required. These companies found that it was much safer to let the farmers take the risks of weather, disease and pests; if the market went down due to oversupply or reduced demand they simply reduced what they paid the farmer and maintained their margins. Once a certain size and amount of market clout was achieved, this proved to be a very workable program and the agricultural commodity markets and the agricultural supply businesses were soon dominated by a few very large companies. Being good entrepreneurs, these companies worked hard at increasing demand for, and price of, their products. One of the early success stories of corporations creating demand by advertising fable occurred just after World War II when the end of hostilities greatly reduced the demand for vegetable oil. The vegetable oil processors were sitting on large stocks of oil and had idle plants; they badly needed to find new markets for their products. At this time most Americans cooked with hog lard, there were breeds of hogs specially bred to produce lots of lard, and used butter on their biscuits and baked potatoes. Corporate whiz kids looked at these products and found that by using a an industrial process called partial hydrogenation they could turn liquid cottonseed oil, peanut oil, corn oil or vegetable oil of any kind into a semisolid material that looked a little like lard. It also smelled like something long dead but they found that steam cleaning and distillation could reduce the stench. They now had a product that could compete somewhat with lard; it couldn't compete on taste but it was cheap. Breaking into the butter market was harder; their pseudo butter looked like a lump of dirty gray fat, had no taste, other than a slight hint of rancid fish, and smelled like chemicals. The whiz kids persevered, however, with bleaches, and dyes and flavors and aromatic materials and eventually oleo margarine was somewhat accepted by the housewife. Widespread acceptance came only after a number of research papers were published (and sensationalized by the media) claiming that animal fats were the root causes of all sorts of human health problems from heart disease to obesity. These early reports, most of which have since been pretty well discredited as paid for propaganda, were publicized far and wide as part of a marketing "blitzkrieg" to sell partially hydrogenated oils as "health foods" while animal fats were demonized. What they could not sell on its' merits could be sold very well with scare tactics. The scheme was wildly successful and a generation of housewives quit buying lard and butter and fed their families the "healthy" vegetable oils. It would be many years before scientists looked at these "health foods" and found them to be severely lacking in several essential fatty acids and loaded with trans fats; compounds created by the hydrogenation process and determined by a panel of US Government scientists to be severe health hazards unsafe at any level in the human diet. Surely it is only coincidence that the increase in heart disease and obesity and cancer and diabetes in the US all parallel the increase in consumption of partially hydrogenated vegetable oils?

High fructose corn syrup was another product of modern chemistry that became firmly established in the American cuisine through corporate promotion. It was aggressively promoted despite disturbing evidence linking its' consumption to the tremendous increase in obesity and diabetes. This manmade "food" has two great advantages: it is extremely sweet and it is cheap. It is now found in a large percentage of processed food products: traditional sweets such as candy, cakes and ice cream but also in breads, soups and even heat and eat casseroles and corn chips. America is being turned into a nation of fructose junkies complete with two hundred pound ten year old kids and early onset juvenile diabetes.

Perhaps the most successful marketing campaign to create saleable "food" products from things that should not be eaten involves soy. Contrary to common belief, traditionally very little soy was consumed in Asia. Soybeans were grown as animal fodder and as a soil improvement crop. The explosion of soybean production, brought on by the advertizing of soybean oil as a health food, created a large supply of protein rich meal which was incorporated into animal feeds. It was not long before this large stock of cheap protein attracted the attention of food manufacturers and today soy protein is present in some sixty percent of all packaged and processed foodstuff and is in virtually all fast food. We even feed it to infants even though there is strong evidence that soy is involved in all sort of human maladies from cancer to infertility to early puberty in girls and lack of puberty in boys. It is also suspected as a factor in several types of neurological disease and is a proven factor in disease of the human and animal digestive tracts. Anyone contemplating feeding soy in any form to their children would be wise to read *The Whole Soy Story: The Dark Side of America's Favorite Health Food* by Dr. Kaayla Daniel.

Modern wheat, at least that part of it created by inducing mutations with chemicals and/or radiation during "The Green Revolution", plays a part in the tremendous increase in obesity, diabetes, auto immune diseases and heart disease. Since these products of mutagenesis (which contain compounds making them both addictive and appetite stimulators) entered the food chain of the United States in 1984, the daily caloric intake of the American people has risen by as much as eight hundred calories. There are types of wheat and other grains that can provide wholesome nutrition but they will have to have their virtues explained to the consumer. Bristol Farms has a lot of work to do on several different fronts.

Jacob was a rare individual; an idealist who was firmly grounded in the real world. It made him happy when he could provide products that provided real health benefits to his customers; it made him doubly happy when he could make money providing these products. It was beyond his comprehension how anyone could put a product on the market knowing that it was harmful, from trans fats to high fructose corn syrup to proven to be harmful genetically modified organisms, the prevailing morality seemed to be "It is only wrong if they can prove it." The evidence as to the harmful effects of pesticides in common use in conventional agriculture is over whelming but the kinds and amounts of poisons used increases every year. The situation is made worse by the drumbeat of companies shouting that their products are safe even though unbiased research proves otherwise. Glyphosate, the active ingredient in the widely used herbicide Roundup is a good example. Company literature assures that the chemical is harmless to animals and to humans but scientists all over the world have linked exposure to glyphosate to human ills ranging from autism to gastrointestinal disease to obesity to cardio-vascular disease to cancer to Alzheimer's to depression to multiple sclerosis and on and on. Mammals do show some tolerance for glyphosate but most microbes are very susceptible to even small amounts of the material; glyphosate has been granted a U.S. patent as an antibiotic and para-site killer. The material is deadly to many of the beneficial organisms that live in both human and animal bodies and play important roles in the health and well being of their hosts. If we damage the populations of these beneficial organisms, we risk very serious damage to both human and animal health. Glyphosate is much less effective on pathogenic organisms such as disease causing varieties of salmonella and clostridia; when glyphosate is present, the pathogens can over whelm the beneficial organisms and cause disease. If this weren't enough, some of these glyphosate resistant organisms can migrate into the soil and cause destruction of the vital soil food web that we rely on to maintain the health and productivity of our soil. The literature is full of studies showing the harmful effects: tumors, abortions, early deaths, etc. etc. to animals fed feeds produced with the glyphosate/ GMO combination. The truth appears to be that glyphosate is one of the chemical poisons most dangerous to humans because its effects are not immediately apparent. Government regulators seem unconcerned; even allowing glyphosate to be sprayed on food crops such as wheat a few days before harvest. http://people.csail.mit.edu/seneff/Entropy/entropy-15-01416.pdf

There are legitimate disagreements about the safety and nutritional qualities of various products but far too many of the arguments aired in public involve one side trying to preserve, or to prohibit, something for their personal economic advantage. The fight over raw milk is an example; the large dairy processers fight tooth and toe nail to prevent raw milk from being sold to the public; not as they claim because it is dangerous but rather because they fear the competition. In their industrial style dairies they cannot hold bacterial contamination down to acceptable levels without pasteurizing their products to kill the bacteria picked up in harvest, transportation and processing. Uninformed, or purchased, politicians aided the large dairies by placing unreasonable restrictions on the sale of raw milk. Some of these restrictions, touted as "protecting public health", were blatantly hypocritical such as allowing farmers to sell the products but not to advertise them or to allow sales to be made only on the farm. If a product is dangerous, it should be banned; if is not dangerous, such restrictions are unwarranted discrimination and pretty good evidence that the purpose of the regulations was to protect, not public health, but the profits of favored corporations. Jacob and his fore bearers had built a thriving business by giving customers good value, both economic and nutritional, and he was proud of their accomplishments. They built their businesses by providing quality products at fair prices rather than seeking advantage through political means.

Time passed and Jacob had more or less put the threatened law suit out of his mind when Henry McCoy called, "I need a few minutes to report on the lawsuit and also to discuss what we have discovered about The Committee for Truth in Food Advertising." Jacob could tell from Henry's tone that this was something more than routine and told him to come ahead; Henry was there in a few minutes. "The lawsuit has been filed in California State Court and surprisingly, it has already been assigned to Judge Albert Castillo and even more surprising, he has set dates two weeks from now for preliminary hearings. These type suits normally see a time lag of a year or more between filing and any meaningful court action. I don't know what to think of this break with precedent but it is highly unusual and in legal affairs unusual normally means political pressure is being applied. That theory is given credence by the fact that we have been able to discover that The Committee for Truth in Food Advertising is funded by a consortium of two dozen or more of the biggest players: factory type farms, chemical companies, etc. involved in food production and processing. They all share one characteristic; they are losing sales as organically produced food production increases.

We have seen some pretty harsh public statements about organic agriculture using terminology like: elitist, dangerous, unsanitary and wasteful of resources needed to feed the world, made by company spokesmen of several different companies. The statements seem to come from the same set of talking points. It appears that this committee was formed to be the vehicle to mount a full blown assault on organic agriculture in the United States."

Yoder Farm

As soon as it was apparent that they would have product to sell Jen Beth embarked on an advertizing campaign; she had Hank make her a set of sturdy metal signs that could be hung on mounting frames set in their fences that paralleled the highway. She and Anna then painted signs advertizing the U-Pick farm and retail store that also had places to hang small removable signs showing what produce was ready to harvest. They put up the signs with an "Opening soon" tape across each one and printed up pamphlets explaining how to pick each type of produce, a lot of people didn't know that pulling the stem out of fruit would cause it to spoil, and also giving tips on how to preserve its freshness. Anna was working on a pamphlet of recipes and tips on preserving produce. They updated their liability insurance to be sure that they were covered for accidents by people picking produce and printed up large signs giving the rules of the business to be posted in several spots in the public area and they arranged for port-o- potties to be delivered and serviced. They printed up flyers to distribute at area farmers markets, took out ads in local newspapers and Jen Beth wrangled an interview on the local radio station extension homemaker show. They cleaned up and installed tables and coolers in the implement shed closest to the orchard and U-Pick field. Jen Beth found a source for cheap woven wood baskets on the internet and ordered three sizes: one bushel, one half bushel and one peck. She had the local printer make up colorful Yoder Farm signs on heavy gauge paper that had adhesive on one side and applied one sign to each basket. All hands turned in to pick roasting ears and samples of the fruit that was ripe and they put the Grand Opening signs up along the highway with "Free samples" signs attached. Cars started to follow the direction arrows and stop at the store almost immediately. Most were just looking but everyone accepted samples of the roasting ears that Anna had cooking in their husks on a charcoal grill and of the fruit that was ready; rave reviews followed and lookers became buyers. They quickly sold out of the roasting ears they had picked at four for a dollar; Jen Beth had never been around corn and was afraid they would be out of roasting ears before they got started. She felt better when Hank told her that there were about twenty-five thousand ears per acre and they had about nine point nine six acres yet to pick. Their advertizing had made a difference as a number of people came prepared and picked large batches of corn to take home and freeze at eight ears for a dollar. Marge Strickland had come over to help on their first day and when she saw the demand, suggested that she bring her Sunday school class of teen agers over on Saturday to pick corn. It would take some of the pressure off of the Weavers and give the kids a way to earn some money. Hank roped off the area where he wanted people to pick and as soon as an area was harvested he shredded the stalks to prepare for summer crops like okra, watermelons and cowpeas and later for fall crops like pumpkins, turnips and winter squash. It was going to take some planning but Hank was convinced that the rolled down living mulch made up of annual plants was the way to go for the U-Pick garden. It appeared that the mulch would deteriorate enough that he could plant the cover crop this fall directly into the residue using Umpa's little ten foot grain drill. If this didn't work, he would have to use some sort of opener to get the seed down to mineral soil; he had best study the no-till drills on the market.

Joe Hendricks stopped by regularly to visit and lately to quiz Hank about large scale organic production; he was fascinated when Hank explained how they planned to use livestock and pasture to build fertility and to reduce weeds, insect damage and plant disease in the crops following pasture. Joe had a young family and lately had begun to seriously question if he wanted to continue to use, and expose his family to, the chemicals that had become standard operating procedure in modern agriculture. "If I can't hug my wife and son without having to take a shower and change clothes something is wrong. I ought not to even bring my work clothes into the house when I have been handling that stuff! Do you remember what this valley smelled like in the summer when we were kids? Now there is a chemical stench over the whole valley from early spring until snowfall. Do you remember how we would pull roasting ears out of the corn patch and roast them in the ashes of a campfire down by the creek? There is no way that I would let my kid eat this GMO stacked trait, chemical soaked crap that I am growing. I don't even want him to play in the cornfield that comes right up to our yard fence." Joe told Hank that he had gone pretty deep into debt to buy equipment and to take over operation of his family farm. Without going into detail, he made it clear that he was very interested in the economics of organic production. Jen Beth had put the records Anna and Henry kept in a form that made it easy to see what happened to them over time and Hank showed these figures to Joe. Clearly they had produced more by farming more acres and by using more inputs but they did not produce more profit per man hour. They were taking in a lot more dollars but were constantly skirting the edge between profit and loss and always with the possibility that, given bad weather or severe market drop, the loss could be catastrophic. Hank did not try to influence his friend but he was very pleased when Joe asked him if he would help him plan out a realistic transition from conventional to organic production.

Their first summer under the new regime seemed to go bye in a flash; the U-Pick garden was a lot of work but it was also lucrative; the sweet corn netted just a little less than two thousand dollars an acre even after paying Marge Strickland's Sunday school class for five Saturdays and a dozen afternoons after school of picking roasting ears. In addition, when the corn that got too tough for roasting ears dried down, Hank hooked up Umpa's old one row corn picker and harvested about fifty bushels of ear corn that they could use for poultry and hog feed. Tomatoes and green beans, especially the pole beans growing on the corn, were big favorites with people wanting produce to can and freeze and as word spread of the taste of Umpa's old varieties of tomatoes and beans, people came from all over the county. Anna organized a group of ladies to can and freeze produce and, when school let out, several of them brought their kids or grandkids to pick whatever was ready for harvest. Hank bought a dozen feeder pigs to use the blemished fruits and vegetables. Anna had increased her flock of laying hens from twenty to one hundred and they now had fresh eggs for sale at the produce stand. The hens too enjoyed all the fruits and vegetables they wanted and as people tasted the eggs it became apparent that they would have to increase production or risk having fist fights over the limited supply of eggs. Hank had already decided that he was going to steal a few acres of pasture to put in small grains for the pigs and chickens. Hanks' biggest fear, that people would not come to the farm to buy, was laid to rest; all they had to do now was keep the products coming. Hank had cleaned and repaired Umpa's beehives and the newly stocked hives were literally swarming with bees coming and going to the alfalfa and clover and other flowering plants. Anna and Jen Beth had cleaned the honey house and had the extractor and plenty of jars ready; they planned to rob hives next week and add local honey to their product list.

The cattle continued to do exceptionally well; Hank was rather proud of what he was learning about grazing management but kept his congratulations to himself. They had started the cattle out, because it was all they had, on very high protein, low energy forage (what cattlemen called washy forage) and early performance was not good; seeing how adding energy to their diet with mature hay improved animal performance was enlightening and Hank promised himself that he would do a better job of planning to have forage at the proper stage of growth when the next batch of cattle arrived. Performance was going to be best when the protein to energy ratio was in balance with the needs of the animals; when this balance was achieved, the pH of the animals' urine would be close to seven; if the pH dropped, the animals were short of protein and if the pH climbed, the animals were short of energy and were burning protein for energy. Since the percentage protein drops and the percentage energy increases (to a point) as forage matures, Hank could test the urine pH of his calves and have an excellent check on whether the maturity of the forage he was presenting to the animals was right to provide the best animal performance. The theory seemed logical and the cattle responded to Hanks' management by gaining like crazy; Jim Bledsoe told Hank that they were doing better than any other set of cattle that his company had out. It was soon obvious that they could carry more cattle than they had, this number could not keep up with forage growth, and Joe Hendricks suggested cutting some of the surplus forage for hay. Hank considered this but decided that since the main purpose of the forage was to improve soil health, he would "waste" the extra forage and let it be consumed by soil life and thus speed up the healing process. They would need to make some hay when they became certified organic but that could wait until their soil was in better shape; for now they could buy what hay they needed.

CHAPTER TWENTY ONE

The Wages of Sin

Joe Meyers called and asked if would be convenient for him to come to the farm the next day to report on the status of their lawsuits against GAI and against Property Management Inc. The family hurried through their chores and Anna got Marge Strickland to mind the store so that they could all meet with Joe Meyers at nine o'clock. Meyers was working hard to keep his "just the facts" professional demeanor but he was obviously excited as he started his explanation with the suit against GAI. "I have held a series of meetings with the GAI legal counsel without accomplishing anything worthwhile. The meetings have been quite acrimonious with GAI attorneys promising to mount a complete and far reaching defense against all allegations of wrong doing of any kind by their clients; day before yesterday they went so far as to put out a press release stating that a major part of this defense, "Though we hate to be forced to speak ill of the dead," would be to, "Inform the court and the world in general of the "criminal history and poor character" of Henry Weaver." They passed out copies of his booking records on the assault charge brought by Gary Doak and photos of Henry being taken to jail in handcuffs. The clear threat was that they would mount a "scorched earth program" to destroy the creditability of Henry and, by association, of his family. This is a tactic that GAI has been successful in using in the past and both Wallace and I fully expected them to attempt to use it against our suit but we were surprised and pleased that these allegations were made public before they were presented to the court. I feel certain that whoever was responsible for the press release is no longer employed since making such information public prior to opening arguments can have no purpose except to attempt to intimate you, Mr. Weavers' family. Most judges will look askance at such tactics but even more favorable for us, it ties our suit to a pattern GAI has used repeatedly to pursue patent infringement suits. This pattern is what we are going to use to convince the court that GAI has gone beyond using the law for harassment to criminal extortion. As I told you before we filed our suit, the Legal Defense Coalition has been tracking what we knew, but were unable to prove, was extortion on a large scale by GAI for at least the last ten years. Since I last spoke with you the Coalition has taken on, as clients, sixteen individuals, partnerships and corporations who have settled lawsuits out of court with GAI. Four of these are residents of the state that you may know. In each of these cases the opening gambit of GAI was the public defamation of their opponents by spreading inaccurate information or downright lies. All sixteen of these entities assert that they were innocent of the allegations brought against them and settled only because the slander was ruining their ability to do business and they were unable to stand the expense of further litigation. After being shown that GAI used the same ploys to force settlement time and again, all sixteen are now willing to testify in our suit and are considering having the Coalition to represent them and others in a class action suit alleging extortion by GAI. The reason that I am here today is to keep you up to date, particularly I wanted you to hear about the press release from me rather than reading it in the newspaper, but more important is the fact that we have had a major shift in attitude by GAI. Somewhere GAI has obtained a list of at least some of the people who are now willing to testify against them. This was bound to happen; too many people are involved for secrets to be kept for long. Anyway, I had a phone call shortly after the press release from the lead counsel for GAI threatening dire consequences if we released the settlement details of any lawsuit involving GAI. I was informed that all settlements by GAI were protected by "iron clad" non-disclosure clauses that they would defend vigorously. I am ashamed of myself but after weeks of abuse from this pompous toad, I snapped back that he should know that contracts signed under duress were invalid and that he had best hire some more lawyers because he was going to have plenty of suits to defend and I hung up on him. I had barely gotten off the phone when District Attorney Jack Roberts, who we have worked closely with so far as sharing information and sources, called to inform me that the Grand Jury had returned true bills against all of the principals and three employees of Property Management Inc. The Grand Jury also returned posthumous true bills against Gary Doak and Jesse Thompson and several indictments against one Harry Gibbons who was replaced as GAI field representative by Jesse Thompson. Gibbons still works for GAI and Roberts let it be known that he was being very cooperative with their investigation. Roberts has filed charges against three people in GAI management and expects that number to climb as underlings give up their bosses in attempts of plea bargaining. It appears that we have accomplished most of what we set out to achieve, prove Henry innocent and see GAI brought up on criminal charges, do we settle for what we have won or do we continue the suit? How do you want me to proceed?" Anna spoke for the first time, "Mr. Meyers, I want: a written apology from the President of GAI acknowledging that Henry did nothing wrong and was falsely accused, I want GAI to donate two hundred and fifty thousand dollars to the American Association for Sustainable Agriculture to be used for teaching farmers to produce without poisons and I want the people who were forced into unjust settlements with GAI to be compensated. I believe the legal term is "made whole". If GAI agrees to these conditions, I am willing to drop the charges; if not, I think we should continue the lawsuit." "Mrs. Weaver, I think that is a magnanimous offer on your part. The only addition that I would suggest is to require that the letter of apology specifies that the persecution of Henry was an attempt at extortion by employees of GAI working with Property Management Inc. and employees of the First State Bank of Cayuga. I fully expect that we will win our suit against Property Management Inc and it officers but it looks as if there is not going to be anything to recover if we do win. Jack Roberts has talked to the previous owners of every farm they have bought since they began operation and vows that he will see that Albert Horning and the rest will make restitution if it takes every penny they own; I think the DA sees this case as his ticket to bigger things. If we are in agreement, I should get back to the office; when I checked in with my secretary, she told me that the office of the GAI lead counsel attempted to call me yesterday afternoon and again this morning early. I suspect that he has found out about the criminal charges filed against GAI and finally understands the extent of the trouble his clients are facing. I suspect that he would very much like to get us out of his hair before he has to defend the criminal charges and the Federal charges that are almost sure to follow; he just might settle on our terms. I will keep in touch."

That night Jen Beth called her parents to report on what Joe Meyers had told them and learned that Bristol Farms had been ordered by the court to remove the label from their dairy products stating that their cows were not treated with bovine growth hormone. In a rather convoluted ruling the court sided with the Committee for Truth in Food Advertising in their assertion that such a label cast doubt as to the safety and wholesomeness of dairy products that did not carry such a label. When Jen Beth asked her Father if he planned to appeal he answered, "Oh yeah, we will appeal and before we are through the whole Country will know who the Committee for Truth in Food Advertising is, what they are trying to do and where they get their funding. These bozos may have won the battle but they will not win the war."

GAI did settle the suit on the terms dictated by the Weavers and the months following saw an almost complete halt of lawsuits against farmers by GAI and a big reduction in suits filed by other companies. It appeared that the corporate world was waiting to see how the criminal charges against GAI would play out. Criminal indictment of GAI employees, a total of six people including a vice president and two heads of departments were charged, seemed to have gotten the attention of a lot of people. The principals in Property Management Inc. had all been sentenced to multiple years in prison and ordered to make restitution to the people they defrauded as well as to pay very heavy fines. When people heard testimony in the Property Management Inc trial that GAI employees had been involved in criminal extortion, evidently with the blessing of at least some in management, GAI stock lost twenty percent of its value over night and was being sold off at a rapid rate even before the criminal trials started. For their part, the Weavers were hopeful that their involvement with GAI and the small town mafia was at an end.

CHAPTER TWENTY TWO

Vindication

Their first season of production came to an end when the cattle, all but six which Hank purchased to try his hand at grass finishing, were shipped to feed yards. Jim Bledsoe came up from Kentucky with a set of portable corrals to load the cattle and was very pleased at how well the animals had performed; they gained 2.15 pounds per head for 184 days and Hank had lost only four animals charting a very acceptable six tenths of one percent death loss. When Jim called his boss to report on the weigh up and ask if Hank could buy six steers, Mr. Wardlow told him to give Hank the six steers and get his agreement to graze more cattle for them next season. The fifty eight cents per pound of gain they had agreed on was higher than the fifty cents Hank used in his planning estimate and the actual gain per day was four tenths of a pound higher than his estimate. These two figures, along with the lower than planned death loss, made their return to management and labor equal $81,219 when the value of the six gifted steers was included. After paying all cash expenses, they had made a gross profit on the 540 acres of pasture of $150 per acre while tremendously improving their soil. This eighty one thousand added to the thirty four thousand they netted from the U-Pick put them at a net return of over two hundred dollars an acre for the entire farm which according to Anna was the highest return in the history of Yoder Farm. When Jen Beth, who was doing the math, announced the final results, Hank whooped and grabbing his Mother around the waist with one arm and his wife with the other went dancing around the room like a kid going to the circus. They were not there yet, they had plenty of learning to do and they needed a better building for the store and a set of pens with a loading chute, but they had proved that the basic plan could work.

Joe Hendricks had been watching the cattle deal closely; he even helped Hank on shipping day. That night he and his wife came over after supper and Joe put a proposition to Hank and Jen Beth. "Would you be interested in developing pasture on the 320 acres that we own on your east and running it along with your pasture? We would have to spend some time deciding who pays for what and how you would be compensated but I think we can make it fair to both sides. It would let you increase your numbers and it would make a start for us to transition into organic production. We can't afford to make the jump all at once but I am certain that we want to convert to organic as quickly as we can. The young couples talked for hours and used up a bunch of note paper but in the end reached an agreement that satisfied both parties. It seemed that Jacob Bristol's idea to create organic farmers by example was bearing fruit.

With the additional pasture that would be available on the Hendricks land, Dr. Carthage suggested that Hank plow down one hundred acres of pasture and plant it to the rye-vetch-crimson clover cover mixture to be rolled down and seeded to test plots of corn, two types of soybeans and two kinds of dry edible beans. He also wanted Hank to plant thirty acres or so of einkorn to follow the bean crop; the world wheat crop is so contaminated with GMO and mutagenic wheat that Dr. Carthage wanted a good supply of the ancient ancestor of wheat to start breeding wheat varieties free of the chemical and radiation induced mutations. None of the produce would be eligible to be certified organic but it would be grown with organic practices and would serve as a test of their program and practices. On this acreage, since it had only one season as grazed pasture, they would not crop it two years but would plant it back, except for the einkorn patch, to their pasture mixture in the fall. Hank decided to include a patch of cowpeas and one of milo as feed for Anna's laying hens and perhaps some pastured broiler chickens; Umpa's little pull type combine with its' six foot header would be ideal for the small acreages. The demand for pasture raised eggs was seemingly unlimited and they planned to have a mobile laying house and movable broiler pens ready so the chickens could follow along behind the cattle next season. As a part of their function to educate young farmers and to get some badly needed help, they advertized for interns to come spend a year on Yoder Farm and were surprised when they were flooded with applicants all anxious to work for what amounted to room and board plus minimum wage. They had room in the Yoder home for two extra people willing to share a bedroom and after reading all the applications and interviewing half a dozen people, they decided on two young men. Tom Kirk, a junior horticulture major with a farm background and Les Browning, a farm boy with a high school diploma who had been working in construction but desperately wanted to farm. When Jacob Bristol was told about the response to their advertisement, he was ecstatic and told them Bristol Farms would provide the temporary housing and support staff needed to house, feed and teach as many interns as they thought they could handle. With the decision to break out the hundred acres, for the first time, Hank felt the need for a bigger tractor and was about to suggest to Jen Beth that they borrow the money to buy a used tractor. Thinking about this as he was riding back to the house for lunch, it hit him that not only was buying a tractor a poor use of scarce capital but that he was surrounded by big tractors and big equipment sitting idle while waiting for the corn and beans to get ready for harvest. One phone call and a quick dinner and he was back in the field marking off the tracts he wanted plowed and disked. Joe Hendricks was busy getting his 320 ready to seed to pasture but his uncle George would be there in the morning with a ten bottom turning plow on a 250 horsepower tractor and his son Greg would come about three o'clock with a finishing disk. As long as he could schedule what he needed to have done to take place in the dead time between the frantic rushes to get corn and soybeans first in the ground and then harvested, he could have the use of big equipment at a minuscule fraction of the cost of owning it. There are some advantages to being out of step with the rest of the world.

After Hank went back to work, Anna was washing dishes as Jen Beth dried when Anna asked, "When is the baby due?" "---I'm not; I mean I don't know --- I'm not even sure I am pregnant. I am late but that is not unusual for me." "Oh, you are expecting all right; you have a glow to your skin that only has one cause. I expect you had best tell Hank and set up an appointment with Dr. Fortner for a checkup."

CHAPTER TWENTY THREE
Storm Clouds

J en Beth had become close friends with Sharon Hendricks; their husbands had been best friends since they were in first grade together and the two young women found that they liked each other and enjoyed each other's company. Joe and Sharon's son, Tommy, at almost three soon looked on Jen Beth and Hank as another set of parents – or at least aunt and uncle – and Anna as another grandmother – one he could always touch for a treat of some sort. Sharon was pregnant with her second child and was delighted when Jen Beth confided to her that she too was pregnant.

Life on Yoder Farm had settled into a busy but pleasant routine when Sharon called Jen Beth and asked if she could keep Tommy for two days; Joe had been sick off and on for months – not sick enough to go to bed but just feeling lousy. Being sick was not normal for Joe and Sharon brow beat him into seeing Dr. Fortner who decided that he needed to go through a clinic in Columbus. Sharon wanted to be with him; she told Jen Beth that being there was the only way she would find out what the doctors said,

"Joe would not lie but he also would not tell me everything that the doctors tell him to do or not do." Joe and Sharon dropped Tommy off at the Weaver home with hugs and kisses and his fat little legs were churning down the hall to Anna's kitchen before his parents got back to the car. Joe and Sharon planned on being home Wednesday afternoon but Tuesday evening Sharon called Jen Beth and asked if she could keep Tommy for another day; the doctors wanted to do more tests. When Sharon and Joe arrived to pick up Tommy, Anna and Jen Beth had supper ready. Anna headed off all objections with, "You have to eat, you are tired and it is foolish for you to go home and cook. Sit down." The young couple was obviously bothered by what the doctors had told them. Sharon was cuddling Tommy in her arms as if he were an infant as he attempted to wiggle loose to better describe his adventures gathering eggs with Anna and his narrow escape from the wrath of a broody hen. The meal was not a great success with Tommy being the only Hendricks that did more than pick at his food. The Weavers were being polite but they were interested and finally Hank said, "Joe what did they tell you? "They have me taking a bunch of pills and they don't want me to be handling any chemicals." Sharon spoke up, "He has serious liver damage and elevated levels of at least four and maybe six different chemical toxins in his blood. All the tests results are not back but the doctors said the amount of damage indicated long term exposure to several different classes of chemicals and he absolutely cannot be exposed to anything that might cause more liver damage. When the doctors got the first blood work back, they thought that Joe must be a long term alcoholic and were amazed when we told them that he does not drink and never has. With alcohol ruled out, they asked him what chemicals he handled on a regular basis and he came up with a list of twelve that he handled regularly and six more that he used occasionally. The doctor that asked about chemicals read the list, pitched it back to Joe and said, "If you are going to be exposed to things like this, I can't help you." By this time Sharon was weeping softly and Tommy was crooning, "Mama. Mama." and patting his mothers face in an attempt to make better whatever was causing her distress. "When they found the liver damage and high levels of chemicals in Joe, they tested me. I don't have liver damage yet but I do have chemicals in my blood stream." Seeing that Sharon was very close to breaking down completely, Anna took Tommy in her arms and started to the kitchen saying, "Let's go see if there are any cookies left in the jar." When Tommy left the room, both Sharon and Joe lost it; they clung to each other weeping and it was several minutes before they were able to carry on a conversation. Joe recovered first, "I don't know how I could have been so stupid; it wasn't enough that I poisoned myself. I had to bring those damn poisons home to my family! I can remember at twelve or thirteen helping Dad mix pre-emergence herbicides or treating seed with fungicide and insecticide and getting nauseous from the fumes but nobody thought anything about it. Sure the labels told you to wear protective clothing and masks but nobody did; I don't know a single farmer who hasn't been soaked a dozen times with chemicals of all sorts. We have to take Tommy in to be tested; little ones are especially at risk of being poisoned because of their smaller body masses and undeveloped immune systems. The doctors also wanted us to get our well water tested. Both Sharon and I have high levels of nitrates in our blood and the doctors told us that many wells all throughout the Corn Belt are contaminated with nitrates from fertilizer and with herbicides like Atrazine. We have the materials to get water samples so we can get the testing done; we brought enough bottles so that you can test your well at the same time.

That night as Hank was getting ready for bed Jen Beth looked up from her computer and said, "Hank I just got an e-mail that made the hair stand up on the back of my neck; do you remember Mary Alice Dotson? You may not have ever met her; she was one of my sorority sisters but two classes ahead of us. Anyway, we have kept in touch off and on; she married a farmer in Indiana and two years ago she lost a baby to miscarriage. She just lost another baby and is devastated. The doctors told her that the most likely cause was the pesticides they found in her blood. She remembered me talking about Mother's work with people affected by agricultural chemicals and wanted to know if it would be alright if her mother, who is a United States Senator, contacted Mother for information on how big a health threat these chemicals pose. Mother has been trying for years to get someone in authority to listen to the horror stories that she hears all too frequently. I gave Mother a heads up just now and sent her e-mail address to Mary Alice.

CHAPTER TWENTY FOUR

Allies Unite

Hart Senate Office Building

Senator Jane Dotson put down the synopsis her staff had prepared for her from the thousands of pages of research reports digitized and furnished to them by Dr. Anne Bristol and pressed the button that opened the inter-com link to her chief of staff. "Rosemary, could you come in please." The door connecting the senators' office to that of her chief of staff opened and Rosemary Billings, Senator Dotson's chief of staff and oldest friend, asked, "What can I do for you Jane?" "How much of this syn-opsis have you had time to read?" "I skim read the whole thing last night and highlighted areas where I think we need more information I have Hillary and Ted doing follow up on some of those areas now." "Is one of those areas the number of genetically modified organisms that have been released on the public without having meaningful testing or environmental impact assessments done?" "It is; I was floored to learn that the food grains that formed the basis of the so called, "Green Revolution", came about through genetic mutations caused by radiation and chemicals.

These grains were evidently released for human consumption with minimal testing for safety; no studies that I can find on the long term effects of consuming this material. From what I have seen so far, even less testing has been done on the various GMO's that have been put into the food supply" "I am disturbed by the magnitude of what Dr. Bristol has shown us and am afraid that I, evidently like most people, have not been paying attention as some very serious changes have been made in our food supply and in our environment. When pesticides are showing up in the blood of newborn babies and there is a dead spot the size of Delaware in the Gulf of Mexico where nothing can live because of agricultural chemical contamination, it is past time that some hard questions were put to the chemical companies and to "Big Ag". From what Dr. Bristol tells us, it appears that the colleges of agriculture and the government regulatory agencies are more interested in promoting what they see as modern agriculture than in promoting a wholesome and nutritious food supply and a healthy environment. I am particularly bothered by the problem of genetically modified organisms being introduced into our food supply with little or no oversight. I would like for you to start one of your bright young people researching what appears to be a revolving door shuttling people back and forth between companies wanting approval of materials and techniques and the regulatory agencies with the power to grant such approval. Have them go back at least ten years; if government employees are being bribed with jobs or other perks to grant approval of corporate requests or if companies are using under handed methods to have their people placed within the regulatory agencies, I want know chapter and verse of how often and by what means it has been done."

Senator Dotson removed her reading glasses and rubbed her eyes with the back of her hand. She was alone in her office and it was late; the clock on her desk read eleven fifteen. She had been reading steadily since the last of her office staff left at six o'clock and she was tired but could not seem to reach a stopping point. When she asked Dr. Anne Bristol to provide her with information concerning the dangers to the public caused by modern agricultural production, Senator Dotson had no idea how much information Dr. Bristol had amassed. The initial response of Dr. Bristol was to ask how in depth the Senator wished to explore the situation. Dr. Bristol had spent more than fifteen years studying the effects of what was now considered conventional agriculture on the health and well being of the American people and had, over time, gathered a tremendous amount of well documented information. She had studied everything from the amounts of insecticide and fungicide residues found on fresh fruits and vegetables, to the effects on farm workers (and their families) handling toxic materials to the steady decrease in nutrient content of foods of all sort. Senator Dotson and Dr. Bristol corresponded back and forth by e-mail and when the senator realized the scope of the problem, by telephone. She finally asked Dr. Bristol to furnish her with as much information as she could on any agricultural practice that had adverse effects on human well being directly or by damage to the environment. Dr. Bristol responded.

"Senator, I have been putting together evidence on a dozen different problem areas for many years; I may overwhelm you but I will send what I have and you can pick and choose. The information is organized by topic and date but as you would expect, there is a great deal of overlap and interaction between topics. As an example, the loss of nutrient density in food is rooted in the loss of soil health caused by reduced organic matter content and loss of soil life due to tillage and heavy toxicant usage. Compounding the problem are mineral deficiencies arising from plant growth being forced with nitrogen fertilizer to the point that the soil cannot give up all needed minerals fast enough to maintain normal mineral content in plants. Also responsible are reductions in plant available mineral content in soils caused by physical factors (erosion and leaching) and by chemical causes (loss of availability). Nutrition has also been lost as plants have been selectively bred to exhibit traits such as uniformity of ripening, long shelf life and appearance rather than for nutritional content. Very little attention is paid to food value by government agencies or by food producing companies; yield, ease of harvest and shelf life are the areas that receive the research dollars. Attention by informed consumers to the overall value, wholesomeness plus nutrition, of our food is the main reason for the tremendous growth in the demand for organic food.

A fairly recent factor affecting the wholesomeness of our food supply is the use of genetic modification techniques to insert genetic material from totally unrelated species such as insects and fish into food plants. Most of the corn grown in the US today has a gene inserted that produces an insecticide to reduce insect damage to the corn plants. Most of the soybeans grown in the US have been genetically modified to be able to withstand being sprayed with a herbicide that acts by making certain trace elements unavailable to any plant it touches and thus disrupting the production of certain essential enzymes; the modified plants have been engineered to be able to grow without the enzymes in question. Even though study after study points to a wide range of maladies in both people and animals as being caused by GMO plants, the use of these materials expands every year. While the people doing this genetic modification spend large amounts of money to convince regulatory agencies and the public that these techniques create no danger to people or to the environment, in truth, they have no idea what the total and long term effects their manipulations will bring about. An example of what could occur happened recently when a common bacterium was genetically modified to convert cellulose – wood – into alcohol. Tests were run and the material was about to be released for commercial production when a curious gradu- ate student decided to see if the bacteria could live outside the fermentation vat. The student introduced the modified bacteria into greenhouse soil growing a number of differ- ent plants. It grew and reproduced very well in the soil and in the process converted all of the organic matter present in the soil into alcohol. Alcohol is deadly poison to higher plants and every plant in the test plot was killed and con- verted to alcohol. If this alcohol producing bacteria had gotten loose, the results would have been horrible beyond belief. It could literally have brought about the end of all life on earth. It was halted not because some agency was overseeing the process but because one student had the intellectual curiosity to do research that should have been done much earlier in the developmental process. That the needed research was not done on an aspect as important as this constitutes scientific malpractice at the best and more probably criminal negligence. I wish that I could say that this was an isolated and unusual occurrence but that is not the fact; similar, though less devastating, mistakes are quite common.

A second dangerous practice in common use is the use of radiation and/or chemicals damaging to genetic material to induce mutations in plants. The purpose of such procedures is to isolate mutations in plant genotypes that produce traits deemed beneficial such as increased starch content or reduced plant stature. Such traits can be fixed in a genotype by these methods but the vast majority of mutations produced are not beneficial but harmful and not enough attention is paid to the destructive effects of damaged genes being introduced into the plant gene pool. Quite often problems of many kinds ranging from poor mineral assimilation to reduced root growth to loss of disease resistance are not obvious until much later after the modified plants have become widespread. It is my opinion that such practices when used as they have been, without thorough testing and rigid quarantine of the material produced, are unethical and perversions of scientific research. Senator, I commend you for your attention to this very important problem and look forward to helping you in any way in my power."

Sincerely,

Anne Bristol PhD, M.D.

What had started out as an attempt by Senator Dotson to understand why her daughter had lost two babies was evolving into a search for understanding of an even larger problem of vital importance that she had not realized even existed. She was intrigued when she questioned Dr. Bristol about the differences between conventional and organic food production. She had never given much thought to organic production; she assumed that the media reports of no meaningful differences in nutritional value between conventional and organic foods were valid. Even the USDA had made such statements and added that organic production practices were completely incapable of producing enough food to meet world demand. Visiting with Dr. Anne Bristol, a very well educated, well informed and intelligent person put an entirely new perspective on the situation. Dr. Bristol's family had been involved in producing organic food since 1849 and she had put together the facts and figures, in the form of peer reviewed scientific research project reports, needed to refute the falsehoods leveled against organic production techniques and against the food grown under such a regime. Study after study indicated comparable yields and superior nutritional quality for the products of well managed organic production and the projects that studied the financial aspects showed it was feasible for profitability of organic production to be higher and more reliable that of conventional production. For Senator Dotson, the most convincing argument for the superiority of organic production was that under organic techniques, the soils became healthier with every passing year. Good organic production practices increase soil organic matter content and as organic matter content increases, the soil can take in and hold more water thus reducing both droughts and floods; as a bonus, each one percent increase in soil organic matter removes approximately 22,000 pounds of carbon per acre from the air and sequesters it long term in the soil. A relatively small increase in soil carbon content spread over the Worlds agricultural soils could reduce the carbon dioxide levels in the atmosphere to pre-industrial levels.

Aside from organic agriculture being good for the environment and both sustainable and profitable, life on an organic farm was a very good way to live and raise a family; people in this environment were not exposed to any of the poisons used so freely in conventional agriculture. Senator Dodson realized, with a black flood of sadness, that she would have a granddaughter coming up on her third birthday and another a year and a half younger if her parents had been organic rather than conventional farmers.

The next morning at staff meeting Senator Dotson announced that her Health and Nutrition Subcommittee would hold hearings starting in three weeks on the state of the national food supply as to safety and nutritional content. She already had a dozen names – suggested by Dr. Bristol of people from all over the country who were involved in various aspects of trying to improve the quality of food and to strengthen the production and distribution processes of good food. These people ranged from academics with multiple degrees through practicing physicians and nutritionists to plant and soil scientists to people actually involved in crop and livestock production and marketing. It was a varied group of people with widely differing skill sets but they were all knowledgeable and all were passionate about wholesome food and its production. All of these people shared two traits; they were very good at what they did and they could explain their field of endeavor to an audience.

The subcommittee would also contact the various commodity groups and trade associations with invitations for them to send representatives to testify.

CHAPTER TWENTY FIVE
The Harvest

Hank sat beside Jen Beths' bed and watched his wife nurse Anna – their newborn second child. His almost three year old son – Henry Jacob or H.J. – sat in his lap busily tying and untying knots in the piece of rope that had become his favorite toy. H.J. was delighted when Anna was born; he had been awaiting her birth almost as eagerly as his parents. He was disillusioned though when he was told that it would be a long time before she was able to come out and play with him. The last five years had been good for the Weaver family; the farm was making money and their soil was improving at a rate that even surprised Jacob Bristol and Tom Carthage. After a slow start in the second year of their program, attendance at their field days and seminars was booming; people might not understand organics but they understood when Hank showed them the figures on what it cost him to produce a bushel of corn. His yields were not as high as those made by the better conventional farmers but his profit per acre (or per dollar invested) was far better and his soil was getting better rather than worse. The years of meticulous records kept by Henry and Anna and the records kept since by Hank and Jen Beth painted a clear and vivid picture – there was money to be made in the right kind of agriculture. Each farm would be different but the principles of improving rather than mining soil, improving water capture and storage and managing for what was desired rather than against what was not wanted are universally applicable. Interest exploded when Jen Beth designed and published The Yoder Farm Organic Project website and posted not only the economic information but pictures and data that they had collected from day one. People were fascinated watching the sequence as Hank took a piece of ground from plow down of pasture to cool season cover crop to roll down and no-till planting to harvest. Jen Beth was getting quite professional with her video camera. Some of the data, like soil test results, she presented in graph form so that changes in organic matter content, pH and mineral availabilities were easy to track from year to year. The biggest stumbling block for most people was bringing animals back to the farms; many of the younger farmers had never worked with animals and most farms had been stripped of all fences and animal buildings. Watching at the field days, how little time Hank spent building temporary electric fence and how simple it made animal handling, started at least some people thinking. One project that attracted a great deal of attention was when Jen Beth videoed the complete sequence as Hank farrowed a set of sows on pasture and then raised the pigs on pasture even down to finishing the butcher hogs by having them strip graze standing corn with an understory of clover. No harvested feed was used and the only buildings used were two portable shades and the little "A" frame portable huts that Hank built and the sows bedded down with hay, for the sows to shelter in when they farrowed their pigs. Hank moved first the sows and then sows and pigs and later the pigs as they grew first to shoats and then to hogs through a series of paddocks each with forage compatible with the needs of the animals at that stage of their life. Jen Beth posted the video on their website; depicting an entire year of hog production in twenty minutes of video. She included an economic break down showing a return per dollar invested that no factory type hog production program could come close to equaling and the website received two thousand hits in three days. People were hungry for information on production practices that made economic sense.

At first only Joe Hendricks, his uncle George Hendricks and the Miller family started the process of becoming certified organic but interest began to build as people watched when these farmers made money even without receiving premium prices for their produce. Jacob sent a team of three experienced vegetable farmers from Bristol Farms to live in the rapidly expanding intern village of trailer houses and teach the resident interns, and anyone else who was interested, how to grow profitable organic produce. Most of the people coming to field days professed to be interested in growing only corn and soybeans but attitudes began to change as Jen Beth showed people facts and figures of what it was possible to make with relatively small acreages of vegetable and specialty crops.

There was opposition from the start; some farmers were unable to comprehend how crops could be grown without regular applications of fertilizer. Some agriculture extension personnel, and more farm supply merchants, even suggested that the Weavers were "mining the soil" and predicted that without herbicides, fungicides and insecticides pests would soon build up to disastrous levels and put them out of business. Hank got Dr. Tom Carthage to write a paper explaining how having a high degree of biodiversity both in and on the soil acted as a natural system of checks and balances which prevented any one species, whether plant, animal or microbe, from becoming numerous enough to become serious pests. Dr. Carthage also wrote a paper explaining how healthy populations of soil life, from bacteria to fungi to nematodes to earthworms, acted to both recycle mineral nutrients and to also make new nutrients available from the minerals locked away in local rock. Jen Beth posted the papers on the website and Hank used the information in his seminars and field day presentations where he quickly learned the truth of the old adage, "If you want to learn a subject, try to teach it."

Hank picked up the mail as he came back from running errands in town and was intrigued to find a letter from the American Association for Sustainable Agriculture addressed to The Yoder Farm Organic Project. They were members of AASA but before mail from the Association had always been addressed to Yoder Farm; Hank opened the letter and, pleased at what he read, started home to find Jen Beth and his Mother. He found the two of them in the kitchen; Jen Beth nursing the baby and Anna supervising H.J. as he tried, without much success, to learn to eat peas with a fork. He handed Jen Beth the letter from AASA, "See what you think of this." Jen Beth read and with a big grin said, "They want us to give a four hour presentation on The Yoder Farm Organic Project at the annual conference and they want you to be the keynote speaker!"

The conference was three months away but Jen Beth went to work editing new video footage to bring the documentation of what they were doing up to date. The cattle taken in on gain still formed the major part of their program but Hank was beginning to finish (make fat enough to grade USDA Choice) a few cattle and the demand for this grassfat beef was very good. Hank found a source of certified organic Devon cattle that finished well on grass and was now offering certified organic grass finished beef as well as chemical free but non certified grass finished. Thanks to the intern program, they were able to produce certified organic eggs, broilers, ducks and turkey and the market for their pastured pork seemed unlimited. The U-Pick program had been expanded to twenty-five acres and Hank had gradually improved the implement shed-store; it wasn't fancy but it was now enclosed, had indoor plumbing and had better lighting. They had eased into the dairy business but now their dairy herd was up to thirty cows and raw milk, butter and other dairy products from organic grass fed cows were so profitable and in such demand, it didn't hurt that the Appeal Court had ruled that they could advertize that their cows were not injected with BGH, that they had been seriously considering building a new dairy barn and increasing their cow numbers. The figures showed that they could cash flow the construction costs and a new barn would be nice but after a lot of thought and number crunching the three of them agreed that there were other places that they could use the money that would yield a better return than a new barn; besides they were out of debt and it felt good. Jen Beth used the question of whether to build a new barn and how they arrived at their decision as part of the financial planning portion in their presentation. The three of them and Jacob Bristol as well strongly believed that teaching the principles of good financial management would be as important to the success of future Bristol Farms cooperators as any knowledge they could convey. Discussing this subject, Anna said, "It is not possible to understand how dangerously seductive credit can be or how destructive debt can be until your every action is dictated by the servicing of a debt load."

The AASA conference was to be in St Louis this year so the Weavers drove down while Jacob and Anne Bristol flew in. The Bristol's quickly asserted their rights as visiting grandparents to monopolize H.J. and little Anna but that night when the kids were put to bed, the adults gathered in Hank and Jen Beth's suite, keynote speakers get perks, to visit. So far, Bristol Farms had signed contracts with only a few Midwest farmers but more were in the process of becoming certified and literally hundreds of people had expressed interest in the cooperator program. The program had created so much interest that the Association asked Jacob to give a presentation on it at the conference. These people did not need to be convinced of the benefits of organic production but there was great interest in the possibility of being able to market their products through a stable and reputable firm like Bristol Farms; more than a few farmers in the group had been hurt when companies either reneged on contract promises or simply went out of business leaving their suppliers unpaid for material they had produced.

Hank thought hard and long about what he should say in his speech. He decided to describe Yoder Farm as it was for so many years under Umpa Yoder and his forebears and then to describe the changes made, the rationale behind making them and the results both good and bad as Yoder Farm transitioned to "modern agriculture." He would describe their struggles to survive as the ever increasing expense of inputs and the rapidly decreasing health of their soils trapped them in a financial nightmare leading eventually to total financial collapse and the death of his Father. Finally, he would describe how Yoder Farm today was financially and ecologically healthy and was once again a good place to live and raise a family.

After a brief but complimentary introduction, Hank looked out at the six hundred or so people present and after expressing appreciation to the Association for inviting him to speak began to tell the story of Yoder Farm. Through all the seminars and presentations he made, Hank had become a very effective public speaker and he held the rapt attention of the audience from his first words. Jen Beth and the rest of the family were sitting on the aisle at the far left side of the hall, in case Miss Anna decided to wake up and serenade, and Jen Beth could see the reaction of many in the audience to Hank's words. As he led them through the story, Jen Beth could see heads nodding in agreement when Hank described how his Father and Mother had worked and struggled before finally being overcome by the situation. When Hank told of his Father's death, there were more wet eyes than dry eyes in the hall.

Hank didn't dwell on the bad times but moved on to the changes that had taken place on Yoder Farm in the last five years and how they had been brought about. After going through a brief description of the practices that they had used to restore the farm to financial and ecological health, Hank said, "Perhaps the biggest change has been to our attitudes; I hope that we now understand that agriculture is a biological rather than an industrial process. We can and should use science to understand nature but it is a severe mistake to try to use science to control nature. Agriculture should be the science and art of promoting life so that we can harvest some of the energy that is surplus to the needs of the system for our own use. Vital to accomplishing this is learning to manage so as to promote what we want: healthy soil, healthy plants and animals and healthy people, rather than expending time, effort and money trying to destroy what we don't want. We must change the culture of death that surrounds modern agriculture to a culture of life. We must make farming the world's best way to make a living and to raise a family."

As Hank concluded his talk the hall erupted with applause so that Jen Beth had to strain to hear her Mother-in-law, with tears streaming down her face, say, "His Father and his Grandfather would be so proud of him. His Father's death was a hideous unnecessary tragedy but perhaps not a total waste if people will take to heart what Hank is telling them."

CHAPTER TWENTY SIX
Epilogue

The first two days of the Health and Nutrition Subcommittee hearings ended and Senator Dotson was fairly well pleased; though she was more than a little bothered by the attitudes displayed by several members of the subcommittee. Even members of her party seemed to look on any criticism of the food production and distribution system as un-American. Quite a lot of time had been consumed by the necessity of giving each member of the committee face time so that they could let their constituents know how important and hard working they were. They finally got into the meat on the second day with Dr. Bristol testifying for over seven hours. She first gave an overview as to the condition of the nutritional status of the American people; she gave her opinions and when these positions were challenged by senators beholden to chemical companies, "Big Ag" or the status quo in general, she gave references to scientific papers that validated her positions. Dr. Bristol concentrated on the changes in the food supply that reduced nutritional content and/ or introduced harmful substances into food. Staffers of several senators went into frenzy when she listed partially hydrogenated vegetable oil, high fructose corn syrup and all genetically modified organisms as harmful materials. Two senators made half hearted attempts to refute Dr. Bristol's arguments but only succeeded in making themselves appear foolish due to their obvious lack of knowledge. One senator changed tactics and with a sneering expression wondered aloud if Dr. Bristol's concern was prompted by anxiety for the health of the public or if her real purpose was to increase revenue for her family's business.

Senator Dotson and Dr. Bristol retreated to the senator's office when the subcommittee adjourned for the day. The senator had apologized for the actions of her colleagues and was pouring them each a glass of wine when her chief of staff came in to tell Senator Dotson that the Majority Leader of the Senate had requested that she meet with him immediately in his office.

The receptionist ushered Senator Dotson directly into the Majority Leader's office where she was surprised to find the minority leader sipping bourbon with the majority leader. "Come in Senator, don't bother to sit down, this won't take long. We want you to cancel the rest of your hearing immediately. I want you to know that I am livid about your conduct; it appears that you have intentionally set out to besmirch some of the strongest supporters of our political system. My phone has been ringing off the wall ever since your hippie doctor started testifying; talk about biting the hand that feeds you! Have you lost your mind? You will cancel the hearings at once and the minority leader and I will issue a joint press release and attempt to minimize the damage of your blunder." Senator Dotson was so stunned that it was a moment before she could say, "I cannot. I will not do that! This hearing is too important; it is exposing real dangers with the safety of America's food!" "You will do it Senator and you will keep your mouth shut on the subject or I will replace you as subcommittee chairperson with someone who will. We are not playing games here; we are talking about real money in the real world. You have enraged a large portion our corporate support base and endangered the funding of the entire electoral process! You will do as I say or you will find yourself back where you came from teaching gobbledygook to idiots at Po Dunk U."

AUTHORS NOTE:

A brief history of Agriculture in America

As in all new lands agriculture in America went through an exploitative period when virgin land was available just over the horizon and the attitude of "break it out, use it up and move on " was more common than we would like to think. This attitude coupled with the tremendous growth in demand for agricultural products fueled by the industrial revolution resulted in widespread and serious damage to agricultural lands on a large scale and a resulting loss of productive capacity. The damaged soils lost not only the ability to produce large yields but also the ability to provide normal nutritional content to the crops that were produced. Large numbers of people were trapped in poverty and in poor nutritional status on these depleted soils in many different areas not only in America but in other areas of the world as well. By the late 1930's, in response to this situation, a movement was under way to develop the knowledge and the practices needed to repair damaged lands and to educate and motivate the people working the land. Ancient practices such as crop rotations, green manures and cover crops, rotational grazing;

water management and combination animal and crop husbandry were researched, refined and given standing in the scientific and academic worlds. Agricultural scientists and a growing number of good farmers began to realize that they could duplicate the productivity of "new ground" by applying these practices and that the productivity of their soils would improve over time rather than deteriorate. In the United States, a great deal of work was done developing long term crop rotations for each area of the country, breeding improved legume plants and the rhizobia bacteria associated with these legumes and in general learning how to make agriculture sustainable and regenerative rather than extractive. The term "grass farmer " came into common use; authors like Louis Bromfield and Edward Faulkner were widely read and articles by William Albrecht dealing with the soil-plant-animal complex were published in the agricultural trade journals of the day. By the late 1940's real progress was being made in educating farmers as to the possibility and importance of soil conservation and improvement. County Agricultural Extension agents and the agricultural press stressed the value of soil organic matter content and taught ways to increase it. Diversity of crop and livestock enterprises was widely recognized as having both economic and ecological value. The well-run farm was seen as having a number of crops which were planted and harvested at different times of the year to spread the workload and to increase the utility of equipment. Pasture was used to build soil productivity and to feed livestock. Livestock was used to give immediate monetary value to soil improving crops, to utilize crop residues, to improve soil productivity and to produce profit from both pasture and crops. On the best of these farms there was no such thing as waste products and inputs from outside the farm were minimal. This period gave birth to that rare and elusive creature "the family farm."

The very real progress that was being made in developing agricultural practices that promote both profitability and sustainability was curtailed and often reversed by the arrival of "modern agriculture." In the last sixty years conventional agriculture has been changed from a biological to an industrial pursuit. The tremendous increase in manufacturing capacity and the explosive growth of the chemical industry brought about by the Second World War changed the very nature of agriculture. Problems occurred almost at once but the prevailing belief was "the answer to the problems of technology is better technology." In less than two generations, agricultural scientists replaced centuries of accumulated knowledge with a totally new concept of what constitutes good agricultural practice. The results of this transition have been tragic. In the name of efficiency, farmers have been urged to specialize in one or two crops rather than using the mixture of crops and livestock that became traditional in each area because it maintained productivity over long periods of time.

Soil is treated as merely a medium useful to hold water and applied mineral nutrients rather than as a complex association of minerals, organic matter and living organisms that, when properly managed, is capable of sustainable productivity. Far too few people realize the true value of healthy soil and how badly we have damaged this most valuable resource. Under continuous tillage, heavy chemical usage and no livestock presence, organic matter content and soil life is lost from soil. For many years this loss was concealed by higher inputs of chemical fertilizers and the development of hybrid crops. Crop yields increased under this regime which made its' menace even harder to recognize.

Today we find that many of our soils are dead and unable to perform their historic function as water reservoirs so that both floods and droughts are more common and more severe. It is common for the water holding capacity of a soil to decrease by a factor of five or more when it loses organic matter content and the soil life that is dependent on soil organic matter. One of the consequences of having precipitation run off the land is the reduction of water stored in underground aquifers. Water that runs off into rivers is available for only a short period of time unless it is impounded in lakes and reservoirs and even then much of it is lost to evaporation and degraded by the concentration of salinity. Water that soaks into and is held in the soil is available to plants and soil life and the portion that percolates into aquifers is available, from springs and wells, to humans and animals over long periods of time. In the long term, the hydrological effects of agricultural practices are of extreme importance to humanity. Throughout history, progressions of cultures have risen to prominence only to decline when they destroyed the ability of their soils to capture and hold water.

In large part we have destroyed the biological diversity, both in and on the soil that once held pest organisms in check so that diseases of plants and animals, insect pests and weeds are all more problematic. The use of pesticides has increased many folds while crop loss to pests has more than doubled and our water supplies, our soil and our foodstuffs are now contaminated with these poisons. The drive toward plant uniformity, to increase efficiency of harvest, has brought about a reduction in the genetic diversity of major crops to the point that all of these crops are vulnerable to catastrophic losses from outbreaks of mutant disease organisms. The use of genetic engineering to create organisms resistant to particular pesticides is an example of technology being utilized for short-term economic gain with very little understanding of the total and long term effects of these actions. The dangers of radical technology are made even worse by the incestuous relationships common between the companies promoting technology and the agencies charged with protecting the common interests. Equally disturbing is the fact that much of the agricultural research done in our universities is paid for by companies seeking approval of some product or technology.

The last fifty years or so has seen a major change in agricultural practice that has never before been attempted on a large scale; we have taken animals out of agriculture. The concentration of livestock in factory style units has created waste disposal nightmares while robbing the soil of the nutrients and organic matter in the manures; the material that once formed the backbone of sustainable soil productivity has been turned into at best a waste product and more commonly pollution. These confinement units create hideous living conditions for the animals, necessitating constant use of antibiotics to suppress disease to sub acute levels, and they give rise to poor working conditions for the human workers. The wide spread low level use of antibiotics is at least partially responsible for the explosion of pathogens resistant to antibiotics and the increase in hard to control diseases in humans. In the new order, soil erosion, frequent drought and flood incidents and outbreaks of pests and diseases are seen as solely natural occurrences while in truth these phenomena are greatly influenced by the practices of "modern agriculture". The monetary cost of the high input technology and its' inherent economic instability has reduced the farmer to the economic status of serf but without the economic protection the serf enjoyed. This statement appears false at the moment due to extreme market distortions caused by political action. The current high prices for farm commodities are the result of illogical government actions. Not even the United States government can long continue to subsidize a product, ethanol for fuel, which requires more energy to produce than it contains. The industrialization of agriculture has been a failure by any reasonable set of criteria that takes into account its' true cost to society.

If the production of safe nutritious food at a reasonable cost while providing decent and stable incomes for family farms and a vibrant local economy is a part of our national goal, we must change our philosophy of agricultural practice. We must realize that agriculture is a biological endeavor and that attempting to practice it in an industrial mode will, in time, destroy the natural resources, the financial structure and the human resources needed by this most vital of pursuits. For many years, farmers and ranchers have been assailed with advice to industrialize agriculture in order to "feed the world". At the present time, conventional agricultural practices are destroying our soil, our water resources and our ecological diversity; who will "feed the world" when, in a few years, the destruction is complete?

The story of the transformation of Yoder Farm from an economic basket case with rapidly deteriorating soil health and poor quality of life for its people (an all too common set of conditions in modern agriculture) into a prosperously productive, ecologically sound and people friendly endeavor is realistically feasible. Sadly it is not a story that is being widely repeated. The forces driving agricultural industrialization come from a wide range of entities: companies wanting to expand markets for pesticides, chemical fertilizer and equipment; misinformed groups pushing bio-fuels; governments wanting more grain for export; well intentioned organizations wishing to make more food available for the poor have all joined forces to greatly increase the amount of land managed with an industrial mindset. Vast areas in South America, Africa and Asia are being converted from traditional uses into farming systems that will, with high inputs, appear to be successful for a short period but will end up degrading soil, water and human lives. Even the highly successful and long running program of rotating land between long periods in pasture and short periods of row crops in Argentina is being scrapped under government pressure to increase grain production in order to increase state revenues.

This trend can be reversed; the technology is known and the economics are sound but this will not happen until we learn to stop taking short term advantages that must be paid for with long term costs. To quote Jin Tan, a fictional character in the book, "It is a rare man who has the wisdom and the balance to be trusted with the ability to deal out death on a large scale."

APPENDIX

The following articles are a small sampling of the hundreds available from news releases, peer reviewed scientific journals and the popular press. Anyone desiring to make their own study of the state of modern agriculture will find an amazing amount of information on the internet. The authors urge people to inform themselves and form their own judgments.

APPENDIX I

1. *The following is an actual news story from BBC News*

14 June 2010

Green Revolution's diet of big carbon savings

By Richard Black Environment correspondent, BBC News

The Green Revolution of the 1960s raised crop yields and cut hunger - and also saved decades worth of greenhouse gas emissions, a study concludes.

US researchers found cumulative global emissions since 1850 would have been one third as much again without the Green Revolution's higher yields.

Although modern farming uses more energy and chemicals, much less land needs to be cleared.

The study is published in Proceedings of the National Academy of Sciences.

"Converting a forest or some scrubland to an agricultural area causes a lot of natural carbon in that ecosystem to be oxidized and lost to the atmosphere," said Steven

Davis, from the Carnegie Institution's Department of Global Ecology at Stanford University in California.

"What our study shows is that these indirect impacts from converting land to agriculture outweigh the direct emissions that come from the modern, intensive style of agriculture."

Hunger tackled

The researchers constructed alternative scenarios for how global society might have developed since the 1960s had the new, high-yielding Green Revolution varieties of rice, maize and other crops that raised crop yields in Asia and South America never existed.

Non-intensive agriculture would mean much greater land clearance

These new varieties turned countries such as India, which imported food in the best of times and needed emergency aid in the worst, into major exporters.

Without the new crops - but with the growth in the human population and all the other socio-economic trends seen since the 1960s - feeding the world at current levels would mean the use of more than twice as much land as is currently used for agriculture, the researchers found.

Farming this way would have required less energy and use of chemicals such as fertilisers, whose production involves emissions of CO_2 and whose use generates nitrous oxide, another greenhouse gas.

However, additional emissions from the extra land clearance, releasing carbon stored in trees and soil, would have been the more important factor by far.

Meeting extra food demand this way would have released about 160 Gigatonnes (billion tonnes) of carbon (GtC) over the decades - which, the researchers note, "corresponds to 34% of the total 478 GtC emitted by humans between 1850 and 2005".

"That's about 20 years of fossil fuel burning at present rates," observed Dr Davis.

Modern gains

Modern intensive agriculture is often criticised over its relatively heavy use of chemicals, which can impact insects, larger animals and plant life in the vicinity of the farm.

In addition, the run-off of excess fertiliser into rivers and lakes can generate blooms of algae and "dead zones" of water where nothing can survive.

However, strictly from the point of view of greenhouse gas emissions, intensive farming appears to be significantly the better option.

"Our results dispel the notion that industrial agricultural with its petrochemicals is inherently worse for the climate than a more 'old-fashioned' way of doing things," said Dr Davis.

He and his team suggest that policymakers keen to reduce greenhouse gas emissions should look towards further increases in crop yields, which they say might be more economical than other innovations.

Existing research shows that curbing production of meat - which is an inefficient user of land and water - would by itself have some impact on emissions, though by precisely how much is debated

APPENDIX II
Sam Devraj Assistant Editor GG2.net

Madhya Pradesh chief minister Shivraj Singh Chouhan

THE AGRICULTURE minister of Madhya Pradesh to-day blamed a recent spate of farmer suicides on over-use of chemical fertilisers and urged the country to embrace organic production. Seven cases of poor farmers taking their lives have surfaced in less than a month in Madhya Pradesh and at least five others are battling for their lives having made attempts to commit suicide by drinking pesti-cide. Harvests are down 60 per cent because of unseasonal rains that fell in September and intense frost in the past month, which has decimated wheat, soya beans, peas, and orange crops, the local farmers' association says. Families of the deceased have blamed the pressure of mounting debts and the prospect of financial ruin, though experts stress that suicides are normally the result of several fac-tors and often stem from mental health problems. State agriculture minister Ramkrishna Kusmaria, in whose con-stituency district Damoh several of the suicides occurred, courted controversy by suggesting the farmers were partly responsible for their financial hardship."The damage to crops is taking place because of our old sins. Regular use of chemicals in fields has weakened the health and resistance and crops are getting damaged," Kusmaria told reporters today. "The farmers should turn to organic farming. "His comments go to the heart of a debate in India about the country's embrace of intensive farming and fertiliser use in the 1970s that led to the country's much-discussed "Green Revolution." This helped boost farm yields, which has helped to feed India's booming 1.2-billion population, but it has also had damaging effects on the environment and has resulted in increased costs for farmers. Despite economic development in cities, two out of three Indians still live and work in rural areas and as many as 150,000 farmers have killed themselves in the past decade, the Tata Institute of Social Sciences said in 2009. The subject was taken up in an acclaimed Indian film last year called Peepli Live made by the production company of Bollywood star, Aamir Khan. The film, directed by first-time director Anusha Rizvi, revolves around two poor farmers who face losing their land over an unpaid debt after poor monsoon rains. A local politician suggests to the farmers that they commit suicide so their families get compensation, but a journalist overhears one of the farmers urging the other to end his own life, triggering a media frenzy. In Madhya Pradesh, state chief minister Shivraj Singh Chouhan has assured farmers of compensation for their damaged crops and has requested a Rs50bn ($1.2bn/£76.2m) aid package from the federal government.

APPENDIX III

Transcript of CBS News Video aired January 4, 2011 10:00am:

(CBS) *American farmers have been growing genetically modified crops for years, from seeds engineered to resist pests and chemicals. These patented seeds produced bigger crops and profits for farmers who bought them from companies like DuPont and Monsanto, but for other farmers the seeds have created a host of problems.* **CBS News Chief Investigative Correspondent Armen Keteyian** *has been investigating.*

David Runyon and his wife Dawn put a lifetime of work into their 900-acre Indiana farm, and almost lost it all over a seed they say they never planted.

"I don't believe any company has the right to come into someone's home and threaten their livelihood," Dawn said, "to bring them into such physical turmoil as this company did to us."

The Runyons charge bio-tech giant Monsanto sent investigators to their home unannounced, demanded years of farming records, and later threatened to sue them for patent infringement. The Runyons say an anonymous tip led Monsanto to suspect that genetically modified soybeans were growing on their property.

"I wasn't using their products, but yet they were pounding on my door demanding information, demanding records," Dave said. "It was just plain harassment is what they were doing."

Today, Monsanto's patented "Round-up Ready" soy commands the lion's share of the genetically-modified soybean seed market, its genetic code manipulated to withstand the company's popular weed killer.

But the promise of fewer weeds and greater production comes with a hefty fee. Farmers must sign an iron-clad agreement not to re-plant the harvested seed, or face serious legal consequences - up to $3 million in damages.

"It's about protecting the patent, defending the patents, so farmers have the protection and can use these technologies over time," said Monsanto spokeswoman Tami Craig Schilling.

The Runyons say they signed no agreements, and if they were contaminated with the genetically modified seed, it blew over from a neighboring farm.

"Pollination occurs, wind drift occurs. There's just no way to keep their products from landing in our fields," David said.

"What Monsanto is doing across the country is often, and according to farmers, trespassing even, on their land, examining their crops and trying to find some of their patented crops," said Andrew Kimbrell, with the Center For Food Safety. "And if they do, they sue those farmers for their entire crop."

In fact, in Feb. 2005 the Runyons received a letter from Monsanto, citing "an agreement" with the Indiana Department of Agriculture giving it the right to come on their land and test for seed contamination.

Only one problem: The Indiana Department of Agriculture didn't exist until two months after that letter was sent. What does that say to you?

"I'm not aware of the specific situation in Indiana," Schilling said.

"I'm just talking in general terms," said **Keteyian**. "Would Monsanto lie, deceive, intimidate, harass American farmers to protect its patents?"

"With farmers as customers I would say that is not our policy by any means."

74-year-old Mo Parr is a seed cleaner; he is hired by farmers to separate debris from the seed to be replanted. Monsanto sued him claiming he was "aiding and abetting" farmers, helping them to violate the patent.

"There's no way that I could be held responsible," Parr said. "There's no way that I could look at a soy bean and tell you if it's Round-up Ready."

The company subpoenaed Parr's bank records, without his knowledge, and found his customers. After receiving calls from Monsanto, some of them stopped talking to him.

"It really broke my heart," Parr said. "You know, I could hardly hold a cup of coffee that morning,"

Monsanto won its case against Parr, but the company, which won't comment on specific cases, has stopped its legal action against the Runyons.

And now four states, including Indiana, prohibit seed suppliers from entering a farmer's property without a state agent, tactics which have threatened a way of life.

APPENDIX IV

Fear on the farm

ET Bureau Jun 15, 2011, 02.27am IST

A special feature in this newspaper on Tuesday points to the terrible mess that Indian farming is headed for, and the ostrich-like attitude that policymakers have adopted towards this. The 1960s green revolution, which boosted the yields of our major food crops — rice and wheat — was based on technology that needs lots of water and chemical fertilisers. The pricing, procurement and distribution mechanism was built around this.

But erratic rainfall and inadequate canal and tank irrigation in many parts of India meant that farmers gravitated towards diesel pumps to pull groundwater to irrigate crops. In the 1960s, canals and tanks supplied more than 60% of irrigation water, tubewells about 0.6%. By 2002-03, canal water was only a third of all irrigation water, tubewells made up nearly 40%. So, groundwater reserves have plummeted, mostly in states like Punjab, Rajasthan, Haryana, Gujarat, Tamil Nadu and UP which are large grain producers.

The green revolution introduced crops that were shorter and grew faster than local varieties, but that meant less fodder for livestock. Much of the soil subject to intensive cultivation has become poisoned by the use of chemical fertilisers and can't sustain lifeform like earthworms, which are necessary to replenish soil quality. If continued, this pattern of farming will clearly push India off an environmental cliff.

The government has to put in place policies that force a change in the way India farms today. The use of groundwater has to be discouraged. The quickest way to do that would be to hike the price of diesel, now kept artificially low. Tank irrigation has to be encouraged, possibly with generous subsidies that could be funded by money saved from fuel sops. Research and development of genetically modified crops, which need negligible amounts of fertilisers and pesticides, has to be speeded up.

Technologies already tested and proved globally should be implemented at home. Finally, fertile east India has to be brought into the farming mainstream by strengthening private transport and storage networks, and dismantling the inefficient state-controlled farm produce marketing committees that prey on farmers.

APPENDIX V

(NaturalNews) As if there isn't enough reason to avoid genetically modified food, new research has discovered GMOs are linked with leukemia and anemia. The study found that *Bacillus thuringiensis* (Bt) used in bioengineered seeds has a substantial adverse effect on blood cells and bone marrow cell proliferation. Even at the lowest dose, the effects were deemed virulent to proper cell health.

Birth of Bt frankenfood

Bacillus thuringiensis is naturally found in the soil and has been used as a foliar insecticide since the late 1960s. Farmers spray their crops with the bacteria, insects consume it and their stomachs subsequently break open. However, use of the toxin didn't stop as a topical pesticide. As reported in the *NaturalNews* article, "Rid the body of dangerous Bt-toxin found in genetically modified food with these tips":

"Monsanto decided it would be profitable to splice a gene of Bt with corn, soybeans and cotton - creating plants that were rife with the bacteria not just on the surface but within the cell wall. Monsanto and the *Environmental Protection Agency* claimed the toxin would be destroyed within the digestive tract of mammals and magically disappear. Guess what? The physicians at *Sherbrooke University Hospital* in Quebec, Canada discovered Bt-toxin in 93 percent of 30 pregnant women, 80 percent of umbilical cord blood of their babies and 67 percent of 39 women who were not pregnant. Considering Bt-toxin is linked with cancer, autism, severe food allergies and autoimmune disease, these findings are downright frightening."

And now it looks as though two more ailments will join the ranks: leukemia and anemia.

APPENDIX VI

Connection between GM food and blood cell cancer

Published in the peer-reviewed *Journal of Hematology & Thromboembolic Diseases*, researchers at the *Institute of Biological Sciences* in Brazil found that Bt is adept at damaging red blood cells along with white blood cell reproduction in mammals. The scientists fed mice varying amounts of the toxin and noted that even after just a single dose, it caused several blood irregularities - anemia and damage to bone marrow cells. According to Sayer Ji of *GreenMed Info*:

"What the new study revealed is that various binary combinations and doses of Bt toxins are capable of targeting mammalian cells, particularly the erythroid (red blood cell) lineage, resulting in red blood cell changes indicative of significant damage, such as anemia. In addition, the study found that Bt toxins suppressed bone marrow proliferation creating abnormal lymphocyte patterns consistent with some types of leukemia."

The research team concludes:

"Taking into account the increased risk of human and animal exposures to significant levels of these toxins, especially through diet, our results suggest that further studies are required to clarify the mechanism involved in the hematotoxicity found in mice, and to establish the toxicological risks to non-target organisms, especially mammals, before concluding that these microbiological control agents are safe for mammals."

Sources for this article include:

http://www.naturalnews.com

http://www.greenmedinfo.com/blog/new-study-links-gmo-food-leukemia

http://esciencecentral.org

http://www.organicconsumers.org/articles/article_27523.cfm

http://digitaljournal.com/article/350126

About the author:
Carolanne enthusiastically believes if we want to see change in the world, we need to be the change. As a nutritionist, natural foods chef and wellness coach, Carolanne has encouraged others to embrace a healthy lifestyle of organic living, gratefulness and joyful orientation for over 13 years. Through her website www.Thrive-Living.net she

looks forward to connecting with other like-minded people who share a similar vision.

Learn more: http://www.naturalnews.com/040721_ leukemia_GMOs_anemia.html#ixzz2VwtnwDOX

APPENDIX VII

GM Wheat May Damage Human Genetics Permanently

Article from GreenMedInfo.com
Posted on:
Thursday, October 18th 2012 at 5:00 am
Written by:

Heidi Stevenson

The Australian government, in the form of its science research arm, is joining Agribusiness profiteering by designing a GM wheat that could kill people who eat it & be inherited by their children.

by Heidi Stevenson

We have not yet seen the worst damage that genetic engineering may do. Australia's governmental agency, Commonwealth Scientific and Industrial Research Organisation (CSIRO), is developing a wheat species that is engineered to turn off genes permanently.

Professor Jack Heinemann at the University of Canterbury's Centre for Integrated Research in Biosafety has studied the wheat's potential. Digital Journal reports that he says[1]:

What we found is that the molecules created in this wheat, intended to silence wheat genes, can match human genes, and through ingestion, these molecules can enter human beings and potentially silence our genes. The findings are absolutely assured. There is no doubt that these matches exist.

The implications are clarified by Professor Judy Carman of Flinders University:

If this silences the same gene in us that it silences in the wheat—well, children who are born with this enzyme not working tend to die by the age of about five.

Silencing the equivalent gene in humans that is silenced in this genetically modified wheat holds the potential of killing people. But it gets worse. Silenced genes are permanently silenced and can be passed down the generations.

Silenced Genes

The wheat genes involved are called SEI. The specific sequences of those genes are being termed classified confidential information. CSIRO, which is part of the Australian government, is developing a commercial application, but refuses to divulge the information that's most significant to the people of Australia! The government is apparently more interested in profits than in the people's safety.

Dr. Heinemann was asked to provide his opinion of CSIRO's genetic engineering on wheat plants and produced the report "Evaluation of risks from creation of novel RNA molecules in genetically engineered wheat plants and recommendations for risk assessment"[2]. He discusses the nature of the genetic entities that are being played with and explains how they can affect human health.

RNA is similar to DNA, which is the molecule that carries genetic inheritance. There are several types of RNA, but a particular group called double stranded RNA (dsRNA) is of concern. Heinemann writes:

> dsRNAs are remarkably stable in the environment. Insects and worms that feed on plants that make dsRNA can take in the dsRNA through their digestive system, where it remains intact.

He delineates research documenting that once dsRNA is taken through an animal's skin or digestive tract, it can wreak havoc. It circulates throughout the body and has been known to be amplified or cause a secondary reaction that:

> ... leads to more and different dsRNAs ("secondary" dsRNAs) with unpredictable targets.

Heinemann points out that a silencing effect on a gene, once initiated, can be inherited. Though it's known to happen, little is yet known about the process.

dsRNA is known to be a tough molecule. It survives readily, even through digestion. Worse, though, it's known to pass into the body through digestion. Then, as Dr. Heinemann writes:

> Once taken up, the dsRNA can circulate throughout the body and alter gene expression in the animal.

That is, gene expression can be altered as the result of eating a food with dsRNA altered by genetic engineering. Judy Carman, of Flinders University, who also provided an expert opinion, wrote in "Expert Scientific Opinion on CSIRO GM Wheat Varieties"[3]:

> In fact, employees from the world's largest GM company, Monsanto, have written at least one paper about how to commercially exploit the fact that dsRNA survives digestion in insects, in their attempts to try to control insect pests of plants. That is, the plant is genetically engineered to produce a dsRNA, which insects ingest when they eat the plant; the dsRNA survives digestion in the insect and then silences genes in the insect to stunt its growth and kill it.

There can be no question that dsRNA can be transferred to humans by eating.

The Risks

Heinemann makes these three points:

1. Plant-derived microRNA [a type of dsRNA] precursors have been detected in human blood, thus demonstrating that they can survive the human digestive tract and be passed into the body through

it. He emphasizes: **"There is strong evidence that siRNAs [a type of dsRNA and the one of particular concern here] produced in the wheat will transfer to humans through food."**

2. dsRNA that have been shown to transmit to humans through food have also been shown to survive cooking! He points out: **"There is strong evidence that siRNAs produced in the wheat will remain in a form that can transmit to humans even when the wheat has been cooked or processed for use in food."**

3. Plant-derived dsRNA was able to silence a human gene in cultured cells. He wrote: **"There is strong evidence that once transmitted, siRNA produced in wheat would have the biological capacity to cause an effect."**

Judy Carman states succinctly:

As a result, there is a chain of evidence to show that there is a risk that the dsRNA from this GM wheat may survive digestion, enter the tissues of people that eat it and silence a gene or genes in those people. There is also evidence that any genetic changes so produced may be stable and become established in many cells of an organ. Furthermore, there a possibility that these changes may be passed-on to future generations.

The wheat genes involved are called SEI. They have extensive similarities with the human GBE gene, which controls glycogen storage. If the GBE gene is defective, it leads to certain death from liver cirrhosis at a very young age. Another defect in the gene results in adult polygluco-san body disease (APBD) in adults over age 40, causing cognitive impairment, pyramidal quadriplegia, peripheral neuropathy, and neurogenic bladder.

Dr. Heinemann investigated and found that sections of the two genes, SEI and GBE, are a perfect match. Because CSIRO is saying that the specific SEI sequence that's modified is classified confidential information, we cannot know for certain what harm might be done to humans. However, it's obvious that shutting down a section of the GBE gene holds the potential of death—yet, Heinemann showed that it's not only possible, it's likely!

Lack of Adequate Risk Assessment

Judy Carman focused more on the lack of appropriate or adequate risk assessment for the modified wheat. She is very concerned that no consideration was given to checking for:

- Whether there are adverse effects on animals or humans who eat it.
- Whether there is any uptake of dsRNA in animals or humans who eat it.
- Silencing of genes in animals or people.
- Silencing of the branching enzyme.
- Toxic effects, such as damage to the liver, kidneys, or any other organ.
- Increase in reproductive problems.
- Whether dsRNA changes are inherited.
- Increased risk of cancer.
- Increased risk of wheat allergies

She is very concerned that the oversight agency, the Office of the Gene Technology Regulator (OGTR), and CSIRO "appear not to be looking for any adverse effects in people, but intend to go directly to look for any benefits." She concludes:

> It appears that neither organisation has appreciated or properly safety assessed this wheat in the light of the fact that the dsRNA produced in these GM wheat varieties may survive digestion, enter the tissues of the body and silence a gene or genes in the recipient. It also appears that neither organisation has "joined the dots" to appreciate that, of all the genes that could be silenced, the most likely one is a similar branching enzyme in animals and people and that silencing it could seriously impair or even kill those that eat it.

The Australian government appears to have become nothing more than another Agribusiness corporate entity. They're using the people's money to fund a massive profit-making venture in genetic engineering without any consideration for the potential harm that may be done to either the environment or the welfare of the people. Not only are they willing to risk mass deaths from products they're hoping to put on the market, they also seem to have no concern for whether they might be doing permanent damage to generations that follow.

Resources

1. Scientists: New GMO wheat may 'silence' vital human genes

2. Evaluation of risks from creation of novel RNA molecules in genetically engineered wheat plants and recommendations for risk assessment
3. Expert Scientific Opinion on CSIRO GM Wheat Varieties
4. CSIRO SEI/SEII SHRNA GM WHEAT FOR PRODUCING GRAINS WITH A LOWER
5. CONTENT OF BRANCHED STARCH MOLECULES, Appraisal of statements by Prof Jack Heinemann and Assoc Prof Judy Carman
6. The GMOs, nature and effect of the genetic modification

APPENDIX VIII

June 20, 2013 in Sustainable Agriculture, by Admin Share with University of Canterbury researchers have found that the biotechnologies used in north American staple crop production are lowering yields and increasing pesticide use compared to western Europe. A conspicuous difference is the adoption of genetically modified/engineered (GM) seed in North America, and the use of non-GM seed in Europe.

The team, led by UC Professor Jack Heinemann, analysed data on agricultural productivity in north America and Western Europe over the last 50 years. The Western Europe and North America make good comparisons because these regions are highly similar in types of crops they grow, latitude, and access to biotechnology, mechanisation and educated farmers.

The findings have been published in the peer-reviewed International Journal of Agricultural Sustainability.

"We found that the combination of non-GM seed and management practices used by western Europe is increasing corn yields faster than the use of the GM-led packages chosen by the US.

"Our research showed rapeseed (canola) yields increasing faster in Europe without GM than in the GM-led package chosen by Canada and decreasing chemical herbicide and even larger declines in insecticide use without sacrificing yield gains, while chemical herbicide use in the US has increased with GM seed.

"Europe has learned to grow more food per hectare and use fewer chemicals in the process. The American choices in biotechnology are causing it to fall behind Europe in productivity and sustainability.

"The question we are asking is, should New Zealand follow the US and adopt GM-led biotechnology or follow the high performance agriculture demonstrated by Europe?

"We found that US yield in non-GM wheat is also falling further behind Europe, demonstrating that American choices in biotechnology penalise both GM and non-GM crop types relative to Europe.

"Agriculture responds to commercial and legislative incentive systems. These take the form of subsidies, intellectual property rights instruments, tax incentives, trade promotions and regulation. The incentive systems in North America are leading to a reliance on GM seeds and management practices that are inferior to those being adopted under the incentive systems in Europe.

"The decrease in annual variation in yield suggests that Europe has a superior combination of seed and crop management technology and is better suited to withstand weather variations. This is important because annual variations cause price speculations that can drive hundreds of millions of people into food poverty.

"We need more than agriculture; we need agricultures – a diversity of practices for growing and making food that GM does not support; we need systems that are useful, not just profit-making biotechnologies – we need systems that provide a resilient supply to feed the world well," Professor Heinemann says.

AUTHOR BIO

Walt Davis was born, and continues to be, a rancher. After studying at Texas A&M, he took over the family ranch in Oklahoma and acted as a management consultant to ranchers and resource managers. He is the past president of the Texas and Oklahoma chapters of Holistic Management.

Davis is the author of How to Not Go Broke Ranching and the novel A Gathering at Oak Creek. His columns appear in Penton Group magazines, the Stockman Grass Farmer, and Acres USA.

Tony Winslett dedicated forty years to a career in marketing. It was during his stint as a marine in Vietnam that he first became aware of the utter environmental devastation that humans can cause.

With Winslett's extensive background in marketing, he understands how foods that are bad for us can still be touted as "health food." He hopes The Green Revolution Delusion will bring awareness of these issues to the general public.

Made in the USA
Charleston, SC
15 June 2014